Sunderland Public Library
Twenty School Street
Sunderland, MA 01375
413.665.2642
413.665.1435 (fax)

The Heart
Has Many Doors

Books by Susan Snively

From This Distance (Alice James, 1981)
Voices in the House (Alabama Poetry Series, 1988)
The Undertow (University of Central Florida, 1998)
Skeptic Traveler (David Robert Books, 2005)

The Heart
Has Many Doors

A Novel of Emily Dickinson

Susan Snively

White River Press
Amherst, Massachusetts

The Heart Has Many Doors: A Novel of Emily Dickinson

First published February 14, 2015.

White River Press
P.O. Box 3561
Amherst, MA 01004
whiteriverpress.com

Cover design by Elizabeth Pols.
elizabethpols.com

Cover photograph:
South Parlor, Dickinson Homestead, Amherst Massachusetts, 1999, Jerome Liebling.
Used with permission.

ISBN: 978-1-935052-69-2

Library of Congress Cataloging-in-Publication Data

Snively, Susan, 1945-
The heart has many doors : a novel of Emily Dickinson / Susan Snively.
pages ; cm
ISBN 978-1-935052-69-2 (softcover : acid-free paper)
1. Dickinson, Emily, 1830-1886--Fiction. 2. Lord, Otis P. (Otis Phillips), 1812-1884--Fiction. 3. Women poets, American--19th century--Fiction. 4. Salem (Mass.)--History--19th century--Fiction. I. Title.
PS3569.N5H43 2014
813'.54--dc23

2014025629

To Peter,
for his wisdom and love

Author's Note

F ew subjects arouse the attention of Emily Dickinson's readers more than her love life, or produce more speculation, hope, and surprise.

The story of Emily Dickinson's romance with the eminent judge Otis Phillips Lord came to light in 1954, when Millicent Todd Bingham, daughter of Mabel Loomis Todd, who had helped launch Dickinson's poems in the 1890s, published *Emily Dickinson, A Revelation*. The book portrayed a bold, passionate woman, unfamiliar to readers who were ensnared in the myth of a virginal shut-in and obsessed by stories of the poet's lost love and fascination with death. Bingham's book received little public attention, despite its disclosure that among the 1,789 poems the poet left behind lurked drafts and copies of her passionate letters to Lord. Many letters were censored—by whom, we don't know. Yet they disclose the candor, courage, and eroticism of a mutual love between a private woman in her late forties and a public man eighteen years older, who had known her since her childhood.

The Heart Has Many Doors is populated by family, friends, neighbors, and servants from Emily Dickinson's and Otis Phillips Lord's households. Because these characters act according to the requirements of fiction, they behave and misbehave in ways that may amuse some readers and appall others.

I accept responsibility for the liberties I've taken, such as giving the judge a tattoo, taking Emily on a secret journey to Salem, inventing several frisky love letters, and allowing the judge and the poet a memorable summer afternoon in a meadow.

At the heart of this narrative lie many of the poet's poems and letters, as well as details of her time and home in nineteenth-century New England. Readers of Dickinson often fashion their own Emily out of both verifiable material and the silken threads that ensnare the heart. I have done the same. A few years ago, when I once more put my ear to Emily Dickinson's writings, I heard the whispers, music, wild talk, wit, hilarity, fury, and tenderness that lie within the life of these characters. Yet I know it is a life I imagined for them. Story outruns certainty.

Emily Dickinson had a huge heart, with room for many people. Her "last great love," Otis Phillips Lord, described by his friends as "cast in a large and heroic mould," matched her in capacity. They occupy a permanent abode in my mind. As Emily wrote of Phil, they have "boundless ways."

Susan Snively
Amherst, Massachusetts
Summer, 2014

A Note on Emily Dickinson's Spelling and Grammar

Emily Dickinson seems at times to have made her own rules in writing. Readers will find apostrophes inserting themselves where they don't belong, and other apostrophes missing where they do. Her spelling, use of capital letters, and punctuation are equally creative. These are evidence of her playfulness, inseparable from her habit of leaping across boundaries. What looks like waywardness—or mistakes by a proofreader—is a clue to the sly authority she gave herself to shape the English language to her needs.

The Heart
Has Many Doors

1.

You cannot put a Fire out
Amherst, September 1847

Her auburn hair floated about her shoulders in the early autumn light. Otis Phillips Lord stopped at the edge of the garden, to watch Emily unobserved. She dug a hole, placed the bulbs, and sprinkled light brown dust over them, then rested on her heels, lifted her head, and smiled at the sun, as though enacting a conspiracy with the element of fire. She swept back her radiant hair and bent over, her hands tamping, her slight body in communion with the earth. He noticed that she had matured physically since a few months before, her small breasts more evident under her apron and dress, her body more rounded.

Lord suddenly didn't know what to do at the sight of his friend Edward Dickinson's daughter. She was not beautiful, but her graceful movements and absorption in her work aroused his wild surprise. He took a deep breath and stepped toward her. Did Emily know that he had watched her commune with the sunlight as he took in her presence? He wanted to lift her up and whirl her around, then collapse beside her on the grass. Yet here he stood, formal and self-contained in his black gabardine suit and high collar, polished shoes and stiff, shiny hat. He tried to control his voice to speak like a plain, familiar man.

1

"Emily!"

"Mr. Lord! Welcome to my garden."

He removed his hat and walked toward her with ease, as though he visited the Dickinsons every week instead of every few months, on business for Amherst College. She held up a daffodil bulb for his approval. Phil Lord was no gardener, but admired the bulb's plump teardrop shape and papery veil.

"Court in Northampton tomorrow. My first appearance here on behalf of Essex County. Your father has promised to advise me."

He sounded young and untried, when he meant to sound confident. He had been a lawyer for over ten years, and felt embarrassed at his gawky self-consciousness. Still, he had managed to speak, and nothing terrible had happened, except that his body was flooded with uncanny heat.

He asked permission to remove his jacket, and watched Emily's large brown-gold eyes taking in every detail of his appearance—the high stock collar, his silk waistcoat, the beads of moisture on his upper lip. Amber sunlight flowed over his head and shoulders. The breezeless, vivid September day felt like mid-August.

"Might I trouble you for a glass of water? I'm—it is warmer than I thought."

When she brought him the glass, he drank the fresh well-water in large gulps, thinking he should have asked for two glasses, so that he could pour the other one over his head, silk waistcoat be damned.

"Please don't let me keep you from your work, my dear. It's a pleasure to see you make yourself just a little bit dirty."

Emily grinned, and Lord admired her white, even teeth. She gathered her hair, searched in her pocket, and fastened pins to secure the thick mass on top of her head.

"You can leave your hair as it was. I have known you since you wore red fur on your pretty skull, like a kitten's."

"Mr. Lord, you utter outrageous things, and you have a way with metaphor. 'Red fur,' indeed." With two quick moves, she removed the pins and shook out her hair. "I wish I could remember when I first met you. It seems unfair that you remember and I don't, simply because I had the disadvantage of being a baby. When I shut my eyes, I can see on my eyelids a whole world before I was born—points of light ascending a blue-black sky, floods of silver balloons, then a warm tunnel and a big shout. I wonder if the silver balloons were December snowflakes. I should ask Father if it snowed the night I was born."

Lord wondered if Edward would give Emily a sharp look for asking such a question. Dickinson had a lawyer's concern about family matters—names, births, deaths—and might remember the details of that night, December 10, 1830. A junior at Amherst College, Lord had been taking a late walk when he saw Edward Dickinson hurrying down Main Street. Dickinson knew every Amherst student, their names and backgrounds. When he slipped on the ice, the younger man rushed to help him. "My wife is in labor," Dickinson panted, as he ran up the steps into the house.

Lord wanted to tell Emily that he had stood across Main Street on the snowy night she was born, listening until past midnight. When he heard the cry of a baby, he retreated to his dormitory on freezing feet. He began to speak, then thought better of it. If he told her about that night, the story would no longer be his to guard until the perfect moment when they could marvel together at the celestial machinery of winter stars that had brought her into his life.

For other reasons, that disclosure would be painful. After his wife's recent miscarriage, talking about newborn babies would upset him. He would ponder that sorrow in his heart alone.

Emily held out her hand, sensing a heaviness in his thoughts. He extended his large palm, inviting her to place her hand in his, like two spoons or shells. He had done this a few years ago, when Emily, proud of her new piano, had played and sung for him, and he praised her clear, musical voice.

"Your hand fits into mine exactly. A happy discovery. If we have past lives, you may have been busy leading your own life during those years I was growing into whoever I am and you were preparing to come to earth as Emily Dickinson. As your elder I'm entitled to pay you certain compliments, even if they make you feel shy. But I'd like to know what on earth you are sprinkling on those bulbs. See, you have left traces of it on me."

Emily plucked a palm-sized leaf from one of her mother's fig trees and delicately wiped his hand. He closed his eyes, feeling her touch work around his palm and fingers.

"I call it Dust of Gnome. It's my own secret recipe." She held out her fingers for him to sniff. Spices, tobacco, guano.

"You trap gnomes and grind them to powder?"

"Of course. I may be a little pale thing, but I, Emily Dickinson, am capable of all kinds of mayhem."

Lord knelt beside her on the old quilt. Wanting to hear more, he hoped Emily had committed some unruly act that would require his secret legal advice. What could it be, he wondered. He checked his own list—drink, raucous behavior, other forms of young male sport—and crossed them off. Not proper subjects.

"When I visit the Northampton court tomorrow, I'll keep an eye out for unsolved crimes that might have your name on them." He raised and lowered his eyebrows like a stage villain. Perhaps Emily could come to court and watch him perform. Would her father approve?

"Father will be pleased at your powers of detection. But tell me the truth. Wouldn't you rather just skip court to stay here and play in the dirt with me?"

He glanced over her shoulder in case Edward Dickinson was nearby. *Yes.* He channeled his mischievous thought into a grin.

He reached out and took a strand of Emily's hair between his fingers. Electricity crackled under his well-manicured nails and traveled up his arm. "You've always told me that spring was your favorite season in Amherst."

"So it is. Busy, hopeful, full of yellow, pink, white, and lavender surprises. Every day is newer and younger."

"When I watch you in your garden on this glorious day, I think that your true season is autumn, as in this strand of hair, with all the autumn colors in it: red, brown, gold. In that brown dress, even with your dusty apron, you fit into the landscape like a late summer bird."

She studied his fingers. "You have beautiful hands."

So he'd been told by his wife Elizabeth, and once, memorably, by his naughty, plump cousin Lucy. He suppressed a vision of his hands gathering Emily to him, holding her face, reading her, tasting her particular flavors.

He tried to transform his desire into avuncular instructiveness. "Emily, now is the moment when we must make a decision about something. In a few weeks you will go off to Mt. Holyoke Female Seminary, and after that you will be a young lady in fact, if not always in manners. That, by the way, is a compliment."

He watched a wispy cloud pass over her face, her anxious look.

5

"To the decision, please, unless you want to see me faint with fright."

"You are your father's daughter, and you will not faint with fright, at least not around me. I have known you all your life, and I plan to know you for the rest of it, if I am lucky. So, to my request, I would like you to call me Phil. You may call me Mr. Lord in front of the ancients, but we must be proper and equal friends, or not at all."

"*Not at all?* How could we not be friends? And what does 'proper' mean? Are we supposed to speak in Latin and bow when we meet each other?"

When he saw Emily's eyes fill and her small chin quiver, he felt guilty and bumbling. He often chided himself for using too-strong language to make his point. He reminded himself once more that he was a grown-up: married, committed, responsible. His wife's miscarriage last March had been his loss, too.

He shook his head. "Of course I'll keep calling you Emily. Hear me out, because I'm feeling inadequate to what I want to say. I think we are closer in age than the calendar indicates. There are people on earth called 'old souls,' not old but wise. While I may aspire to be one, you already are."

His heart lurched as Emily brushed her cheeks with the back of her hand, then plucked hairpins from her apron pocket and swiftly coiled her hair into a Grecian knot, snug against her nape.

"I thought I was used to seeing women manage their hair, but you could perform that trick for me every day of my life, and I'd never tire of it."

She turned her changeable eyes on him. "Now you have made me forget my next sentence."

"I can wait."

"My father calls you Otis. And your middle name is 'Phillips,' as I suppose you know by now."

He chuckled. "Yes, Elizabeth also calls me Otis, as she has done since we were children growing up in Ipswich. 'Phillips' would be a bit odd, don't you think? As if I had two heads. Even though it's a family name."

"Who calls you Phil?" She resumed her work in the dirt.

"I was Phil as a schoolboy, and for a time at Amherst College. But I'm not trying to go backwards in time, and I wouldn't be a schoolboy again for hard cash. I want to hear a different name from you than from others."

It was as close as he could come to telling Emily that he had a private bower for her in himself, where he could visit her without anyone knowing. If she discovered the bower, he would hand her the key. But such a discovery would take years, and in the meantime, anything might happen. She was poised at the beginning of her womanhood, as he was poised to advance his career in law and politics.

She laid her hand on his arm. No gnome-dust could conceal the elegance of her long narrow fingers.

"I'll call you Phil, then. At least until I stop being a young lady, and become something else. *Phil, Phil.* That name trips off my tongue, and makes me happy. And lucky, too—calling you by a secret name. By the time I grow up, I may have one too. I hope it's as wild as yours is proper."

He smiled, thinking of some wild names for women—all French or Italian. *Celeste. Belladonna.* "I'll wait to see what you become, Emily. Whatever it is, you will always be—you will always interest me."

She stood up and shook out her apron. He held out his hand, and she helped him to his feet. He buttoned his black coat closely about himself.

"Do you think we should sign this new agreement into law, Counsellor—Phil? Or do we make our own law without needing to engrave it somewhere official?"

"I think that we need not answer this question, or even ask it. Some things stand outside the law. I have long known that. It makes me nervous, but I have to put my faith in law, since that's what I've chosen to do with my life."

Caught again, he thought. Blundering into a human truth that defied reason and judgment, and turned even an innocent-seeming conversation dangerous.

She gave him a triumphant smile, looking as though she'd beaten him at chess. Or perhaps it was just her play-acting. She was the most dramatic female he had ever known, and had a way of leaping across boundaries with unexpected words and lightning wit.

"Surely, Phil Lord, you have nothing to fear from our compact with each other, however interesting I may become."

Her eyes held his with such intensity, he feared that if someone witnessed this moment, he would have to explain himself to the local magistrates. Used to the rules of reasoned argument, he felt helpless in the glance of this girl who was no longer a child.

What age was Emily? No age, and every age.

He almost feared to see her again, and to come closer to the point where he would simply reach out and claim her, whatever the consequences. He felt the imaginary key to the private bower, alive in his pocket.

Edward Dickinson approached them across the lawn, carrying two bridles and a pair of boots. He wore the air of a man released from work and eager for exercise. He had changed into riding gear, which always made Emily's tall father look taller.

"Otis! Let's ride for an hour before supper. These boots ought to fit you. If we're late, the women won't mind, will they, Emily?"

He watched her smile up at her father.

"I hope you won't be too late, Father. I've made a fine berry tart for dessert, and I expect compliments and requests for second helpings."

Emily curtseyed to Phil Lord, and he winked. Edward led him toward the barn.

As she watched the men ride off down West Street, Emily thought how handsomely they rode, with an easy confidence that made her heart beat faster. Men like Phil and Father were so lucky and free. She would have liked to go with them, but she would have to ride sidesaddle as girls did, when she wanted instead to press her knees into the horse's warm sides. When she asked Father to show her how, he said that females simply did not ride like that, it wasn't proper. Her tomboyish friend Helen Fiske had told her that riding astride was thought to cause damage to women's lady-parts, as she called them, although Helen didn't believe it, because men had more obvious parts in that region than women did, and yet they rode all the time. Emily had amused herself for days with this valuable bit of information.

Through the parlor window flapped the notes of piano-scales, heavy and thick. It was her sister Vinnie's hour to practice, unwelcome to both player and listener. She'd told Vinnie she should give up the lessons and spare the household, and her sister agreed. But Father wanted Vinnie to continue the discipline. Restless, her mind on men and horses, Emily pushed away the thought that her mother might need her in the kitchen to peel carrots and turnips.

9

She opened the barn door and edged inside. A few golden motes of sawdust rose and scattered in flakes of light. Besides the two sleek horses Father and Phil were riding, the Dickinsons had a black and white pony named Folly, whom Austin sometimes rode. But her brother had grown such long legs that he claimed to feel ridiculous when he rode Folly. Emily felt sorry for the pony.

She wanted to chase something—not a person or an animal, perhaps the air itself. To speed forward, not look back, and let the road-dust fall on her, wherever it might.

"Folly, would you like to help me? I can help you, too."

A snuffle, two warm brown eyes.

Folly whickered as Emily bridled her and led her out of the barn. She put a flat saddle on the pony and climbed on the mounting stool. True to her promise to herself, she gathered her brown skirt into a bundle and positioned herself astride, then set forth, amazed that no one from the house had witnessed her escape. Emily lifted her knees and pressed them inward, to feel the pony's muscles moving underneath her. The sensation of being one with Folly made Emily almost shriek with joy.

In two weeks, she would be at Mt. Holyoke Female Seminary: proper, confined, on the way to being an educated woman. But today she was a reckless young creature. She had talked with Phil Lord as she had never talked with anyone, male or female. He'd played with her hair, held her hand, looked into her face with an ardent candor she now believed she understood. It was frightening and glorious.

Emily clucked to Folly and gave her a gentle kick, until the pony picked up her hooves and cantered down the Sunderland Road.

"Think of it, Folly," she sang to the pony. "We are now *outside the law!*"

2.

The Judge is like the Owl
Amherst, March – July 1862

March 22

P hil stood between Austin and Emily, watching Frazar Stearns's funeral procession move past the town common. The drum tattoo, a noise both sharp and flat, beat out a numbing agony. *Tap, tap, tap-tap. R-r-r-r-, tap, tap, tap-tap.*

The war was not going well for the North. Even in Amherst, hundreds of miles from the battlefront, a feverish patriotism masked a fear that the fighting could sweep northward, and people would have to run to Canada, or the sea. Edward Dickinson rallied citizens to help Massachusetts fill its quota of soldiers, an effort that hoarsened his voice and brought visitors to the front door at all hours. The sound of drums from the nearby town common made Emily grind her teeth. Vinnie and Mother retreated into the kitchen or the barn. Emily wrote her cousins Loo and Fanny Norcross that she could feel sorrow everywhere, in the shops and streets, even the wind in the trees.

And now this after-horror, far worse than the death of her cousin Francis Dickinson, the first of Amherst's war dead. Frazar Stearns, twenty-one years old, beloved by everybody in town, killed in a place nobody in Amherst had ever heard of: New Bern, North Carolina. In a swamp! Emily wanted to stamp her feet and shout.

In her unbecoming gray dress, Emily looked paler than ever. Her gloved hands clenched and unclenched as her head swayed in time with the drums. She had been to many funerals, Phil knew, but this was different: the rows of Frazar's Amherst classmates in formation on either side of the catafalque, the closed coffin covered with a pall of white flowers. She reached over him to grasp Austin's hand, but her brother drew it away as he reached for his handkerchief. Phil put his arm around her shoulders.

"Look at how young they are. Not much older than children," Emily whispered, just as the prayers began.

He heard Austin mutter, "Frazar is murdered. Murdered," his voice full of angry tears.

War is a crime, a necessary crime, Phil thought. By what violent means is our nation preserved: prisons, armies, the minié ball that knocked out Frazar's heart.

Phil recalled Edward Dickinson's eloquent words, written in 1855, after he'd lost his seat in Congress, words that had made him proud to have Edward as a friend: *"By the help of Almighty God, not another inch of our soil heretofore consecrated to freedom, shall hereafter be polluted by the advancing tread of slavery."* He wondered if Edward had repeated them in church or at the dinner table, his dark eyes intense.

Later, when Emily served Phil tea in the parlor, she put a drop of brandy in it, and dared to do the same with her own. She opened the velvet drapes and looked next door at Austin's house. No sign of Sue or their little boy Ned.

12

"The sun has gone into hiding, or mourning. It almost seems as though winter has set in again, or told the spring to retreat. The leaves are too shy or ashamed to unfurl."

"You are a barometer, and you know New England weather."

She sighed into her half-full cup, then recited part of a poem:

"Great Clouds – like Ushers – leaning –
Creation – looking on –"

Phil raised his eyebrows. He wanted to hear more, but Emily looked shaky.

"Austin is a wreck," she said. "Colonel Clark, whom Frazar served, is broken down as well. His father Reverend Stearns is suffering. They blame themselves for letting him enlist, but he was so eager to be of use, so determined to do good. I can't get his ruddy face out of my mind, or his blue eyes, or his freckled forehead, or the way he looked in his uniform when he came by the house to show us, and offer Austin a proud salute."

"A true son of the Republic. Idealistic, eager. What would he have done, I wonder, if he hadn't been so intent on soldiering?"

"Married his sweetheart, Ella. Become a missionary, I think." She tried not to slosh her quivering tea. "Austin saw Frazar in his coffin. Dried blood stained the front of his uniform and his strict gray face. The doctors wouldn't let his father see him. Austin wishes now that he had joined up, and says it's not too late. Sue and Mother are frantic for him to procure a substitute."

"I shall have to talk some sense into him. He is now a young father, too busy and not always robust. Austin shouldn't

13

be a soldier." Phil rose and paced around the parlor, then sat down beside her. His large eyes looked so serious that she felt alarm.

"Emily, I will tell you something that I want you to promise not to tell another soul. I am thinking of enlisting in the Army myself. Despite what I said about Austin, and despite what I know to be true about war, I think I could be of use. At the very least, they could use my voice as a trumpet in the military band."

When she dropped her teacup and saucer on the carpet, tea soaked into the flower-pattern. The cup's rim broke, as if she had bitten a slice from it, and the saucer cracked. When she bent down to mop up the spill, she felt her face redden and her eyes fill with panicky tears. She used the tea-stained napkin to wipe her eyes and dab at her nose.

"Please don't say things like that to me, Phil, even in jest. I can't bear it." Emily wanted to lie down on the carpet and howl.

He took the broken cup and saucer and wrapped them in his napkin. Then he gently helped her onto the sofa, and held her face up to his own. "I am not in jest, dear. I am forty-nine years old, and in good fit. I am rarely ill and seem to need little sleep. More to the point, I am feeling useless on the bench. The same old stupid mischief, week after week, when this country is heading into a bloody chasm. How can I sit by and watch?"

"Does your wife agree with you?"

A weary look, a sigh. He hadn't expected her question. "Elizabeth respects my feelings on the matter. But of course she does not agree. And I can't say to her that since I am not . . . the father of children, my life would be less of a sacrifice than a younger man's life. It would cause her pain."

She grasped his sleeve. "When would you—have to go?"

"I don't know. Arrangements would have to be made for my replacement in the Salem court, and that could take months, even a year."

"I doubt if you could be replaced, Phil."

Hearing her father's voice in the hallway, Emily started to gather up the tea things.

"Please," she began, and held her hand up. "Just, please."

"Let us put this subject aside, and think of Frazar."

She hung her head. The deluge was almost upon her. "Frazar is complete, now. Bit by bit"—she paused to swallow hard—"we have to restore him to the young man we loved, not a ruined body in a box."

As the north parlor door opened, she hurried out the south door, hiding her face from her father.

July 10 – 11

The Dickinson garden boiled with visitors. In white dresses with lacy sleeves, Emily and Vinnie moved among the guests, carrying trays of lemonade and sherry, ginger cakes and cucumber sandwiches. The Amherst College Commencement party, an annual event almost as important as Thanksgiving, was hard on the Dickinson women and their servants. This year marked the fortieth Commencement of the college that Emily's grandfather had helped to found, and that her father had served for decades.

She couldn't remember what hour she and Vinnie had climbed from bed, washed up, and hurried to the kitchen. Perhaps she hadn't gone to bed at all, but spent the night grating ginger and creaming the butter and sugar. Her tray of treats was heavy, the smell of the sherry too rich. The garden buzzed in the warm day. Carlo the dog lumbered

15

among the guests, sniffing the hems of lavish, bell-shaped skirts. Emily felt hot and dizzy.

"Vinnie—could you help me?" Her sister, trying to catch Reverend Henry Ward Beecher's attention, didn't hear her. Emily thumped her teetering tray onto a garden bench. Suddenly Phil Lord was beside her, grasping her elbow. He seized a glass of sherry that threatened to tip over.

"Sit down here, this minute. You mustn't sacrifice yourself to Commencement. It is only a party with too many speeches. Would you like a little sherry?"

Emily shook her head and said, "Lemonade. Sherry might make me behave disgracefully."

"Is that a threat or a promise?" he asked in his rogue's whisper.

Either a threat or a promise would give me a thrill, she thought. After a few sips of lemonade, she felt better.

Phil saw Emily's mother walking away from the garden with Elizabeth and Sue Dickinson, who was pushing her one-year-old boy in a carriage down the path between the Homestead and the Evergreens. He turned to Emily and put his hand on her shoulder.

She spoke in a low voice. "I just need a few minutes before I resume my duties. I'm not used to making so much small talk or trying to remember which of these grandly dressed ladies is Mrs. Doctor Professor So-and-So. My brains have tangled up."

She didn't want him to leave her side until she gave him the piece of paper she'd tucked in her pocket. If she couldn't contrive little plots for herself, reading the woeful daily news would strain her to breaking.

Phil surveyed the company. "I've been to dozens of Commencements, but this year's crowd is larger than ever. It's the war, more than the college's anniversary. People don't know when they'll see each other again. Even the sky is warning us about the future." He pointed up.

Emily followed his glance and shivered in spite of the warm day. "That is one of the strangest clouds I've ever seen—a large loose rectangle with several protruding hooks. Look how it descends slowly, then rises and moves off, changing its mind, or circling around waiting for a chance to pounce." It was like the war itself, she thought: sky and earth tangled in conflict, no certain God to make peace among the mortal factions.

"You always describe ordinary things in unforgettable ways. I think you're a secret animist, and believe that everything has life, even stones and clouds."

She couldn't help but smile at Phil's speaking the truth about her private religion.

Phil did not mention again his plan to enlist, nor would she bring up the subject, which kept her awake at night. She wanted to persuade him that he was needed in court, not in the cavalry, although it would be daunting to argue with one of the Commonwealth's most impressive arguers. Meanwhile, the rumor of the judge's intention to resign traveled among lawyers and judges, appeared in the newspapers, and sparked talk about probable replacements.

"An appalling array of political hacks," Father had sniffed at the dinner table, when he read the Springfield *Republican* to the family. "Trust me, this will not happen. Otis is a romantic, but he has a reputation for common sense."

The cloud with hooks moved eastward, and the afternoon sun shed a moist brightness on the lawn. Visitors gathered in chairs under the trees. Emily cast her mind back over the events of the long day. In their Commencement speeches, the famed minister Henry Ward Beecher had surpassed Lord in metaphor, even in theatrics, displaying a white owl on the lectern, shot and stuffed when he'd been an Amherst College student. During the speech, filled with storms from the Book of Revelations, Emily almost expected the owl to rouse itself and take off into the heavens. Beecher's words could make thunder visible and give lightning its own rapturous music. Lord's speech, by contrast, praised traditional institutions and argued for a return to past greatness. His audience offered only tepid applause. She felt an embarrassed sympathy for him and Father, moving with gingerly dignity around the wreckage of the Whig Party. She sipped her lemonade and tried to think of a tactful compliment.

"There you go, reading my mind again. My speech was not right for this ceremony. I would not have made a good man of the cloth, and my eloquence, such as it is, sounds better in the paneled courtroom than anywhere else. I should have known better than to out-glib Beecher." He sighed. "It is always instructive to know that power has limits."

"Mr. Beecher obviously believes that the power of his words can keep back the raging evils. You are more honest, Phil. We do what we can, and tell the truth." He gave her a look of grateful surprise, and she went on, "Mr. Beecher is moved by his own eloquence. My experience sitting on a hard seat in church, waiting to be knocked silly by a blast from a long-dead prophet, makes me resist him."

Phil was glad that he could respond to humor after the difficult morning. Emily nudged his arm and nodded toward the minister, surrounded by admirers. Vinnie was still trying to edge up to him, and the sight amused Emily, who knew her sister would want Beecher to notice her. Of course, since Vinnie was pretty, he would do so, and she'd talk about it all week. Emily did not find the great preacher attractive. He had the kind of face that lost its youthful refinement to a heavy sensuality. He touched women as he talked to them—stroking a hand or a shoulder, raising their fingers to his lips. Phil often touched her hands or wrists or shoulders, even her hair. But if Beecher had tried the same thing, she would have recoiled.

"How you put things often amazes me. I do hope you write down your wild remarks."

Phil fingered her sleeve, and she gave him a slow, cat-like blink. She liked to hold his coat for him, and sometimes imagined running her fingers through his brown-gray curls.

Emily's father always brought out his best drink for the annual Commencement party. Phil helped himself to another sherry. "I'll be fifty years old tomorrow. Think of it! One foot dangling over the abyss." He loved hyperbole as much as she did.

"Judge Owl, you are filled with nonsense." Teasing him revived her energy.

"What did you just call me? Judge Owl?"

When he gave her a piercing glance, Emily thought Phil looked more like an owl than ever. She drew forth the poem from her pocket.

"Please read it to me, Emily, if you dare."

The Judge is like the Owl –
I've heard my father tell –
And Owls do build in Oaks –
So here's an Amber Sill –

That slanted in my Path –
When going to the Barn –
And if it serve You for a House –
Itself is not in vain –

About the price – 'tis small –
I only ask a Tune
At Midnight – Let the Owl select
His favorite Refrain.

19

"'Amber sill. Midnight. Favorite refrain.'" He shook his head. "I'll study it for deeper meanings."

He liked the way she rhymed "vain," and "tune." The poem fashioned an intricate landscape with the Dickinsons' oak tree, the barn, and the house. Familiar things, given a quirky playfulness. But there was more to the poem than playfulness, and it intrigued him.

She waited to hear him speak about deeper meanings.

"I don't want to patronize you, of all people. I'd gladly read more of your poetry. It's not like anything I've ever read, but you know how old-fashioned I am. Shakespeare, and more Shakespeare."

She told him about her habit of taking her Shakespeare book up to the cupola, where she read passages aloud to the trees and hills.

"I wonder if both of us could fit into that cupola. We could read scenes together, and startle the passersby. You could play Romeo, and I could play Juliet. Ah, at last, a smile from you, just for me. I like owls, and I'm proud to be in your poem."

If she showed Phil her poems, she would have to select carefully, concealing loss and desire in favor of puzzles, wry philosophy, snakes, deer, snow. She would copy the poems and give them to him, then endure the exquisite nervousness of waiting for his response.

He squeezed her hand quickly. His face wore his Honored Wife Nearby expression.

Looking over his shoulder, she saw that they were about to be interrupted. "I must resume my role as hostess, or whatever I am." She picked up the tray, a lighter burden than before.

Elizabeth Lord and Emily's mother, in pastel silk dresses, walked toward them, their wide skirts swaying above their hoops and crinolines. Phil folded her poem into his pocket, and she winked, a wren daring an owl to breach her territory.

*

He hears the church bells striking twelve. Now it is July 11. Sleep is a country for the young. His legs twitch. Time for a stroll. He pulls on his clothes. When he kisses Elizabeth's long braid and tiptoes out, she doesn't stir.

Main Street is quiet, except for some brawly noise from the campus. Even after the exhausting day, Phil doesn't feel tired. He adjusts his eyes to midnight, as he does in Salem on his late-night walks past the courthouse, full of plots and dramas. Amherst exudes the odors of grass, horse-manure, and fertile valley soil—as welcome now as when he was a young man who debated his ambitious classmates by day and walked or read by night. When he walks past the Evergreens, he notices a light in the library window—Austin, examining a recent purchase for his art collection. He walks on toward the Homestead, with the owl poem brooding in his pocket.

Emily can be ardent, coy, irreverent, mystifying. In conversation she capers around like a fencer, then thrusts at him with a joke or metaphor. Is her invitation to sing at midnight a code for some outlaw act? He pauses to look up at her dark window. He could go back to the hotel, but a magnetic force urges him on.

Fifteen years before, he and Emily had made their compact. So far, she had never slipped and called him "Phil" in front of others. Names were masks for emotions, kept like prize horses in separate stalls. He thought of that afternoon, when he had ridden out with Edward toward Sunderland. He'd learned later from Austin that Emily had been punished for her escapade with Folly. Excluded from the dinner table, she'd spent several hours in the barn, grooming the pony and Edward's two noble horses. He thought that Emily preferred this punishment to making awkward conversation under her father's glaring eye. The berry tart, he remembered, had been delicious. He'd scribbled a note to Emily—one word, "Excellent"—and asked Vinnie to take it upstairs.

Now Phil's hair is turning gray, and he is a judge, known all over Massachusetts for his brilliant arguments and unforgettable voice. He and Elizabeth have never, after all, had living children. Settled, busy, and content, he holds his fantasies close. But every now and then, the imagined bower springs up before him, a green mossy place, secreted in familiar woods. Elizabeth often teases him about his daydreaming over breakfast, or late at night in front of the fire, an unread book in his hands.

He is indeed an owl, curious to see what happens next. Walking into the garden east of the barn, he smells lilies, roses, and hemlock. Emily sits on the bench. She seems fashioned out of light and air, dusk and flesh.

"Welcome to midnight, Judge Lord. It is my best hour."

"I hope you don't mind."

"Mind?"

The varied tones of her voice are too tightly braided to unravel. She sounds nervous, expectant, even seductive.

"My accepting your invitation. I found myself walking at midnight. A restive sleeper, I'm afraid. And my legs twitch, so up I get."

A corner of her mouth curls up in a naughty smile. Perhaps she'd like to watch his legs twitch.

"I don't issue invitations unless I mean them. But the question is, can you pay the price?"

"For having—this restlessness? I have no choice."

22

"No. A Tune at Midnight. Your 'favorite refrain.'"

He is turning back into an awkward eighteen-year-old, his age when she was born.

"First, please, and remember I am a jurist, not a poet— what is the Amber Sill?"

"Owls build in oaks. An oak branch. Or a slant of light on the barn roof. Owls inhabit unexpected places."

"Are those the amber sill?"

"You are speaking like a jurist, who likes things definite. And I like doors to stand ajar."

This slim fantastic woman continually metamorphoses into different versions of herself: shy daughter, restless spirit, mischief-maker, sensualist. Her face appears moonstruck in the near dark, and her voice is husky, as if she has drunk a cup of fog. "You are a man of property, are you not?"

This is a lawyer's trick from Emily, the daughter and sister of lawyers. The poem specifies a legal arrangement, combining hospitality and allure.

"And I'm being offered more property."

Her invitation seems to come from a desire to provoke him. He likes the friction that scampers up his spine and down to the root of his body.

"And the price is a tune. Emily, I am no singer, although I can carry a tune. I'm pleased that you associate me with wisdom."

But if I were truly wise, he thought, I would not be sitting in the dark with you when I should be tucked up in bed next to my wife.

"Owls need perches for singing, whatever song they choose." She sounds pleased with her powers of observation.

She tries to restrain her leaping heartbeats under her thin shift and dimity dress. The windows of the house behind them are dark. Father has the gift of swimming in a deep sleep, not emerging from the waters until dawn.

"Emily, I don't want to sing a hymn. Have pity on an old man, and pick something else."

She lays a hand on his sleeve. Frock coat. Shirt underneath. Then skin, blood, nerves, bone. Himself. "You are only as old as your wisdom. And the tune is whatever you fancy."

He takes hold of her wrist, where her pulse is thrumming. They sit in a charged silence. The town is quiet. No animals prowl the grounds or snuffle in their stalls, no aimless drunks weave up the street, not a bird or a breath of wind stirs in the trees. In a few hours, the dew will fall, the birds begin their resistless chorus.

"I choose Stephen Foster. You know him?"

"He's like Poe. Dead, but alive. Inescapable."

"Do you know 'Hard Times Come Again No More'?"

She carries the notes in her ear, as she carries poems in her pocket.

They begin, his voice trolling along the bass part, her treble fluttery, then true.

While we seek mirth and beauty and music light and gay,
There are frail forms fainting at the door.
Though their voices are silent, their pleading looks will say
Oh! Hard times come again no more . . . .

"Do the poor sing about the poor, I wonder?"

"You knew to prolong the '*Oh.*' I wonder how often you've sung this song. And in what company." The question is one of dozens she has about his life, his youth, courtship, marriage, losses, and triumphs.

24

"My wife at our piano. It's a good song for judges. To '*pause in life's pleasures and count its many tears.*' There's nothing about the law in it, only suffering. I find it instructive. And you?"

"I've played it for Father, and sung it by myself in the woods and the garden."

"You have a fine voice," they say at the same time.

Underneath their voices, tambourine, piano, flute, wind, drum, lightning. Underneath their feet, the edge of the earth.

"One of us is a liar."

"Only one?"

"I never lie."

They rise from the bench as if summoned by a chorus master. Phil puts his finger under her small chin. "You have blessed my fiftieth birthday, Emily Dickinson."

The crowd musters in her heart. Now and only now, and perhaps forever, she will get her wish. "I'll stand here quietly, and you will lean down and kiss me. And then you must go."

How has he resisted her voice, all these years? A trail of sweet smoke, luring him further into the darkness.

She lifts her face, he moves his hands to her waist, gathers her lips in his, releases her.

It will take them a long time to come to terms with this moment.

3.

A Secret Told
Amherst, Boston, Cambridge,
February – June 1864

Amherst, February 1864

6 February, 1864

Dear Phil,

There are things you need to know about me. My work is to love, and to sing, and to tell the truth. But I have a Fear, long harbored, that I can no longer keep to myself. My Eyes are not what they should be. I am often in pain, which I won't describe here. Vinnie asks that I seek help. You are the first Candidate, Father a close second. I am electing you. You have known me long enough to understand why decorum eludes my grasp.

If you stood before me I would show you what my eyes are like, unless we were in the dark together, where I would rather be, seeking safety and comfort. The Doctors nearby are insufficient, and make me nervous. If you know of a Doctor for Eyes, please write Vinnie and tell her. She is better at negotiating with Father than I am, although I don't mean to call my Sire untrustworthy.

My shyness is my affliction.

I pray that you can read the White Spaces, for in them lie all my Courage and all my Hope.
And more besides.

Emily

*

Sunday 14 February, 1864

My Dear Emily,

I am worried about your eyes.

Vinnie wrote me that you avoid the sunlight and often suffer headaches. You must concentrate on getting better, and I must concentrate on helping you do so. That is part of the pact we have made between us. You would do the same for me if I asked.

I have made enquiries. Dr. Henry Willard Williams is a noted ophthalmologist and professor at Harvard. He has offices in Boston, on Arlington St. I shall write him, and copy my request to your Father, who will make all the arrangements, with my help, if need be.

Dr. Williams is to be trusted. His sisters live in Salem, and are talented artists. He would be especially sympathetic to you.

The Courts are full of mayhem, more than usual. Runaway soldiers, drunks, divorce-seekers, men overcome by anger and fear. At times even judges are helpless. Should you be required to stay for a time in Boston, I pray that you find a safe and quiet harbor. Please tell me what I can do.

It is apparent that I am going to be a jurist for the duration, since no suitable replacement agreed to take the job. I had a few regretful days about not becoming a military man, but I believe it is for the best.

    Be brave, Emily, and if need be, choose your sight over your writing for a time. Your eyes need cherishing. Include me, please, in the list of those who cherish you with all their heart.

As ever,
Phil Lord

*

Boston, April 1864

W hen she arrived at Dr. Henry Willard Williams's office, Emily wore a shawl and a deep bonnet. The train trip from Palmer had nearly undone her: stares, pain, and the fear of the doctor's probing instruments. Shortly after Worcester, Emily dropped to sleep on Vinnie's shoulder, and dreamed that Phil met them at the North Station, then carried her in his arms up to the doctor's office. Instead, she was lifted off the train steps by a large red-faced porter whose breath smelled of beer and onions.

    In the station's waiting room, a tearful Vinnie surrendered her sister to their cousins Loo and Fanny Norcross. For the next few months, Emily would live with them in a Cambridge boarding house. She wondered how she could manage to write. She would miss the spring and summer in Amherst, and her beloved Carlo. At home, green wheat was pushing up through the dry blond stalks, tulips nosing among the daffodils, early peas perfecting themselves in their infantine pods. The most beautiful time of year in Amherst, and she had to dwell in a strange country for an indeterminate time. She imagined her big dog wandering in the meadow, then settling at the foot of her bed, patient and confused in her absence.

28

In Dr. Williams's offices, a small reception room held two deep leather chairs, a couch, and a small table with a stack of folded handkerchiefs. Emily was relieved to find no other patients there. While they waited, Loo massaged her stiff shoulders and tried to distract her with views of the unfinished Public Garden across the street.

The doctor was a large man with a long face like a handsome mule, and huge hands.

After the necessary fact-taking, he fitted her head into a frame, lit a lamp, then trained the ophthalmoscope on her eyes. His fingers, gentle and capable, helped her lift her eyelids. The bright light hurt her, and she tried to keep from whimpering as she held her head still.

"What do you do with your eyes, Miss Dickinson, except the plain act of seeing?"

"Why do you ask, Dr. Williams?"

"Only because I always ask."

"I read. And I write."

"Letters?"

"Yes," her slow reply. "And poems."

"Ah, poems."

She could tell he was being tactful. Heat swept up the back of her neck and into her scalp. If this man was going to be in charge of her sight, she wanted him to know who she was. The eminent ophthalmologist was engaging in his life's work, with her eyes as an experiment. Emily would not hide her life's work from him.

"I could recite you a poem, if you would like to know what I do."

"Yes, please."

His voice held forbearance.

"They dropped like Flakes —
They dropped like stars —
Like Petals from a Rose —
When suddenly across the June
A Wind with fingers — goes —

They perished in the seamless Grass —
No eye could find the place —
But God can summon every face
On his Repealless — List."

"Please turn your eyes toward the light, Miss Dickinson."

She vowed never again to speak her poems to strangers.

Dr. Williams peered into the machine and wrote in his notebook. Then he put a finger under her chin and turned her face toward him. She tried not to think of Phil Lord in the garden, the soft spice of his kiss. She would think instead of the war, and young Frazar Stearns, Austin weeping, and the million villages of the dead.

"You are a poet."

His matter-of-fact voice aroused her gratitude.

"You write every day?"

"Yes."

"And in what medium?"

"Pen and ink. Sometimes pencil. On the backs of letters, the margins of newspapers, whatever scrap I can find."

"Thrifty daughter of New England."

She felt herself bristle. "I need to be ready to write at a moment's notice. My life is full of interruptions."

Henry Willard Williams took note of her dignified, soft voice.

"Miss Dickinson, your eyes are seriously troubled, as I think you know."

"Yes. I have known for some time."

"I would not have you give up writing poems such as the one you recited. If you have other such treasures, a mere doctor would be wrong to advise you to bury them."

Emily couldn't speak. She ordered the tears back into her skull.

"If you want a writer's life, then I must do everything in my power to heal your eyes. It will not be easy. But I know from my sisters how art claims the artist's time and energy, as it must."

He wore a doctor's impassive expression, but his eyes were gentle.

"Please tell me the truth, Dr. Williams. The friend who commended you to my father would expect nothing less."

He adjusted the ophthalmoscope and wrote in his notebook.

"I am also originally from Salem. Judge Lord is fierce, but trustworthy. I have never dealt with him in court, but I know those who have, and they describe him as unforgettable. He and your father wrote to me in persuasive terms, about taking on your case. I suspect that in matters close to his heart, like your family, Lord has the highest standards. So I must do my best—better than my best."

Emily's heart lifted, until she felt another flash of pain.

"What will you do?"

"I'll treat you every week with aconite drops. They sting, but they'll do you good. I will also have to subject you to the glare of my machine. These methods will produce tears, but you must try to think of them as carrying away your affliction, like a river running to the sea. And Miss Dickinson, I must also ask you to change your habits."

Dr. Williams's mutton-chop whiskers seemed to stand out from his jaws as he blotted her wet face with a soft cloth.

"What habits?"

"It burdens me to say this, but reading and writing offer temporary pleasures that will come to torment you. Your eyes are suffering from enormous strain brought on by overuse. The strain has aggravated an earlier condition that arose from the mild case of consumption you had years ago. We must now try to reverse the course with calm, quiet, medicine, and darkness."

Even if the hundreds of poems she had written had made her eyes sore and dry, Emily could not un-write them. She'd sewed them into little packets, stored them in a bureau drawer, and written more poems. By now they numbered in the hundreds. If she did not write, she thought she would go mad, like a caged animal.

Emily's head and feet felt numb and cold. If only she could close her eyes forever. She remembered her case of consumption as a holiday from school, daily doses of foul-tasting fish oil, and an order from her doctor to ride horseback several times a week. The freedom to read and ride gave her life a sweet bloom. Those months when she was fifteen were among the happiest times she could remember.

As she tried to come to terms with Dr. Williams's orders, phrases from her poems and letters appeared behind her eyelids, written in scrolls of fire.

"How can I not read or write?" She gripped the arms of her chair.

"Miss Dickinson, as painful as it is, please look into my eyes. I will shut out the light to make it easier. Please hear me as your doctor expressing his care for you and the future of your vision."

The doctor pulled a chair close to her and folded her hands in his. Emily felt a deadly surge in her heart. Her pulse felt audible. She forced herself to look at him directly. Light gray eyes, not as blue as Phil's. A curiously shaped nose with a broad turned-up tip. She wondered what he looked like when he smiled, and whether, unlike Father, he still had all his original teeth.

"Your eyes will improve, with my help. But the healing requires that you give your eyes a long rest, longer than the time you spent in your mother's womb."

She imagined herself a tiny speck of life whirling around the universe in a dark red wind, waiting to find a place to grow and become herself.

"How will I live?"

"The months will pass, as they always do. You are living with your cousins, in Cambridge?"

"Louisa and Frances Norcross. They are kind and sweet. And very young. I don't want to imprison them."

"Miss Dickinson, your personal circumstances are more fortunate than others'. Some of my patients live alone, some are too far gone to recover, especially veterans of the war. Some, alas, are mad. I can treat their eyes, but not keep them from raving, drink, or terrible memories and dreams."

Self-consciousness and shame flowed over her, as the doctor returned to matters of fact.

"You can dictate letters to your cousins?"

She wandered into the bramble of her thoughts.

"I advise you to keep writing to a minimum, and use a pencil, which requires less concentration than a pen, and fewer small movements of hand and eye."

But I cannot speak my mind. How can I write to Vinnie, or Sue? Or Phil?

I'll have to contrive a special language. Trust my memory. Hope for visitors to rescue me from myself.
And use a pencil instead of a pen.

*

Cambridge, June 1864

Every morning, Loo or Fanny applied cool compresses to her eyes, and Emily wrapped a soft bandage around her head. They read to her. Reports of battles, Lincoln's speeches, and stories of lost young men from small New England towns lifted her from herself. Men and women younger than she were suffering—bereft, ill, mortally wounded.

As dusk settled on the crowded Cambridgeport streets, Emily would scratch out a few lines to Vinnie, Austin, or Sue. Sometimes she'd manage to write Phil a careful note, trying not to expect a reply. Austin wrote that the judge's crowded court term required him to stay in Boston rather than traveling the seventeen miles back to Salem. This news gave her hope that he would visit, but he never came.

One morning, a month into her ordeal, she had a caller.

Seated in a chair near the parlor window was Elizabeth Lord. Mrs. Lord rose and embraced Emily, then kissed her forehead, which she had never done before. Emily uttered the sound Carlo made when he slept and twitched at the foot of her bed.

"I could not come to Cambridge without seeing you, so that I could report to Otis. He is holding court in Boston this term."

Emily's head crowded with forbidden thoughts. Was Elizabeth staying in Boston with her husband? Her soul batted at her cage.

Mrs. Lord slowly peeled off her ecru lace summer gloves. She was dressed in light gray, which suited her gray-green eyes and pale complexion.

"Tell me about Dr. Williams. Otis and I know him, mostly by reputation. We hear that he has invented new ways to treat the eyes. If anyone can help you, he can."

Emily flinched at "if."

She described the doctor's use of the ophthalmoscope, but couldn't give more details of his examination without feeling faint. Bright morning sunlight hovered outside the curtains, a vendor with fine, dangerous wares.

She had not often talked one-to-one with Elizabeth Lord when the Lords visited Amherst. The women seemed to communicate best through music, taking turns at the parlor piano with Mendelssohn, Schubert, and Haydn. Emily feared blurting out "Phil" at the wrong moment, and had to fight her truant curiosity and desire. A garter snake of pain pushed its sharp head behind her ear.

Elizabeth asked polite questions about her life in Cambridge.

Mrs. Bangs ran a clean and proper place, but with her sight impaired, Emily's hearing grew more sensitive. Cambridge produced sounds she'd never heard in Amherst: soldiers and their brazen-voiced commanders marching down the street, songs and shouts filling the air, whinnying horses and creaking wheels from the nearby horse railway. Acrid dust blew into the windows. Once, trying to sleep, she heard a load of coal rattling into a nearby cellar. The noise made her dream of being trapped in a villa in Pompeii as ash fell from Vesuvius.

To mention these complaints would be improper and repellent.

35

"Otis and I would be happy to have you come to us in Salem, when his schedule permits, and sit beside the sea, under a shade. We also have a conservatory. I'm not as skilled a plantswoman as you are—just think of your growing jasmine in Amherst!—but I find it comforting to be among sweet quiet things."

For a moment, Emily was tempted to accept. She had never been to Salem or sat beside the sea, except in dreams. Sometimes she heard it, a low changeable voice between a whisper and a roar. She imagined Salem as a moving gallery of people from all over the world, silks and spices pouring into the hands of prosperous merchants, ordinary citizens bowing as Judge Lord passed through the streets like a royal personage.

Speak to me about your husband, she wanted to say. *What low-lifes and buffoons he is frightening in court. What he thinks of the war and the young men of Salem, eager to join up. What you thought of his wild idea to enlist, two years ago—the separation, the danger, the thought that he might not come back.*

"Otis had an amusing case the other day. A lawyer for the defense showed up in court drunk, can you imagine! When Otis was asked for a ruling, he said, 'You are drunk.' And the drunk said it was the best verdict Judge Lord had rendered yet!"

"That is a story to make me happy in the dark."

The garter snake made a quick lick behind her ear.

Elizabeth moved across the sofa to grasp her hand. Her fingers were long, cool and dry, exquisitely manicured, but with a look of suffering.

"My husband has known you since you were a baby. Long before I had the pleasure of meeting you in—when was it? 1860. I suspect that he feels a particular closeness to you. He has often said that you are more like your father than Austin is."

"I am probably too wrapped in the family to notice. But Father and I share a sense of humor, as he does with Ph— with Mr. Lord. We rejoice when Father lets it out."

Elizabeth rubbed her fingers together as if stroking lotion into them. Her knuckles appeared puffy and sore. When she lifted a fine dark eyebrow, her austere beauty wore an odd asymmetry.

Emily saw Elizabeth's mouth tighten into a smile, and her eyes turn greener with a sharp knowledge, as green eyes did. She could almost guess Elizabeth's unspoken words: *You can't fool me, so don't even try.* She remembered meeting her in 1860, when she could scarcely speak at dinner except to thank the Lords for praising her seed-cake. Mrs. Lord's serene, winsome face had surprised her. She had not changed much, but the serenity seemed frayed.

"You must miss Vinnie."

She sighed, feeling a longing for her sister. "If Vinnie and Carlo were here, I think I could bear anything. But Mother needs her at home, and Carlo would die here, without the woods or the garden."

Elizabeth squeezed her hand, but her brief touch was not comforting. "I am close to my sister Mary, too, and if I don't see her for a couple of weeks, I worry and fret." Her voice softened. "Otis remembers you and Vinnie playing in the garden, in ruffled drawers with bows. Your bows were yellow and Vinnie's were pink, I was told."

Sisters, baby clothes—the conversation had sailed into milder waters.

"I wish I remembered the underpinnings, Mrs. Lord. We must have looked rather comical."

37

"Otis and I would have loved daughters, if it had pleased God to give us any. Both our families bore rafts of sons, but daughters . . . ." Her voice trailed off.

Elizabeth's eyes filled with tears, and Emily's started to sting. There was no way she could ask about lost or unborn children.

"Mrs. Lord, I have forgotten my handkerchief. I'll go fetch it."

"Take mine, dear. I have others. And please call me Elizabeth."

She offered her a dainty lace-bordered square embroidered EWF—Elizabeth Wise Farley. The judge is like the owl, Emily almost blurted, but she is Wise.

"It's too pretty to use. Did you make it?"

"All Ipswich females made lace—some into their very old age. My sister Mary and I made a lot of pillow lace while waiting to be married."

So Elizabeth's life before marriage had its daily tedium. And now? Emily wondered what she did, with no children and her husband so busy and often absent. She mused on what the pair talked about when Phil rested his feet before the fire, a glass of good claret in his hand. The Lords, high up in Salem's elite, would host elaborate parties, like those at Austin and Sue's house, teeming with powerful, important guests. Phil knew everything about her small world, but she knew little about his mighty one. Perhaps he had flirted with the idea of soldiering because he needed to test his strength to the limit, and found his home life somewhat restricted.

I should be ashamed to be thinking this.

Elizabeth was kind, sensitive, worthy of her remarkable husband, and she apparently resented God for denying her the gift of children. Underneath layers of prickly thoughts, Emily sought an affinity with Phil's well-bred wife, who wasn't pious or perfect, however impenetrable her history.

"Otis has shown me some of your poems, dear. They are not like anything I have ever read, but I do believe you are a real poet, not a mere versifier. Did you know that Otis's father, Squire Nathaniel, wrote poetry?"

Wondering whether Phil wrote poems too, Emily's face grew warm, and the back of her neck felt sticky. If Elizabeth had read the poems she had given her husband, she had read the owl-poem, and she meant for Emily to know it—and more besides. She felt oddly suspended, as though hovering above Cambridge in a balloon.

"You love my husband, don't you?"

The gray-green eyes looked deep into her own. No sharpness, just penetrating candor.

As she thumped back to earth, Emily could scarcely breathe. Elizabeth Lord had stopped massaging her fingers and drew herself up straight, as though preparing to hear what she already knew.

"Yes. How could I not?"

She had vowed to Phil to speak the truth—a vow inseparable from her poetry. She couldn't break it now without violating her heart.

"He is so like your father. And yet not."

I never wished to wrap my arms around Father, and kiss him on the lips.

"My father never plays."

"Ah, yes. I can see why you say so." Elizabeth did not say whether her husband played, or what he played, but Emily believed she knew.

"If you love my husband, that is a joy to me."

39

Her finely cut lips turned up in a slight smile. This is one of life's duties for women, Emily thought—placing a small hook at each corner of the mouth, lifting the heart that trailed underneath.

She vowed never to disclose what happened in the garden two years ago, but forever stand outside of that memory as if it were a finely sculpted statue she could see only through a hole in a fence.

I am such a little piece of work. But I have my own work to do.

4.

So we must meet apart
Boston, Cambridge, Salem,
June 1864 – January 1866

Boston, Suffolk County Courthouse, June 1864

J udge Lord regarded the thin, long-faced man on the witness stand and felt his right knee twitch, as it always did when his suspicions were aroused. Mr. Uriel Woodcock, head of the South Boston Asylum for Girls, had a superior air and spoke in a dry, scratchy voice. Lord fixed the witness with his sharp blue glance. Cases about children always aroused him to his full power.

From the back of the courtroom, a murmur rolled forward like a wave. Good, Lord thought: I want this witness to feel nervous in my presence. I want him to sweat in that expensive black suit. Ah, there he goes: fingers to the tie, a furtive loosening. Soon he will wipe his hand across his upper lip. When the witness stroked his moustache, the judge smiled. A ray of sunlight drove a lance through the tall west window and picked out a spot on Mr. Uriel Woodcock's neck.

Today, it seems, I can move the elements. Let us see if I can do the same with people.

41

The case was ugly and painful. Mrs. Mary-Ann Crowe had petitioned the court for custody of her ten-year-old daughter, Annie. Mrs. Crowe's estranged husband, Jeremiah, had seized the child, placed her into the asylum, and ordered the asylum's administrators to forbid Annie's mother to visit or communicate with her daughter. Petitions for custody were nothing new to Judge Lord, but this one carried the poison of pure spite.

The husband's and the wife's lawyers rose and sat, like marionettes. Paid lackeys, Lord thought, who asked only routine questions. The wife's lawyer looked like a college sophomore; the husband's he had long known to be a charlatan. Twice so far, Lord had scolded them for unpreparedness. The judge himself would have to exercise the probe, to uncover the truth.

Now, Mr. Woodcock, let us see what you have to say about this sickening matter.

"How long has Annie Crowe been held in your institution, Mr. Woodcock?"

"Two months." Woodcock spoke with the bland confidence of someone who had a heart made of leather.

"'Two months, *Your Honor*' would be a more appropriate answer, Mr. Woodcock."

"Two months, Your Honor." The voice truculent, unsteady.

"And what was the reason for her admission? She is not an orphan. She has a mother and a father. Nor is she suspected of delinquency of any kind."

"Ah, yes, Your Honor. But her parents are separated from each other, and Mr. Crowe . . ."

"That is, Mr. Jeremiah Crowe. Would you point out this person, if he is in court?"

Uriel Woodcock pointed to a ruddy man in his late forties, with flat black hair parted in the middle. Lord gave Mr. Crowe a long appraising look, and nodded slowly, as if he were inspecting a horse and finding that it had a swayed back and rotten teeth.

Woodcock burst forth, "Mr. Crowe argues that his wife, who is considerably younger than he, is ill-suited to be a mother. She asserts her right to take her daughter to her own church, and in other ways has proved unfit—" Jeremiah Crowe rose from his seat, and Lord gestured for him to sit down.

Although Lord could hammer the air with his large voice, he picked up the gavel and rapped it louder than necessary. The witness jumped, and several people in the courtroom tittered. Mary-Ann Crowe's lawyer attempted to squeak out a protest.

"Mr. Uriel Woodcock, I remind you that Mr. Jeremiah Crowe faces a possible charge of unlawfully detaining his daughter—a charge close to kidnapping. Mrs. Crowe, who has every right to petition this court for justice, is not accused of anything. Taking one's daughter to the church of one's choice is within her rights, unless that church permits human sacrifice or heathen dancing."

Raucous sounds flew up from the audience. The judge's bench hearings drew large crowds hoping to see him drill into an incompetent attorney, or quote Shakespeare, or turn a case inside out and send the lawyers scurrying.

Lord dropped his voice a few notes down the scale and made use of his impressive eyebrows. He spoke with menacing gentleness, stressing each word.

"And now I am going to direct some further questions to you."

43

Scattershot laughs rattled around the courtroom, from spectators who knew Judge Lord's methods. Restless in his chair, Lord prepared to launch himself at Woodcock, now mopping his forehead with a handkerchief.

"By what authority did you refuse to allow Mrs. Mary-Ann Crowe to see her child? And to keep her daughter for two months without a chance to see her mother?"

Woodcock tried to summon up an officious dignity. "Why, by the authority of the father, Your Honor. The legal guardian of the child."

Lord rose from his chair and leaned down. The ray of sunlight had moved from the witness's neck, and lit up the judge's right hand. The seal ring on his little finger gleamed like a beacon. Jeremiah Crowe's lawyer arose and stuck his thumbs in his vest pockets, as if preparing to make a speech. Lord leaned forward and motioned for him to be silent.

"The legal guardian of the child! Do you pretend to know the law, Mr. Uriel Woodcock? Do you believe that a father has the right to deprive his child of her mother's presence, or use an asylum as a prison? Do you set yourself above the courts of Massachusetts, Mr. Woodcock?"

"I—I believed I was acting in the best interests of Mr. Crowe. Your Honor."

"And what about the interests of Miss Annie Crowe, ten years old? What about her mother's bond with her child? The kindly attention that only a mother can give? Bedtime stories, advice, a tender hand on the brow when the girl has a fever?"

Lord knew how to emphasize a story told in court, as he picked up the strands of testimony and wove them into a drama. As he often did, he felt the weight of his lost hopes for daughters of his own. He had watched his young cousins and the children of his friends grow up, lucky and cared for. But what if their lives had skewed into another path? If Emily or Vinnie had suffered as young Annie Crowe had suffered, who would they be now?

He glanced at the back row of spectators, where two women, one in brown, one in black, held each other's hands. Sisters—Annie's mother and aunt. Pale, pretty in a mild way, with sorrowful faces. He guessed that the mother was the one in black, her hand a fist against her chest, her eyes fixed on the judge's face.

"You may step down, Mr. Uriel Woodcock. God help you if I ever see you in my courtroom again. But before you are ushered out, you will turn and look me in the eye. I promise you will never forget this moment."

"Attorneys, please rise," the bailiff announced.

Woodcock's face had turned greenish-white. Lord hoped the man would hold off fainting until he pronounced his judgment.

For thirty years, Lord had endured all the emotions a judge could feel: compassion, anger, disgust, hilarity, amazement. But rarely this degree of bitter pain. He wanted to fling off his robes and shepherd Mrs. Mary-Ann Crowe into Court Square, where he could seize a cab and hurry to rescue Annie from the South Boston Asylum.

"I am tempted to assign you, Mr. Woodcock, and you, Mr. Jeremiah Crowe, a course of reading in Dickens, but his novels would test your imaginations beyond capacity. You should not be running an asylum, Mr. Uriel Woodcock, nor should you, Mr. Crowe, have any authority over your daughter. Woodcock, I order you to return Annie Crowe to her mother, Mrs. Mary-Ann Crowe, and to do so swiftly and safely. I will send two court officers to accompany you and see that it is done, and two more officers to escort Mr. Jeremiah Crowe back to his residence, so that he stays there under their watch until Annie Crowe is safe with her mother. If the child has been harmed, or starved, or sickened, I will make sure that every inhabitant of your so-called asylum is given a decent place in some other institution. And that its doors clang shut forevermore."

Handkerchiefs waved in the courtroom, and people muttered approval, until the judge quieted them.

In the back row, Mary-Ann Crowe wiped her eyes, then rose from her seat and bowed to Judge Lord. Uriel Woodcock and Jeremiah Crowe were shouldered out of the courtroom by four Boston policemen.

Lord rapped the gavel, then hurried from the bench before the applauding crowd could see him cry.

Cambridge, late September 1864

After months of confinement, Emily received a note from Phil, proposing a visit the following Sunday. No need to answer, he would simply arrive at tea-time. Like a god from a cloud, Emily muttered to Fanny.

Four o'clock passed, then four-thirty. She sat rigid in the boarding-house parlor, the cloth around her eyes, only her thoughts to keep her company. The hallway clock was striking five when she heard carriage-wheels, then the judge's unmistakable voice introducing himself to Mrs. Bangs. She untied the cloth, smoothed her hair, and wriggled the knots out of her shoulders. She tottered to her feet, numb from sitting still.

When he walked into the room, the space shrank around him. He seemed taller and mightier, like an afternoon sun. Squinting up at him through the veil of throbbing pain, Emily felt that she had lost inches as well as pounds.

"I am glad to see you, my dear, and I apologize—"

"Please, Phil. My life is Swiss—still and cool—and yours is full of crimes and shouting, like something out of the Wild West."

A long clasp, stroking fingers, his thumbs tickling her wrists—their cherished language—a secret dictionary in her mind. She knew all its pages by heart and turned them in the darkness. A book of images and whispers, like the strange melodies she improvised on the piano and never wrote down.

"No crimes for me today, praise God. I am still and always Phil, even if I am a poor correspondent."

The fervor of his voice surprised her. He wore a new watch-chain and a fob with a red stone. Ruby, his birthstone. Over the years, the judge's clothes had become more formal and important-looking. She wished she could spirit herself to Salem and prowl around his house, invisible. She could examine his books and paintings, taste his brandy, hide in the wardrobe, stroke his robes of ermine and inhale the aroma of his winter coat.

Emily requested tea, which she didn't want, but Phil made her drink a cup and eat a few bites of shortbread. His mock-sternness made a sly parody of Father, but his eyes were gentle. She could feel the tense band on her forehead begin to loosen.

The tea and shortbread made her feel better. She could do nothing about her rheumy eyes, or her parched complexion. At least she was wearing her best dress, light blue with blond lace trim, and Loo had filed her pretty nails and replenished her supply of rose-water. Her cousins had gone to Concord for the afternoon, so that Emily could receive her company alone.

"In some ways you remind me of Father." Speaking frankly made her emotions raw and urgent, especially when she noticed the difference between home-feelings and the mighty towers of her private sky.

47

"Friends are often alike. I think you mean something else."

"Your caretaking instinct. Making me drink tea and eat cookies, tastier than the fish-pills Father fed me every day when I was fifteen. You must have kept a pet bird when you were a child." In a rapt trance, Emily floated back to her childhood days, when she would finger Mr. Lord's watch as she babbled stories to him. She reached out and rubbed the fob's red stone with her thumb, to memorize its smooth shape.

"No, I had a pony named Tilda and a dog named Jacky. You're rather like a bird, a song-sparrow. Or a bluebird, in that pretty dress. You eat like a bird, as I suspect your father often said."

Aware of what Phil did not let himself say, Emily thought she would like to put the cloth over her eyes and take nourishment from him, spoon by spoon, clasping his hand and guiding it to her mouth.

"If Father were here, he'd be feeding me nasty-tasting medicines, for my own good. The two of you are co-conspirators in helping to save my eyes. Such powerful men I know," Emily said, half to herself. "No wonder you're all co-conspirators. You can't help it." She wanted to know what he knew about Dr. Williams, and their connection in Salem. She pictured Phil and the doctor walking on the Boston Common, children and small dogs falling quiet in fascination and awe.

"Elizabeth told me that you have frequent company here."

Emily barely suppressed a sigh. She wondered what else Elizabeth had told her husband about her visit. *Baby drawers. Games in the grass. Her father. Sisters. Childlessness. Love.*

"Not so frequent that a visit from you seems ordinary. I wondered whether you would—"

She feared that her voice would melt into a whisper. Phil cupped her face in his hands and searched her red-rimmed eyes.

"Not a day has gone by without my thinking about you. Much of my time has not been my own. It's the life I chose, but it has a price when people I cherish have to suffer. This summer has been brutal—war makes a wreck of the law— and I don't know what this fall term will bring. Elizabeth meant it when she asked if you'd visit us in Salem."

He fastened his eyes on her, inquiring.

Yes, she thought. No. How would she bear the familiar weight in her heart?

She groped for his hand and placed it in her lap. "I'm grateful to be invited, even if I suspect I'd be a useless and not even ornamental guest. But I keep hoping, week after week, that soon Dr. Williams will allow me to go home."

The word "home" made her voice crack. Salem seemed as far away as the Klondike. Amherst held her family, her gardens, and Carlo. Her eye-trouble had imposed restrictions, but even a restricted correspondence could not quell her feverish need to write. She sighed.

"It would help if you would tell me a story from your real life."

Phil told her about Mary-Ann Crowe and her daughter Annie, the thuggish father and the contemptible Uriel Woodcock. Knowing she would want to hear of his role in the drama, he quoted—with some pride—his sharp judgments and witticisms. As she murmured and gasped and applauded, he leaned back in his chair.

"Talking with you, I feel the burden of the case lift from me. I should attach you to me as an extra ear, but you'd probably miss the rest of you, as I would. There's a coda to this story.

After the Crowe hearing, as I left the courthouse, I caught a glimpse of the young girl, fetched from the asylum by two speedy policemen. And—" He hesitated. Emily's wriggly smile faded.

"Please go on."

"She could have been you, at age ten, as I remember you. The chestnut hair, the slim form. She had on a white apron, the institution uniform, and her little figure glowed as her mother held her. I have rarely been so moved by a display of reunion. I almost approached them, but then thought that my part in their lives was done."

Emily swallowed the dangerous tears. "You will be their hero forever, because you restored them to each other. You gave back Annie her childhood. Now they have the rest of their lives to heal the damage."

There, she thought, was her verdict, undeclared: *How much more powerful is serving as a merciful judge than being a soldier running a bayonet through a Rebel farm-boy.*

When he mopped his face with his handkerchief, she rose and asked in a desolate voice if he would like to be excused from visiting her until a more convenient time. If he had more such cases in the docket, he would need to prepare.

Phil stood up and drew her close. The watch fob pressed against her face. She wrapped her arms around him. Holding her cheek against his gabardine vest, she made a shadow-whisper: *this is the middle of his body, just below his heart.* She could hear it, steady and a little fast, and felt dizzy at the mysteries that lay beneath. *My ear is a stethoscope, my hands are as inquiring as a doctor's hands, my ears could hear his voice from blocks away. My heart is a twist of white thread that could unroll itself from here to Salem as quickly as a wind-pushed tide.*

He sat down again, facing her. "I have been inexcusably rude, my dear, not visiting you until now. The fact is, I feel helpless. I want to bang a gavel and order your pain to go away and never come back. Also, forgive me, I find this parlor, well-furnished as it is, a bit stuffy. Are you allowed to walk outside? Would you like to take my arm and find a shady bench somewhere nearby? It is almost six o'clock, and the evening shadows might be cool and comforting."

For the first time in days, Emily smiled with unexpected joy.

As they walked, they noticed the smell of rain in the air and the buildings hung with dusty bunting left over from the Fourth of July. The early evening light gave her a sense of freedom, anchored to his elbow. Being outside lifted her spirits. The crowds were the usual mix of people she observed from Mrs. Bangs's window: tired-looking soldiers—some with missing limbs—matrons and children, busy citizens quick-stepping around them. Phil held her arm and walked slowly. Every few steps, he stopped and lifted the veil from her bonnet to inspect her face, until she laughed.

"Did you think I would disappear, or that you'd look and find that my head had turned backward on my neck, like someone possessed by a devil?"

He led her to a bench in a little park near a Roman Catholic church. The door was always open for worshippers, or strangers, who needed help in time of war. Emily and Phil watched the sun, veiled by light clouds, descend behind the buildings near the Charles River. From inside the church came the sound of a choir practicing.

"Would you like to go inside, for a few minutes? In case you anticipate being possessed by Satan. We could sit in the back."

Oh, to be teased like this, several times a week. Emily wondered if she could be instantly cured that way. If teasing were a religion, Phil would be its Pope.

As they stepped into the church, she removed her handkerchief from her sleeve and dabbed her eyes. The dusky sanctuary was lit with dozens of candles. Her eyes responded to the wavering brilliance with a spill of tears. Frowning, he peered into her face.

"Don't worry, there's no pain this time, it's just the change of light from dusk to candle-flame. It will pass."

She sat close to him, listening to the dozen male choristers as they sang a few lines of a Latin hymn, then stopped as their leader corrected the pitch. Phil whispered the words— *Ave verum corpus, natum de Maria virgine*—familiar to Emily from her schooldays. A black-clad woman slumped in a nearby pew, her arm around a young boy with his face buried in his hands. Emily had rarely been inside a Roman Catholic church, but she liked the feel of it, like a market, with people entering or leaving, to take whatever they needed. She shut her eyes and sent up a silent plea of hope for the woman and the boy, and a thought-prayer of gratitude for the comfort of the big man beside her and the soothing darkness that had become the most welcome part of every day.

Words from her secret dictionary curled across the white scroll in her mind. *Joy. Pain. Release. Paradise.* Next time, when she put the bandage on, she would imagine him tying its knot, as carefully as he had tied the strings to her life.

He helped her down the church steps, counting them and guiding her feet. The street-lamps were lit, making easier their way to the boardinghouse.

"Phil, you are treating me as though I might break apart at any moment. I am not Humpty Dumpty, you know, even if my eyes sometimes feel like overcooked eggs with thin shells."

He harrumphed, a sound that only he could invest with charm. "Right foot, left foot, my dear. You are a soldier in a battle for your eyesight, and I want to help you win it. Since I have given up my grand and foolish idea of being a soldier, I wish I could metamorphose into a doctor, or perhaps a wizard. I thought of being a doctor, you know, in college. That lasted about two weeks, until I had to help set a friend's broken ankle and—well, never mind. My sense of theatre still finds the wizard idea appealing."

"Citizens would shriek to see their noble Judge Lord wearing a pointed hat with stars on it and waving a wand instead of a gavel."

This time his laugh was hearty and surprised, the one Emily liked best. "That's my old Emily I hear. I am glad to have you back."

"Have you missed me? I have missed you, Phil." They were almost at the boardinghouse. She had hours of talk left in her, but had to obey the summons from the god of darkness or suffer the consequences. Only a few more steps, and he would walk away, find a cab, and resume his life. Her days would proceed, a sad, dull calendar, one by one. Visits to the doctor, Fanny's reading to her, careful walks, her clumsy attempt at knitting, and every now and then a burst of courage that helped her write the first lines of a poem.

I felt a Cleaving in my Mind —
As if my Brain had split —
I tried to match it — Seam by Seam —
But could not make them fit —

Despite her determination to keep her strength, Emily needed the safety of her room. Phil's visit had given her joy, and now the joy would fade into her dreams until she heard again his voice at the door.

He looked down at her. In the half-light he appeared sorrowful, older than he had a few hours ago. His eyes held dark shadows.

"I have missed you more than I can say. I have probably said too much already. Careful, here's a step up. Drat these wooden sidewalks." His big voice grew rough. "Emily, I want you to promise me to take care of yourself, and to guard your precious eyes. I want to see you sitting in your garden, with the sunlight on your brave, comely face."

"My afflicted, hazel witnesses."

"Then let them bear witness to my request."

At the door to the boarding-house, she reached for his hand. "I won't ask you to come in. Only to come back one day, and read Shakespeare to me. Your selection."

He sighed and stroked her face. A light rain had started. "Shakespeare. I would like that." He cleared his throat and held his hand over his heart.

"The strong necessity of time commands
Our services awhile; but my full heart
Remains in use with you."

He bent and kissed her on each cheek, and on the tip of her nose.

"And all the gods go with you," she whispered. They both knew the play well—*Antony and Cleopatra.* Her favorite.

*

Salem, January 1866

From the morning's mail he unfolded a letter and deciphered the scrawl.

"Oh, Emily's old dog is dead. Dear Carlo. Poor Emily. That dog had many friends. She should put a death notice in the *Republican.* I bet the charming Sam Bowles would do it for nothing."

Elizabeth, who preferred cats to dogs, dug out a fresh skein from her knitting basket. News of the Dickinsons, he noticed, did not often evoke much response. When she did murmur something, her politeness seemed stiff.

He remembered the spring of 1850, when Edward had brought the puppy home to protect the females when he was away. The two men watched Emily and Vinnie romp with the dog in the garden. Emily tried to shoo Carlo away when the wiggly beast sported with the men's shoelaces. Watching the puppy climb on her dress, nuzzle her neck, and receive a hearty kiss on his nose, he had felt an unexpected surge of jealousy. She was nineteen, and had a young woman's bounteous affection for anything alive—human, plant, or beast. He knew he was included in her capacious heart, but at times he wanted more. He couldn't give voice to that desire without despising himself, but there it was, a familiar flower with a rich scent and a thorny stem. He knew her mischief, as she knew his teasing ways. That day, it seemed the world lay all before her, her education complete, her home life content. Perhaps she anticipated a happy prospect of marriage. Who could suit her, he'd wondered. Emily was not like anyone else. He'd been tempted to advise Edward not to let her throw herself away on an ordinary young man.

He asked himself why he would have wanted to speak so boldly. It was a long time ago, and Emily was now thirty-five, still unmarried. Intact, no doubt—except that she was likely to make her own rules. As she owned her spirit, so would she own her body.

Reading and remembering, he was lost in the firelight, and startled when Elizabeth spoke. He was conscious of her watching him wander around in his thoughts.

"Her cousin Fanny told me privately that in Cambridge she missed her dog so much, she couldn't speak his name. I wish I could have persuaded her to come here for a few days."

He almost laughed at the familiar ploy, Elizabeth tossing out a line to see if he would snatch at it, exposing a ripple of his fantasy-life. He got up to place another log on the fire, well aware of what he had not said—that he was relieved Emily had not visited Salem. He would have been tempted to invite her to sit in the library and talk with him late at night, in front of the fire. He would have given her a glass of port, and watched the firelight play on her hair.

"I'm sure your visit to Cambridge was a comfort, Elizabeth. You are good at comforting, as I well know." She wouldn't dare accuse him of dissembling. They both knew what kind of comfort they liked.

"So are you, Otis, in your own way." She gave a little laugh as she burrowed again in her knitting basket.

"What a noisy place, that boarding house," he said, "even with everyone trying to make the best of it. Too much company wore her out, especially Edward's relatives nearby, and Vinnie's old beau Joseph Lyman, and the charming Colonel Clark. Emily was hanging on by her nerve-ends."

"Yes, I saw that myself. And she has more nerve-ends than most of us. But as you well know, she is not a child. There has always been something uncannily grown-up about her. And yet—not. There is some passage she has yet to go through. Not marriage, I think, but the movement from her own world into the world of others." Elizabeth's voice carried sharpness. No doubt she believed Emily led a self-indulgent life, writing in her room when she could be out and about her village, doing good works. Without children to

56

raise, his wife sustained herself by taking care of her Farley relatives—and her busy husband.

He allowed his silence to speak for him. He did not want to hear her pass the slightest judgment on Emily's character, which he would take as a judgment on himself. He had never told Elizabeth that he had stood in the snow, on the night Emily was born, and that he had made a vow to watch over her as best he could.

Hearing Elizabeth clear her throat, he fastened his eyes to the paper.

"Well, she has suffered a loss, and should be pitied."

He lowered the paper and regarded her thoughtfully. Instead of reading, he remembered last fall. After his first visit to the boarding house, he had managed to pry open a few more hours—a Sunday in November, just before Emily went home, another late the following spring, after she came back for more treatment, and one at the end of August, just before court reconvened. The arrangements required his cancelling appointments and delaying his return to Salem. He did not mention these visits to his wife, reasoning that they were as justified as meetings with lawyers and state officials—if only for his mental health. On each occasion he read Shakespeare to Emily, as she sat next to him and kept her eyes closed. Her sighs and whispers floated in the room like feathers he wanted to catch and keep in his pocket . . . .

Behind the newspaper, Phil retrieved a few unbearably beautiful lines from *Antony and Cleopatra*, and spoke them in his head:

Stay for me:
Where souls do couch on flowers, we'll hand in hand,
And with our sprightly port make the ghosts gaze.

57

Elizabeth dropped a stitch and tried to retrieve it. She sighed, and he looked up.

"She is in love with you, you know."

A log shifted in the hearth, sending up a pop of sparks.

He folded the paper and put it aside. "I think she is given to hero-worship, Elizabeth. It's a Dickinson habit. Austin worships his father, even if he kicks against the traces now and then. Vinnie reserves her adoring glances for the young law clerks of Amherst."

"Neatly put, dear. But this is something more. Emily has an attraction to powerful men."

"Like hundreds of women in the world, including you, Elizabeth."

He arranged his face to look both serene and enigmatic. Being a judge was like being a Shakespearean actor without face-paint or change of costume. Perhaps, after all, he had satisfied his wish to tread the boards.

She smiled. "I remember that when I knew you, so long ago, I wanted to know everything about you."

He looked at his wife with surprise. She rarely spoke about the early days of their long courtship, or expressed such sentiments. By their late twenties, they had known each other for years, and felt that their maturity was a mutual gift. He had been gratified by her acceptance of his overtures, and she praised his vitality and wit. So much between them was understood—his ambition, her devotion to her family, her response to his bold sexual maneuvers, his admiring of her soft skin and the blue veins of her breasts. Most of the time, he found her sweetness and dignity comforting, a balm for his stressful days.

"Even though you already knew everything about me! I still think our fathers worked secretly to bring us together.

Quite dynastic of them, I must say. And rewarding, I hope for you as much as for me." He reached out and squeezed her knee. It was time to let his private thoughts retreat, and resume his domestic self.

"But of course even a devoted spouse can't know everything. You are a complex man, Otis Phillips Lord."

She rarely used his full name unless she wanted his whole attention. He found it hard to explain himself. He had not crossed the line with Emily, and did not intend to. The bower in his mind was still a sacred space.

"Whatever 'complex' means."

Images rushed into his head, and he tried to shoo them away, like inadmissible witnesses—he and Cousin Lucy, skinny-dipping in a pond, then frolicking in the grass; Emily's face as he kissed the tip of her nose; his hands drifting across Elizabeth's smooth belly, on their wedding night.

They sat in nearly companionable silence.

Later, after Catherine O'Leary served them a light lunch beside the fire, Phil put down the boring legal screed he was reading and raked his hands through his hair, leaving a slight trail of soot from the fire poker. He needed to confess something, to ease the thick feeling in his head.

"I made Emily cry once, when I lost my temper. I was completely unjust, and I still regret it."

"Tell me."

He went to the window and drew aside the velvet drapes. The scrim of snow obscured his view of North Street.

"Still snowing?"

"Yes. It will last all day, I think."

Just for today, he liked being enclosed in his house. The bower lay hushed in white.

59

"You know how Edward's wife fusses over guests. Always with the best intentions. A sweet woman, but sometimes she drives me to distraction."

"Yes, dear. I feel it too. She's very anxious, I think."

"I was talking with young Emily in the parlor. She often asked me to explain some point of law, so that she could square up to her father and take him by surprise. And in bustles her mother, and asks if I want tea—no thank you—or a rug for my knees—still no—or a pillow for my back—again no—or would I like to come into the kitchen where it's warm. On and on. And young Emily breaks forth and says, 'Would you like to have the Declaration of Independence read, or the Lord's Prayer repeated, or the Preamble to the Constitution, or would you like me to attempt an imitation of Jenny Lind, or show you one of Carlo's parlor tricks?'"

"Otis, that is outrageous. She has such a wicked wit. You must have laughed yourself silly."

"Not quite. I caught sight of Emily's mother's face, stricken with embarrassment. Poor woman, she was doing her best, as always. And here was her brilliant daughter showing her up, and showing off. A behavior I am quite familiar with."

Elizabeth's expression was unreadable. He noticed that a corner of her lips turned up, as she kept her eyes on her handiwork. Whenever his wife knitted by the fire, she seemed to be fashioning her thoughts into socks and scarves.

"So you turned brilliant Emily over your knee and switched her little bottom?" Elizabeth's voice was peppery.

"Great Heavens, wife!" He felt his face flush, but went on with his confession. "I took her out into the garden—despite its being a cold day—and gave her the Judge Lord treatment, full of thunder and lightning. She ran off and didn't reappear.

Later she wrote me the most abject letter I've ever received. All about wanting to be 'my best little girl,' and not being banished. She already had one heavy, if very loving parent, and she didn't need to hear this kind of thing from me."

He didn't mention that when he saw Emily's face collapse in tears, he wanted to fold her in his arms and beg her forgiveness.

Sitting with his wife of twenty-three years, he found it impossible to disguise his tenderness for Emily. She had a curious power in those aching brown eyes and her breathless voice.

Many women were attracted to prominent men. He had occasionally fended off mild advances—a hand squeeze, a cloakroom kiss—from the wives of some of his colleagues. Elizabeth had once referred to his "force field," a phrase he liked because it flattered his sense of power. But he hoped Emily did not worship him. Mere men should not be worshiped.

Emily's golden-brown eyes appeared in his mind, candid and merry. Her full, pale lips, her graceful fingers working among his own. Her face, upturned under a streetlight in Cambridge, touched by rain as he lifted her bonnet-veil and kissed her cool cheeks. On this quiet Sunday, he imagined her as a white-clad spirit hovering near his big house, standing alone in the snow as if it had become her own element.

He gave his wife a rueful look. Her comment about spanking had embarrassed him, but he could mine it for private amusement.

"When did this happen, Otis?"

"I suppose about five years ago." He knew exactly—early 1861—but thought it best to be vague. Yet he hated using

61

words like "I suppose," and tempting the gods to expose his evasions.

"I don't remember your mentioning this business with Emily."

The confession had brought no relief, only embarrassment and a faint sense of falsity. "I was ashamed of myself. And the worst of it was that Emily's performance made me want to laugh, if only she had picked another target."

"When I visited her two summers ago, I told her that we would have loved daughters, if God had given us any. Today I believe that more than ever. For you more than me, I think—since I am an honorary mother to nieces and nephews. But I think you would have taken a special delight in being a father to females." Elizabeth reached to clasp her husband's hand, as sorrow passed over his face.

"You told her—? Elizabeth, we never—it is too painful, even now."

"I did not supply details. She did not need to know then, or ever, that when we married we were a few months from being parents. No one knew that except Mary, although I often thought others suspected. And then, of course, we lost the twins in March."

He let out a long sigh and felt for his handkerchief. A lump rose in his throat. Since March 1844, he thought of his stillborn twin daughters at unexpected moments: as he got dressed, walked to court, paused over a letter from Amherst. The twins' lives, forever incomplete, stirred him to think of Emily's life. In a sense she was kin to them, because she also inhabited his soul and body.

"Emily sometimes displays the power to guess others' secrets, I suppose because she has a few of her own tucked away. But that one stays with you and me. I have said that I hate the month of March, but I let people think it's because of the weather."

They stayed quiet for a time.

Elizabeth put down her knitting. "Speaking of uncanny things, I remember that poem, 'The Judge is like the Owl.' What do you think it meant?"

He twitched in his chair and spent some time placing a bookmark in the brief he had been trying to read.

"I told you when I showed it to you that I didn't know. An invitation to sing. She once said that her business was to sing. Poetry, I suppose. Or music."

Or love, their smoldering common ground.

He wished he had taken up pipe-smoking. It would give him something to do with his hands.

His "favorite refrain." He knew that Elizabeth had noticed the provocative phrase. His wife had probably guessed that Emily would not have known his favorite refrain unless he had told her.

"Did you ever ask her?"

Not for the first time did Phil believe his wife would have been a good lawyer, with her talent for frank questions. Her excellent posture, fine figure, and high white forehead would have made her a perfect Portia.

"She told me nothing I could make out. Something about a home for wisdom. My hide-bound legal mind doesn't stretch to such things."

Elizabeth, counting stitches, made a wry smile but did not look at him. He guessed that in mentioning the poem, his wife had given him a gentle warning. She had done so before, when a wayward unhappy wife came too near the judge at a dinner party and leaned her deep cleavage into his helpless gaze.

The long winter afternoon stretched before them. He needed a rest from his thoughts, from talk that stirred a squall of unruly fantasies. He rang for Catherine to have a cozy fire lit in the big bedroom upstairs.

Elizabeth looked tired, but gave him a smile when her husband suggested a long winter's nap.

5.

Let my first knowing be of thee
Salem, Amherst, Boston, December 1872

Salem, 20 Nov., 1872

Dear Emily,

I am writing to propose a special occasion to honor your Father's seventieth birthday, and hoping to persuade you to join in a conspiracy with me. (I know you are familiar with conspiracies.) The celebrated Russian pianist Anton Rubinstein will be performing in Boston at the end of December. He is passionate and dramatic, with an impressive repertoire.

I propose that you and your Father attend a matinee recital on December 27 with Elizabeth and me, then come to Salem for a night or two, returning to Amherst for his New Year's Day birthday celebrations. It would be an honor to have you visit our home.

I know you are not in the habit of leaving Amherst, but I hope the prospect of both hearing the great Rubinstein and giving your esteemed Father a musical treat will persuade you. I trust that your Mother's present indisposition will pass quickly.

Your Father's years of hard work on behalf of Massachusetts surely warrant such a gift from me, a friend of many years. I can think of no better person than you to accompany him—you who *love music. Your Father takes much pleasure in your company. He writes me that your eyes are now recovered, so the trip would place no undue strain on you.*

I would make all the arrangements about the concert, train tickets, hotel, carriages, and so forth. All you would need to do is inform your Father that these things have been taken care of, and then have Mr. Tom Kelley place you and your Father on the first morning train to Boston.

I have enclosed an envelope readied for your reply. Please allow yourself to be persuaded to come, listen, and enjoy the occasion among old and trusted friends, and to give your Father a much-deserved happiness.

> *Faithfully yours,*
> *Phil Lord*

E mily's hand trembled as she read the letter again. She had not been away from Amherst for years, and the prospect of train travel, slushy streets, and an oppressive crowd of elegant Bostonians seemed almost like a nightmare. Her refusal to mingle with strangers had become a way of life.

When Sue complained that Emily would not visit the Evergreens to converse with famous men like Henry Ward Beecher, Frederick Law Olmsted, and Ralph Waldo Emerson, Emily wrote her that she was happier among weeds than among important guests who made her feel small and shy. She did not like conversation about Topics, but what she most disliked about such packed and perfumed events was seeing her brother's headache roll over him like a thundercloud as Sue became more scintillating.

Still, she told herself, a seat in the Music Hall was not a drawing room. No conversation with famous strangers, no filling of sherry glasses, no serving of elaborate sweetmeats, as at dozens of Amherst College Commencements. No man would say "What?" to her gnomic words. This voice in her head—sensible, reassuring—puzzled her. It almost sounded like Vinnie.

From the large southwest window, the clotted sky appeared sunless, the hemlock trees witch-black. The weather often turned surly just before Thanksgiving, as if giving a warning of the coming winter punishment. It was not an afternoon for brooding on the landscape's metaphysical messages.

She read Phil's letter again. Formal, graceful, careful, with just a few touches to let her hear his familiar voice. "I can think of no better person than you . . . ." He understood her devotion. "A much-deserved happiness." He was right. Father would love the music, and the judge's robust presence might cheer him. Mother's headaches and depressions came in waves, and November, tough and colorless, always turned a key in her inner lock. Father felt helpless to lift his wife's low spirits. What if he were to take time off for pleasure?

Anton Rubinstein! She had read of him, heard her friends talk of the Russian's phenomenal playing, and wondered if he would ever visit the Evergreens, so that she could hide in the rhododendrons and hear him perform Beethoven.

Oh, to listen unseen. But who would notice her in the mighty Music Hall throng? It would be like the church she and Phil had visited, years ago, where people gathered not to inspect each other, but to be uplifted for a while. She would be a pale, unremarkable face in a firmament of faces. People might recognize Edward Dickinson and Otis Phillips Lord, but not a small fortyish woman. Emily envisioned Mrs. Lord's shining dark hair, with its fashionable dusting of gray, braided and adorned with lace. Nervousness clenched her stomach. If only a tornado could pick up her and Father and deposit them in their seats in the Music Hall. Then it could whirl them back to Amherst, with their clothes neatly brushed and only freshness in their faces to suggest they had witnessed an act of genius.

Her thoughts full of music, dresses, carriages, Father, Phil Lord, Elizabeth, and herself, Emily paced in her room. She imagined sitting in a plush seat, the lights slowly lowering, the romantic scowling face of Rubinstein poised above his hands as he summoned up thunder. She could steal a look at Father, or brush his hand with her own. He might even treat her to one of his rare, beautiful smiles. She would see Phil in his evening clothes, his big frame magnificently decked.

Going to Salem would be like visiting the sun or the moon. She imagined alternating between bouts of burning and freezing, sensuous thrills and self-consciousness. Phil's witty, affectionate letters always warmed her blood. Remembering how gently Elizabeth lifted the veil from a fact she could not hide, she still felt awe at the older woman's candor.

"You love my husband, don't you?"

"Yes, how could I not?"

She would be with both Lords together, away from Amherst. A man and his wife, long married, making the little gestures that signal togetherness. Long ago, when she and Elizabeth had played Haydn at the Homestead, she saw Phil place his hand on his wife's shoulder, and his wife pat his fingers. For a few days, sleep and appetite disappeared.

That event had been years ago. She was older now, more confident in herself. Her bureau drawer held hundreds of poems and a box filled with letters. She had endured near-blindness and recovered her sight. Now she anticipated Father listening to Rubinstein, Phil Lord's elegant hands applauding, and the great Russian pianist supplying the music to accompany a passion she had long learned to conceal in public while releasing it in writing.

Emily held the letter up to the winter light, imagining that it gleamed. For over twenty years she had traced Phil's handwriting with her fingers, and listened to his spirited clamor. The bold, handsome cursive asserted an irresistible force. Sometimes she tried to reproduce the way he wrote her name: the large, looping M, his classical spelling of Miss as Mif's, the k and s in "Dickinson" peeking above the other letters, the flourish on the t of "Amherst," like the curl of a buggy whip.

This has been carefully planned. Not for the first time, she envisioned Phil as a military strategist, wearing a general's uniform and seated on an enormous horse. He had said exactly those things that could make his plot succeed.

If Phil wanted to rob a bank or steal a railroad train or command troops, he could do it. He should have been a soldier, after all. He had the voice, the build, the talent to command. Persuading her to leave Amherst was also a tricky campaign.

24 November, 1872

Dear Phil,

Thank you for your generous invitation to come to Boston with Father and hear the great Anton Rubinstein. I accept with pleasure.

I shall choose my own birthday, Dec. 10, to inform Father of the forthcoming adventure. In the meantime I hope to acquire suitable raiment, so as not to embarrass the noble company.

Gratefully yours,
Emily

*

The huge Music Hall was too hot. Emily buried her face in the programme, and prayed for the dimming of the lights. Phil tried to distract her. More dressed up than she had ever been since her visit to Washington in 1855 with Vinnie and Father, she vibrated with nervousness.

"Do you know, that awful fire, over a month ago, missed the Music Hall by one block? I could smell it from the Courthouse."

"I could almost taste the half-dead embers as the carriage approached. But now I am so overwhelmed that I can feel only awe." She wished she could clasp her arm in his, as they had in the Cambridge church. She gazed at the mighty organ dominating the hall. "The organist must feel like a tiny spider crawling among giant redwoods."

Phil whispered, "Custom will never stale your infinite variety, Miss Dickinson." She felt her face blush. No one had ever compared her to Cleopatra.

He pointed out the hall's coffered ceiling and the remarkable space, twice as long as wide. With its world-renowned acoustics, it made a perfect place for a fury of sound. The Dickinson-Lord party occupied seats in the first balcony on the left, so that they could see Rubinstein's fingers on the keys of the large Steinway piano.

Emily reached across Phil to pat her father's hand. The train journey had tired him. She hoped he would be able to stay awake through the concert. Rubinstein was famous for his long recitals, with heroic encores—Beethoven's *Waldstein* sonata—that could tax a weary listener. Already, before she had heard a note, she admired the pianist's largesse. An artist with a great gift took joy in its abundance.

She wanted to whisper to her father, *You are with me and your best friend, and you are safe, as I am safe with you. We have long been in the habit of each other.* She wished she'd thought to conceal a small vial of brandy for him in her evening bag.

In their rooms at the Parker House, where they would stay overnight before going on to Salem, she had changed out of her brown traveling dress into a gray-green silk concoction with a small bustle and sleeves that fanned out at the wrists. The seamstress had reconstructed one of her mother's Paris gowns, adding modish touches and modeling them to Emily's petite frame. The neckline was lower than Emily was used to, so she wore a light corset that pushed up her small breasts, revealing a soft dent of cleavage. She could hardly believe her transformation. Before Tom Kelley took them to the train, Vinnie, excited about the chance to make her sister look fashionable, had braided her hair and swept it back and up, and fastened a bit of lace to it with a handsome ebony hairpin.

"I've never had the chance to decorate my sister before. You have to stand in for a Christmas tree. Our judge will want to kneel at your dainty feet!"

Emily shushed her, while Vinnie danced and hummed. Now, when she looked into the long mirror in the hotel, she beheld herself as an odd bird whose neck and limbs stuck out of curious molting plumage. Father, unexpectedly kissing her on the forehead, muttered his approval.

"You look right amazin', my dear."

The compliment made her laugh. Father didn't know how funny he could be when he talked like a country-man.

Elizabeth Lord was arrayed in a rich dark purple velvet gown, trimmed with black lace. Long coral earrings swung from her earlobes. She looked like a Lord's wife, Emily observed, as she indulged in amused contemplation of Phil and her father, barbered and polished to a fine sheen. She stole shy looks at the audience, surprised that they were not much different from Amherst citizens, except that their clothes were more expensive and the women wore lashings of jewels. Otherwise, they were ordinary people, plain, handsome, lean, fat. One gentleman sported a monocle; another, a Union veteran, had an empty sleeve. A matron in the next balcony accompanied four little girls, dressed alike in lavender and unflattering gray lace. Several patrons came over to greet Judge Lord and shake her father's hand. Elizabeth accepted some compliments and turned to Emily, who praised her regal velvet dress.

Elizabeth squeezed her hand. "You do look quite lovely, Emily. That color suits your hair, and I like this thick twist and the lace, too. But none of us mortals will command the slightest attention when Rubinstein takes over the stage."

"I am much happier not to be noticed in such company. Anonymity gives me leave to enjoy my senses."

"Anton Rubinstein is the most dramatic man I have ever seen."

Emily smiled. Dramatic men were the only kind worth knowing. "You have heard him before?"

"Yes, with my sister Mary and my niece Abbie, a few weeks before the awful fire. I'll be interested to note your response to him. Mary thought he was quite—barbaric. Abbie . . . well, I'm afraid she's at an age to be distracted by the latest fashions. In any case, the *barbaric* would not appeal to her."

Emily thought, now I can be at ease, with a true barbarian on stage. She glanced at her father. He appeared tired, and wore his customary cloak of loneliness.

"Otis, why don't you and Emily exchange seats, so that she can sit between you and Edward? Otherwise we women might indulge ourselves in tittle-tattle."

72

Phil raised a skeptical eyebrow, but stood up so that Emily could claim the seat next to her father. As he helped her settle her elaborate skirts, he whispered "enchanting" into her ear. She noticed his quick glance at her bosom. Patting her father's arm, she whispered into his ear, "My cup of anticipation is full tonight." She hoped Phil had overheard her.

Then she lost herself in a glorious tempest. Rubinstein's huge hands took over the keyboard and wrestled it to his will, then quieted the frenzy into a melancholic, barely audible softness. His feet on the pedals, like a dancer's feet, slid, capered, mashed, caressed. Emily's feet moved to the rhythm, catching the pianist's restlessness as her hands crept forth like butterflies from a cocoon, to open and close above her green silk skirt. Heat and chill spread up her neck. Her breastbone thrummed. She wanted to cry out when the music took hold of her, a sound both familiar and as strange as volcanic eruptions from another planet.

Behind Me – dips Eternity –
Before Me – Immortality –
Myself – the Term between –

He knows, she thought. He knows all the secrets I have ever had.

She closed her eyes as the pianist eased into the second movement of Beethoven's *Pathétique* Sonata. She moved her hand down Father's arm and allowed herself to grasp his fingers. His hand was cold, but slowly grew warm beneath her touch, as the notes broke open the hymn-like cadence, and she watched the pianist command the bass line as though playing a song.

"When he first strode on stage, I thought he was Beethoven, come back to life," Emily remarked to Phil during the interval, after she regained her voice.

"I expect he is rather more well-groomed than Beethoven ever was. He carries that raw power straight from the frozen North, and somehow sets it on fire. You were listening with your whole being. I have heard that every Rubinstein concert takes a toll in fainting women."

He handed her a glass of champagne. Having rarely tasted champagne, she felt her cheeks grow pink and her tongue quicken. Her eyes twinkled. "I have never fainted in my life, Phil Lord, and I don't intend to miss a minute of this concert by casting myself into a stupor. But here is my review, since you didn't ask. Rubinstein commanded all the emotions a piano can express. I have never heard a piano used as artillery, or seen a pianist bursting through his clothes to grow leaves from his fingers. The gods have been mere myths to me. Now I have seen and heard one. I have you to thank."

Unable to reply to this remarkable verdict, the judge hovered near her, warm and protective. From time to time his eyes swept across her bosom.

Who would have thought my childish breasts could rise to this occasion?

He touched the lace adorning Emily's braid. "I can't resist commenting on your handsome costume. Is it possible that I spy a discreet little bustle on that remarkable green dress?"

Teasing and being teased combed her nerves into a happy calm. "Is it possible that you, sir, have been reading *Godey's Lady's Book* and are now prepared to discourse on the evolution of the bustle? Do you keep the latest issue near your judge's bench? Never mind, Judge Owl, just remember that I have caught you looking at my backside."

Phil's explosion of laughter caused a few heads to turn.

She savored her mischief. The matron and two of the little lavender girls passed by, and Emily threw them a wink, producing giggles. The presence of children always made her feel joyful. She wanted to lean toward Phil and inhale his bay rum scent and sneak her hand into his. She looked up at him and blinked slowly, then gave him a full, fresh smile.

Emily heard her father's voice talking to someone about the unfinished railway project that obsessed him. *Poor man, he has heard a miracle, but still stays rooted in the earth, the only home he believes in.*

"Oh dear. He's heading into the Hoosac Tunnel again, and I'm afraid he'll never come out. It's his own Northwest Passage. Could you—?"

Phil caught Elizabeth's eye and she worked her way over to them so that the judge could rescue Edward's colleague.

Elizabeth talked with her customary diplomatic grace. At last, used to the habits of her heart, Emily felt at ease with her. "Have you played any of this repertoire? Rubinstein seems to know everything. I expect him to produce a piece by a composer from Mongolia."

Elizabeth removed a glove and held out a hand, which still appeared older than her face. "Alas, I can't play the piano as I used to do. The cramps of old age are upon my fingers. Don't look shocked, dear, I have just turned fifty-eight. Otis is now sixty. Think of it."

Ten years since Phil's unforgettable fiftieth birthday.

"'We turn not older with the years, but newer every day.'"

"Is that Emerson? It sounds like him. Ah, our gentlemen are returning."

75

The house lights flickered and dimmed.

As the pianist struck the first notes of Schubert's *Moments Musicaux,* Emily smiled, hoping Elizabeth would guess that she had been quoting herself.

After the concert, Phil told Emily that he could not hear Chopin's *Tristesse* without shedding tears. They talked about Rubenstein's light-hearted Handel, tempestuous Beethoven, tuneful Schubert, and Chopin, unbearably delicious. Taming his large voice to a whisper, he grasped her wrist.

"I am grateful to you, Emily, for agreeing to my plan. I know your father will remember this evening for the rest of his life. As will I."

"And I." Finger by finger, she removed her evening glove and let her hand rest in his, then touched his watch fob, as if to seal her good fortune. If Elizabeth saw her, so be it. She felt ageless and brilliant, a bird soaring from peak to peak. Eight years before, in constant pain and fear for her eyes, Emily could never have imagined hearing the sounds Rubinstein made. The pianist, Phil, and her father blended in her teeming consciousness. Poised on her dressy shoes, she kissed Phil's cheek, a chaste kiss, befitting the elder daughter of his good friend. She breathed warmth on his skin, tempted to nibble his pink earlobe. For a moment, they were safe in the crowded hall, its brilliance another form of seclusion, the counterpart to midnight in her garden, twenty years before. She saw Father helping Elizabeth into her cloak. He still looked tired, Emily noticed, but handsome, even courtly.

She had behaved properly, wrapped in the magnetic field where a genius struck fireworks from his machine. Bowing to the audience after playing Chopin's *Barcarolle,* Rubinstein, his mane streaked with perspiration, his hands hanging from his sleeves like lion's paws, raked his glance over the audience.

For a second, his narrow, intense eyes fell on her—a small woman in a gray-green dress, holding her fingers together prayerfully, without applauding. One of the most famous men in the world, he too had suffered, loved, survived, and found his soul in art. *"To be alive—is Power,"* she telegraphed to him, without the help of words.

*

The next day, the threat of a blizzard prevented Emily and her father's visiting Salem. Despite a fervent desire to see the Lords' house, she was relieved to be going home, although the journey would take hours through the snow-covered stations. The porter on the train told them that the blizzard would not arrive until evening.

The past twenty-four hours had given Emily too much to take in. Sleep had eluded her in the Parker House bed, as she relived the sumptuous concert, Phil's light touches, her father's fragile smiles. Rubinstein, she would later write her cousins Loo and Fanny Norcross, made a fascinating chill along her spine. In the half-sleep of travel, she saw herself standing in a Northern winter wood, watching a forest-god play a huge black instrument. Soon the forest-god would ask her to sing, and she would rise among clouds and feathers, as Rubinstein propelled her into the glassy weather of minor keys. Together they would move from ice to ice, until the floe they stood on broke open to the sound of cornets, and the pianist's hands became Phil's hands, then Father's, then her own narrow fingers, and a cornet—a silver hammer in the air—the conductor's whistle.

Jolted awake in her thick, tuffeted seat, Emily looked at her watch. Later than she thought, and less than halfway to Palmer. She longed to be home, to write alone at her table, as the year turned and her father moved into the deep straits of a new decade.

When the train hit a bump, her father, sitting across from her, roused himself, blinked, and regarded her expectantly, as though there had been no break in their conversation. To distract him, she asked what part of the concert he had liked most.

"Sitting beside you was like hearing an Aeolian harp respond to the elements. I know you have always loved Schubert's *The Erl-King.*"

Emily had emitted a small squeak when the great pianist almost levitated off the bench, his long hair flying, as his rapid staccato chopped at the air. Her father wiggled his hand up and down. "It was impressive. I wonder if Mr. Rubinstein gets paid by the note."

"Did you notice our good judge making use of his handkerchief?"

"Where can a judge weep if not in a concert? Besides, Otis has always been quick to laughter and to tears. Like someone else I know quite well."

Emily wouldn't mention that she had seen her father steal his own handkerchief from his pocket, during the Chopin. Like Phil, her father held both winter and spring in himself—a bare winter maple, stripped and defiant, or an oak tree coming into leaf.

Snowflakes flew past the train windows. Emily noticed the porter, a gray-haired man with a bluff, dignified air. His blue uniform sported a black velvet stripe with gold trim, which meant that he had senior status, and might be able to arrange refreshments. She got up and swayed down the aisle to find him, and passed by a narrow door, slightly ajar. The closet emitted a faint whiff of disinfectant.

"That's a privy, Miss. It's small, but it'll do. There's one like it at the other end. We keep it quite clean."

She thanked him and asked about tea.

"Yes, we can do that. My wife bakes the gingerbread, special."

When the porter accompanied her to her seat, he tipped his cap to Edward Dickinson, well known to the railroad staff. Emily knew Father was pleased by the gesture.

She didn't want to read, just talk. She asked when he'd first met Otis Phillips Lord, and hoped Father would not detect her tremulous joy in speaking his full name. He rarely offered confidences, but they had a long journey ahead of them.

Edward took a swallow of tea and leaned his head back. "Otis came to call on me when he was a freshman, in, let's see, the autumn of 1828. Hat in hand and a stiff collar and tie. A proper young man of sixteen, bearing a letter of greeting from his father, Squire Nathaniel Lord, Register of Deeds in Ipswich. Amateur classicist, I believe. Also a poet. Wrote about astronomy, or some such thing."

He signaled to her with his mighty eyebrows. Father took pride in his ability to retrieve distant facts. She wondered whether he knew that she had written poems about the stars and the Northern Lights.

"What did he look like then? Otis, I mean. I was too young to notice."

Her father gave her a deep studious glance. "Surely you would not call him Otis, Emily. Or would you?"

Phil, Judge Owl, my Lord, Your Grace, Master, Dearest Jurist.

"No, Father, I've never called him Otis. But please resume."

She hid a smile in her teacup and offered him a biscuit. Not as good as her gingerbread, her father said, brushing dry crumbs from his coat.

"He looked like himself, only younger and thinner, of course. He had those vivid blue eyes, which have now acquired a reputation for the way he flashes them at lawyers and witnesses. A strong, mobile face. Otis loved to talk, as he still does. I knew he was headed for a career in law. Since I am not much of a talker, I found the young man's company quite agreeable. As did your mother. In time, Otis became quite affectionate with you and Vinnie, and brought out the scamp in both you girls."

For a wild moment, Emily wanted to tell her father about the pink and yellow bows on their drawers. He went on, "Without meaning to, he made Austin feel shy. But it was an instructive shyness, teaching him to curb his impulses. He had a happy effect on your mother, too."

She felt a surge of joy.

"One day I came home and your mother was in the garden, laughing as I have hardly ever seen her laugh. Otis was chasing you and Vinnie around, or vice-versa, and Vinnie kept falling down and getting up and falling down on her little fat legs. Your mother sometimes said that children were the funniest things on earth."

"How old was I?" She anticipated a sleepless night trying to relive her days as a scamp.

"Vinnie had just learned to walk, or rather totter. I suspect you were three. You were very quick, and you kept bumping into Otis's long legs and then running away, then charging at him again, like a tiny wild horse. He was a fit, well-built young man, but your mother said that you gave him such a merry chase, he needed about a quart of water to restore himself."

"His Little Playthings."

"What? Come again?" Edward leaned toward Emily and cupped his ear.

"He said that he called me and Vinnie his Little Playthings." Her father's dramatic eyebrows twitched.

"Oh, did he now? Well, I don't remember that, and I would advise you not to repeat that phrase into any ear that might make sport of it in a newspaper."

She waited for him to say more, but in a few minutes, her father nodded off, and Emily felt her own eyelids droop. Needing the lavatory, she eased out of her seat carefully, so as not to disturb her father, and sought out the little closet the porter had shown them. By the time she returned, the train had slowed to a crawl, and the snow pasted itself to the windows. The lights flickered out, and the train stopped. After a few tickings and wheezings, the engine fell silent. Awake again, Father looked at her with consternation. A wave of cold air swept down the corridor. The porter leaned from the car and looked up and down the tracks. Emily stood up to peer out the top of the window. The wind was blowing from the northeast. Her discomfort yielded to fear. Nor'easters, as every New Englander knew, could devour trains, as maelstroms could swallow ships and tigers feast on a man's dainty bones.

"I hope you are warm enough, Father."

"The storm has arrived early. Nothing we can do."

They waited for news from the porter, but heard only shouts and footsteps running down the aisle, and a forlorn whistle. Emily rubbed the cloudy pane and found an opening between daubs of white. Snow piled up along the rails. A flicker or two from lanterns propped between the cars showed nobody with shovels, no lights outside. They were stuck in some uninhabited region of the state, not even on a map, she imagined, except for the scar of railroad tracks.

"*Here Be Dragons,*" she whispered.

"Say again?"

"My mind, Father, playing silly games. Shall I sit next to you, so that we can warm each other? The end of my nose would chill a specter."

"Yes, Emily, that would be welcome." She moved to the seat next to his, then wrapped one end of her thick shawl around his coat, encasing both of them in paisley. Groping around the dark seat, she found his hat and settled it on his head, then found her gloves, put them on, and felt for her father's hands. It was too dark in the train to hunt for his gloves, which he was probably sitting on. In a few minutes, he seemed to have fallen asleep again. She placed his cold bare hands between her knees and packed her heavy skirt around them. Praise God, she had tucked winter underthings in her case.

The train seemed to be nowhere. She tried to remember if she had ever been nowhere. No small houses nearby, no town or factory or farm. On a Saturday night between Christmas and the New Year, the whole state slumbered. Cows, chickens, and famous pianists had retired to their rooms. She and her father might have been harbored in Salem, comfortable among quilts, savoring the fires lit in every room. The men in leather chairs in Phil's library, sipping brandy and talking late. The women reading, retiring early. How could her heart, stoked with kindling, have borne two days near Phil's ruddy fireside? She might have spilled her wine or stayed awake, her eyes pasted open and her ears pricked for any domestic sounds—laughter, murmurs, the clink of glasses.

Or Salem might have been more like home than she assumed. Conversation, firelight, comfort.

She drifted off to the sound of her father's light snores. Snow multiplied itself, white on white. She conjured up Phil's blue eyes above his white stock and tie.

In the middle of the night, Phil opens the door to her room. She is still awake. He climbs into the bed and wraps her in his arms. At last she sleeps.

"Emily. My dearest. My own wife." Father's hands climbed out from between her knees to gather her against his chest. He slept deeply.

She dared not disturb his dream of Mother. How long, she wondered, since her parents' bodies had realized this dream?

Back and forth, half asleep, she crossed from world to world, home to elsewhere, nowhere, anywhere. Her mind was a boat, a carriage, a train, a sled, a cradle, a bed in a town near the sea, or a room guarded by snowy hemlocks. Hours passed.

The porter's footsteps awakened her. Her father unwrapped her shawl from his shoulders and placed it around her, tucking in the ends.

"It appears we are to wait out the storm. Are you afraid, my dear?"

"Not yet. This is not the Yukon, or the High Sierras. It is little old Massachusetts."

She didn't want to say that her worry was for him, not herself. He was older, grayer, not altogether well. But he was still Edward Dickinson, and irreplaceable.

"All will be well, Emily. We won't starve or die. We'll stay on the train and wait. There are provisions, and sooner or later they'll re-light the lamps to alert the rescuers. Remember, I am still involved with railroads in this state."

She took pride in the pride of his voice.

Father could stir the snow with his finger, and make it melt.

Safe in our alabaster chambers, we'll wait until the snow has reached our lips and covered up our names.

The storm howled around the train, its tail miles away in the North Atlantic. *Hurry inland,* she telegraphed the beast, and *curl yourself in a cave.*

6.

My House is a House of Snow
Boston, Amherst, 1874

June 16

E dward Dickinson staggers in the noon heat, his boot-soles steaming. The State House shimmers behind him. His speech in the House chamber—arguing for more and better railroads—fades from his memory. Suddenly faint, he'd had to sit down and put his head between his knees. His colleagues' voices slammed around the room, breaking into echoes.

"I am old, I am done with speeches." His legs scarcely hold him up. The three hundred yards to the Tremont House, where he boards when away from Amherst, stretch and buckle, as though an earthquake trembled under the Boston Common.

Near collapse, he pushes the dead-weight door into the Tremont House lobby. When his eyes adjust to the dark, stuffy interior, he wanders into the dining room, where he orders a beer and a cup of clam chowder. The chowder tastes like wet sand, the beer is piss-warm. The headache that started in the House chamber throbs around his skull like a war drum.

In his room, his heart thudding and his skin clammy, he starts to pack for home. He can hear the panic in his lungs as he gasps for air. When a breath of wind rustles the window curtain into a slim white column, he thinks Emily has appeared to take him back to Amherst. *Put your hand in mine, Father, and I'll lift you up.* But she is only an apparition induced by heat. In the mirror, his own grim mouth and hectic dark eyes tell him he must get home as soon as possible.

He lies on the narrow bed, trying to calm his nerves. Every breath brings him less oxygen, more heat. One of his eyes goes dark, as he gropes for the porter's bell. His brain whirls among strange stars, while his body descends, a train to nowhere, through gray space.

At home, Emily sets the table for four before she remembers that Father is away. Overcome by an odd feeling of dread, she sits down and puts her face in her hands, then gets up and looks eastward out the window. The last train to Boston has just left Amherst, its horn-blast whinnying away. It is too hot to eat. She slides into Father's chair and shuts her eyes. Wetness trickles from the back of her neck down her spine, as she dozes on her folded arms. Trailing sparks from her sleeves, Emily pursues her father from Beacon Street to the hotel, to his room. Her ear is at the door, her eye searching for the keyhole. She calls his name, but her voice is useless. She whispers to him across the hundred miles from Amherst to Boston. "Wait, Father, wait . . . ."

"Doctor," Edward Dickinson whispers to the porter, who leans toward him and cups his ear. "Doctor." It is his last word on this earth.

*

"Doctor, murderer," Emily sobs against Austin's chest. Nightmares wrap her in a bristling caul.

"We are lost," Austin repeats—almost his only words since the fatal telegram: COME AT ONCE TREMONT HOUSE YOUR FATHER APOPLEXY

Too late for the train. The barnyard a chaos of horses, rushing men, Austin snapping orders.

Then another telegram: EDWARD DICKINSON DIED SIX P.M.

"He was not a doctor, but a stranger. To give him morphine! To take him away, like a kidnapper!"

"He is somewhere else, Emily. No doctors now."

Only undertakers, weeping relatives, neighbors bearing inedible hot food. Helpless kindness.

Father has no feet, no face, no body. Emily burrows through a long tunnel into Father's new house, cool and lonely. In dreams, when she reaches for his hand to help him travel from his sweaty seat in the Statehouse westward to his green island in the Amherst grass, she finds his fingers, crisp, bony air.

She refuses to go to the funeral. Her eyes are almost swollen shut, her throat raw. Austin totters like an old man.

Phil will come when he can.

June 19

Emily hides her face against his coat. Phil thinks it is like holding a weeping flame. He has never seen her in such a helpless state. She looks as though she has eaten nothing for days, and she has no size to spare.

Through her cracked-open bedroom door, they hear the minister's voice from the front parlor. Reverend Jenkins's words are full of tears, as he reads from the Book of John.

In my Father's house are many mansions. If it were not so, I would have told you.

I go to prepare a place for you.

The words, read long before at his own father's funeral, remind Phil of Emily's remark, "Home is a holy thing," one of her out-of-the-blue utterances at the dinner table, years ago.

Emily has left her hair loose from its customary Greek knot. The soft waves carry a delicate scent of jasmine. Phil had no time to pack a change of clothes before rushing to the train from the Cambridge court. Late, distracted, and uncomfortable, he cannot not make time to grieve openly. As he has done so many times, he calls upon his sense of propriety to help him through the shock of Edward's death.

He wants to comfort her in some simple way.

"Would you mind if I used your hairbrush?"

She points to the bureau. "I'm not sure it's suited to your hair, but please use it if you need to."

He sits her down on the bed and brushes her hair back from her forehead, down to the middle of her back in a deep auburn wave. She leans her forehead against him, and he removes his watch chain and fob. After a few minutes, he gathers his coat around him, embarrassed to be aroused at a time like this.

Phil brooded on Edward's last days. Hurrying from Amherst to Boston for a legislative meeting, his friend must have weakened hour by hour until he collapsed. The heat and the cigar smoke in the State House chamber would have made it hellish. Within a few hours, having been given morphine by a doctor unfamiliar with Edward's previous bad reactions to the drug, he was dead.

He recalled the 1852 Whig convention in steamy Baltimore, when they exchanged confidences late at night over brandy: Edward's embarrassment at his father's bankruptcy, Phil's battles with his father about religion, their fears of radicalism, their worries about impending war. Using the abstract code of men, they scarcely touched forbidden subjects from their earlier lives—Edward's frantic desire to marry the lovely Emily Norcross; Phil's foolish adolescent romance with his second cousin Lucy; the sense of purpose won only through hard work.

Mellowed by the brandy, Edward confessed his hope that Austin would marry the fascinating, dark-eyed Susan Gilbert, and Phil his sorrow that he and Elizabeth had failed to produce living children. As the two friends talked of the bitter fractiousness between South and North, they feared that the future would be a tilting rock, likely to fall if the earth trembled. Their families and careers depended upon maintaining their beliefs in the old ways of the Republic, however unfashionable.

The next day they resumed the shouting and the speechifying. Years later, after each man had lost political influence in Massachusetts, Dickinson and Lord could count on each other to know the secrets of their hearts.

*

When Phil reaches to enfold Emily in his arms, he also embraces her father. He had never told Edward his feelings for his daughter. Comforted and sustained by Elizabeth, he was able to move away from a temptation to act outside convention. It was easier when Emily wasn't near him, giving him enigmatic smiles and little touches like sparks from firecrackers.

Lifting his hands from her slight shoulders, Phil catches a sleeve button in Emily's hair. Trying to untangle the strand, he botches the job, and she takes over, making a small whimper. Her smooth hair seems to have wound itself around the button of its own will. Two or three long bright strands trail from his sleeve.

Later he will wrap them in a handkerchief, unable to throw them away.

"Isn't it odd, Phil, how little things can bring us back to earth, even when we want to fly into space?" Emily takes his hands in her own as she reads the universe, her swollen eyelids shut. "I can hear muffled talk, the whistle of teakettles from the kitchen, Father's horses in their stalls, the lazy hum of bees in the honeysuckle. Nature keeps on delivering its own mail, in its own time, no matter what has happened to mere people. My human senses are both numb and alert. Death makes us more alive. It will take me the rest of my life to understand this, and by then it will be too late to send messages back to earth."

He kisses her hair and leads her to the window. They watch the funeral procession move off down Main Street on its slow trek to the graveyard.

Now is the ultimate goodbye—the undertaker closing the coffin, the pallbearers shuffling forward. Emily sees Austin stumble, then grasp Sue's arm. As if in quiet respect, the wind drops away.

"It would comfort me to tell you a story I have kept in my heart all these years." He points across the street. Emily gazes at the grassy corner of the Dickinson meadow, where she used to walk with Carlo, now a large, blunt-nosed shape visible only to her. There are too many words for death and birth.

"I stood in that very spot, the night you were born. I was eighteen years old." He tells her about the December night when he saw Edward slip on the ice, rushed to help him, and heard him gasp that his wife was in labor.

"It didn't seem right to go back to my room. Hours after midnight, I heard a newborn baby cry. Shadows passed back and forth across this very window. Then I saw the silhouette of your father, looking out at the wintry dark. I trudged off to campus just as dawn broke. The baby was you, of course, uttering your first word, saluting the sunrise, as you like to do. I am a witness to your arrival in the world."

"No wonder I feel so connected to you."

"I am responsible for you, Emily. It was written in the stars. Those silver balloons you talked of, long ago? It snowed that night, for hours. I almost froze my legs off, my dear. But here I am, not at all frozen."

She pours water into her basin, and wets a handkerchief. Sitting Phil in her reading-chair, she loosens his collar and dabs his face, then her own tear-streaked cheeks.

In his damp shirt, his grief exposed and his body throbbing, Phil is at the mercy of the story he told her. She manages a whisper. "All the birthdays remaining to me I'll celebrate with you at midnight on July 10, your birthday-eve, whether you are in my garden or elsewhere."

"My claim and yours. Settled and firm. Not law on the books, but our own law."

"The Sunday before he took the train to Boston, Father spent the whole afternoon with me. A rare occasion, except for our trip home from Rubinstein, when a snow-beast held us captive."

He imagines Emily and Edward in the library, the smell of heliotropes drifting in from her conservatory.

91

"I will go to my grave wondering if he had worries about his health, or Mother's travails. I am ashamed to say that I brought the conversation to a close, proposing that he walk with Austin, who was pacing in the garden. I should have let Father stay to talk with me, because I wanted it too. Now I always will. The future is a mystery, because we'll always wish the past was otherwise."

"Your father was a mature man, not a needy child. He wouldn't want you to feel distress."

Their shared wisdom feels right, part of her business to love and speak the truth.

"That afternoon I read to him, from Psalms. Played 'All Things Bright and Beautiful' and 'Believe Me, If All Those Endearing Young Charms.' When I played it, Father's face turned soft around the edges. Once, years ago, when I sang the song, I caught a reflection of my parents in the portraits above the piano. A handsome couple, and they still knew it."

Their voices drop to whispers. His silk tie is askew, still moist.

"Father's life was as lonely as his death. What happens to men who work too hard and simply fall off the earth? Why can't they rest?"

He remembers his own father, Nathaniel, who had also died suddenly and alone.

"I would like to hold you, please, if you would let me." Sorrow and love twine around each other.

He sits in the chair and gathers Emily onto his lap. Phil unbuttons the top two buttons of her dress, and kisses her throat. Quiet sobs, a spill of tears. He has gone too far, but she holds his face in her hands and kisses one ear, then the other. A brilliant sliver of light wavers toward him from the bower in his mind. He watches until he can no longer bear it.

"It is a marvel and a horror to be alive at this moment, isn't it, Phil?"

Outside, the day's unreal sunlight dissipates into the hemlocks.

Edward Dickinson is beyond the privileges of earth and air.

7.

We talked with each other about each other
Amherst, April – September 1876

P hil climbed the stairs to the Evergreens guest room,
where he found his traveling case and clothes neatly laid
out. Sue Dickinson always took good care of her visitors.
The handsomely decorated room had a reading chair, a bed
with a thick double mattress, a commode in the dressing
room, and carafes of brandy and soda water on the dresser.
It was like a room in a fine hotel.

Still, he would have been happier, while presiding at
the Northampton court, to stay at the Homestead in the
bedroom that faced the garden. The furniture dated from
forty years ago, the mattress needed turning, and the dresser
held no carafe of brandy. When he had stayed there, with
or without Elizabeth, Emily would knock gently to offer
morning tea and toast. He liked getting up early to watch the
birds sport in the trees while the rest of the world awakened.
In the Homestead kitchen, he'd find Emily, already dressed,
her hair in a braid hanging down her back, slicing her
homemade bread and spooning jam in pretty dabs on her
mother's best china.

Since Edward's death, daily rituals had helped the family
through their grief. Every day, Austin would go next door for

breakfast. Emily baked, Vinnie cleaned, and Maggie Maher turned visitors away. Emily told Phil that she dreamed of her father nearly every night. He imagined Edward striding into the dining room to place his papers in the empty soup tureen, where he could be sure to find them.

By contrast, the atmosphere in the Evergreens oppressed Phil. Tension roiled in the air like the smoke of Austin's little cigars. Sue and Austin moved in their separate spheres during the day and met only at the dinner table—a normal arrangement for a busy couple, but he sensed that man and wife had never reached accord. Ned, Mattie, and Gib, such different ages, moved in their own worlds, although Ned liked to pull his little brother in his wagon. Ned's awkwardness and Mattie's petulance sometimes made meals a trial. Gib liked falling in the grass, rolling around, and repeating the performance on his little drunken legs. The child reminded Phil of Vinnie when she and Emily were his Little Playthings, over forty years before.

After supper, Austin strolled with the judge around the neighborhood, and they talked in the Evergreens library. He still struggled with his father's death.

"Otis, I never dared to kiss my father until he lay silent in his coffin. When I told him so, he wasn't listening."

"That makes me sad."

"Was your father affectionate with your family?"

Lord added water to his brandy glass and swirled it around. "I remember when he truly became my father in feeling as well as biology, when my baby brother Isaac died, at twenty months. I was almost three, bewildered at Isaac's sudden disappearance. He was a lovely little boy, and I liked to curl up next to him when he napped. One day I touched his forehead and found him burning up with fever. I ran to my mother, and was whisked out of the nursery and confined to my room. The end came quickly. I was restless at Isaac's funeral, which took place in the spring, and distracted by the birds and squirrels in the Ipswich Burying Ground. I leaped about like a wild kid, until my sister Mary slapped my hand and I started to cry. Papa picked me up and held me. I remember patting his wet cheek."

Sipping his brandy, he felt for his handkerchief. "It's odd to remember something that happened before I learned to read, but the scene remains with me. And then he said—my blue-eyed feisty father, whose face is the model for my own—'You are my treasured boy, and I never want to lose you.' He was the same age as Edward when he died of a stroke almost twenty years ago, and, like your father, he just toppled over and disappeared from this earth. He was alone, not even my stepmother with him. Unbearable. But we all die alone, I suppose."

He thought of Edward, Emily grieving in his arms, and Vinnie wearing herself out with usefulness. Austin carried his grief in an unreachable place. He and his father were both close and not close, depending on the family weather. Phil guessed that Austin's difficult marriage produced inadmissible frustration. Edward had admired the elegant Sue, with her talent for décor and her scintillating manners. How could Austin have spoken frankly to his father about his home troubles, and risked severe judgment?

They sipped their brandy and listened to the sounds of Amherst putting itself to bed. Horses, children, wagons rolling into their barns. Phil always found the rhythm of country life a comfort.

He saw the misery in Austin's face, and made his voice quiet. "I detect unhappiness in this house. Please let me know if I can help."

"I'm sorry you have to bear witness. I hoped that Gib—unexpected, but for me entirely welcome—would bring about a change. Sue is a devoted mother, proud of her children. She loves them more than she ever loved any member of her family, or my family, or me."

Austin had never been so open with his father's best friend.

"That is sometimes the case with women. The attachment is so close."

"I appreciate your ways with my children. You're kind to Ned, who is sometimes slow and has odd vacancies in his speech. Emily is more patient with him than Sue is, and keeps him well furnished with apple pies. Still, he is too thin."

Phil touched Austin's knee. "I would advise you to take him to a children's specialist, as soon as you can." He hoped he had made his big voice sufficiently persuasive.

They heard a rustle of skirts. Sue strode in, a sleepy Gib in her arms like a young emperor. She had combed his blond hair in a Roman style around his forehead.

Austin dandled his small son, and the judge made friendly noises at the little boy, trying to remember whether he had ever seen Edward hold any of his children, or swing them around in the garden. Austin's face softened as he bounced the radiant Gib on his knee.

When Phil retired to the guest room, he hoped the serene tableau he had just witnessed would last.

Late that night, he awoke to agitated voices, feet rushing on the stairs, the sound of Sue weeping, and Austin hurrying upstairs to Ned's room with a basin and towels.

Phil knocked on Ned's door. "It's me. I'm here to help."

The boy lay unconscious on his bed, his nightclothes streaked with vomit. His chin was red, his face ghost-white.

97

"He's had some kind of seizure. I think he bit his tongue. I don't know what this is. I heard thrashing coming from his room. When I came in he was being sick and moaning. Could he have eaten something poisonous?"

"Let's get him cleaned up. I think I know what this is. A friend at school had it." He helped Austin unbutton Ned's soiled nightshirt and together they washed him. The boy moaned but didn't wake up.

He raised a window to let out the sour smell.

Austin asked in a rough whisper, "What is it?"

"Epilepsy, I believe. Is this the first?"

"As far as I know. Epilepsy! Pray God it's a temporary horror. He looks so wasted. He's only fifteen."

Phil didn't want to tell Austin that the seizure was probably not the last, and that there might be many more. What a sorry thing for a fifteen-year-old.

"Do you want to fetch his mother?"

"Sue couldn't bear the thrashing and the vomiting. And it would be too much to ask one of the servants to keep watch—they are run ragged already. I can't ask Vinnie or Emily—they are too busy with Mother."

Austin would take care of things, as always. The two men sat by Ned's bedside until his breathing grew more regular and color returned to his face.

"You go back to bed, I'll watch here."

Austin stretched out on the carpet. Phil covered him with a quilt and placed a pillow under his head. Poor man, he thought, isolated in his own house, without much wifely comfort. He bundled up the stained nightclothes and left them outside Ned's door.

Returning to the guest room, he saw no sign of Sue, no light from Emily's window.

September 1876

When Phil returned in the fall for another round at court, Emily noticed the dark pouches under his eyes. Ill for weeks, he had taken a long rest cure at the Crawford Hotel in the White Mountains. Some days he would hike if he felt well enough, but he spent most afternoons sketching on the hotel porch. He avoided company, except for a few old pals from Salem. Gossip about his incapacity and probable retirement echoed throughout courthouses all over the state.

"It shows, doesn't it, Emily? My age and feebleness."

"You may call yourself feeble, but I know better. I hope you are now on the mend, from whatever—"

"Inflammatory rheumatism. I could think of several other names for it, but they are not for your tender ears."

Alone in the parlor, they talked about Edward.

"I still dream about Father, every night a different dream. I suppose it's a form of conjuring. He is always silent, so I talk to him through a crack in a rock."

Phil rested his head on the mahogany sofa-back. The teapot sat untouched, although he nibbled a piece of her gingerbread. He asked her to play a tune on her piano.

She had told Loo Norcross that after hearing Rubinstein in 1872, she found it difficult to resume the piano. But now she played Mendelssohn's *Elegie*, one of her favorites. Phil glimpsed Sue pausing to listen outside the open French window. As the echoes faded, Emily sat motionless. When Sue walked in and gave her a swift kiss on the cheek, Emily shook her head as if she'd been sprinkled with cold water.

"That was a treat. I haven't heard you play in ages! You must come over and play it for the children."

Sue's party-in-the-parlor voice made Emily recoil. "If music leaps out of the windows, that is simply what music

does. The children are always welcome to come and listen."
Phil, catching the emphasis, saw Sue purse her lips.

"How is my friend Austin?"

"Oh, about the same. He complains of a headache, but
I trust this will pass. He plans to take Ned to the Centennial
Exposition in Philadelphia in a few weeks. Austin never
wants to leave Amherst, but I think Ned would enjoy the
sights. The boy needs to broaden his horizons."

"I pray he is well enough to do so. A change is as good as
a rest, they say."

Phil wondered about Emily's coolness to Sue. While Sue
chattered about Philadelphia, she slipped out of the parlor.

Emily did not intend to sit at Sue's table, even with Phil
there. In ten minutes, she predicted, he would peek into the
kitchen. When he did, he looked embarrassed.

"I promised Susan that I would test my juridical powers
by asking you to tea. Could you spare a moment?"

He sneaked her a wink.

Emily wiped sugar and berry juice from her hands and
followed him into the parlor.

Sue's dark eyes swept over the red stains. "Your apron
gives the appearance of battle!"

Emily recognized the mixed messages of playfulness and
criticism. "I choose my battles so well, Susie. Judge Lord said
you wanted to confer with me? I must have hatched into a
strategist."

Sue grasped Emily's wrist. "Please, darling, do come over
to tea. I know it is hard for you to leave your aerie. But it
will just be the four of us, and the children." She swayed
seductively back and forth in her rich skirts.

Emily drew back. "So that makes six, assuming Ned and
Mattie. What about Vinnie?" She did not intend to make

this easy. Sue seemed frustrated that she couldn't outsmart her. As Phil watched them talk, he thought that Emily indeed resembled a strategist.

"Yes, of course." Sue said in a clipped voice. She and Vinnie were not close.

"I can't leave Mother."

Emily wondered how often she had been obliged to utter these bleak, necessary words. Sue seemed to forget the invalid upstairs, except when she brought Gib to be admired, if he was freshly bathed and not too wiggly.

"Yes, darling, of course I understand. But—"

"I shall stay with Mother, and Vinnie will come to tea, if you will have her. Maggie has Sunday evenings off, as you know. Vinnie needs relief from her long watches, and it would be a kindness to include her."

Phil added "lawyer" to "strategist," and suppressed an admiring smile that might irritate Sue. When Emily met an obstacle in her path, she could be as sinuous as a garden snake. Sue turned a look of wavery brilliance on the judge. After she left, Emily touched Phil's arm.

"Please don't think I am declining your cherished company. I don't go next door for any social occasion. The children come here often, Sue sometimes, and Austin breakfasts with us every day. I send bread or pies or a chicken, slain and plucked for chicken-Heaven. I can't explain my stubborn behavior. It has deep roots and draws from frosty springs."

"You don't need to explain, dear. Now go tell Vinnie about the plans, and I will stop back here after tea, if you'll have me." The promise lifted her heart.

*

Phil was sorry that Austin, fighting a cold, was in bed. When the guests were seated around Sue's elegant table, baby Gib made a ritual appearance in his nurse's arms, to have his tiny damp toes wiggled and his silken blond hair stroked. He was a beautiful child. Phil hoped that the little boy could put off wearing the Dickinson face—thoughtful, tense, and sad—that Austin had acquired over the years.

Vinnie poured Ned a generous glass of her homemade currant wine, and Phil mentally saluted her. Somebody had to help the boy into the social world and assure him that he didn't have to parade as a young Prince Dickinson. Perhaps the wine calmed the boy's nerves and staved off his seizures. Pleading schoolwork, Mattie escaped to her room, and her mother didn't protest. He knew the girl had never found him amusing. On a long-ago visit to Salem, she had frowned when the judge teased that she might like to come and live with the Lords in their big lonely house. When the six-year-old displayed a pre-tantrum flush, Elizabeth took her upstairs to let her rummage in her jewelry box. Emily called Mattie "the North Wind."

Phil sensed that everyone at the table wished to be somewhere else. The conversation flapped around and threatened to land with a thud in the berry trifle. Then Vinnie raised the subject of grim Calvinist hymns no one sang any more. With a solemn air, Phil laid down his fork and began to recite: "*My thoughts on awful subjects roll, Damnation, and the dead.*" Ned tried out various faces. Phil let forth a short humorous bark, and a frowning Sue poured her guests more wine.

"Do you remember the choir in the old First Church, when they allowed people to keep their pigs and chickens in the cellar during the winter months?" Vinnie asked the judge.

Ned broke into helpless laughter. "I can't imagine my sober Grandfather herding chickens into church!"

Avoiding Sue's glance, Phil grinned. "I dare you to bring forth a hymn that I can't sing, Vinnie. Remember good old *Watts and Select?* We were all raised on it." He adjusted his silk stock. He often parodied his own dignified courtroom manners, although Sue never got the joke. Vinnie would always accept a dare. She could mimic anybody, even a whole congregation of hymn-singers and whatever farm animals they herded into the church cellar.

"*Broad is the road that leads to death,*" she sang in a warbly soprano, as Phil seized the lower line and produced a woeful imitation of a bass viol. Vinnie faltered on the high notes and switched registers, to add a lugubrious touch.

> *The fearful soul that tires and faints,*
> *And walks the ways of God no more,*
> *Is but esteemed almost a saint,*
> *And makes his own destruction sure.*

*

"Oh, Emily, you should have heard it." Vinnie slapped her knee. She and Emily sat with Phil in the parlor, drinking Father's port.

"Our friend the judge reminded me of Father when he mocked that preacher who mixed up 'cherubim' and 'terrapin.' Sue was not happy, I can tell you. And Ned looked as though he'd swallowed a live cricket. Then Austin banged on his wall to tell us *it's a Sunday night!*" Vinnie caught Austin's imperious baritone, and Emily clapped approval. She guessed that their brother was feeling better.

103

Vinnie's went upstairs to check on Mother, her laughter ringing out behind her.

Emily walked her fingers up Phil's sleeve and gently tugged his earlobe.

"Judge-Lord-Sir-Honorable-Supreme-Esquire. Was that a contrivance? Did you dip your toes into the river of plot and parody?" For a bright second, she wondered about his toes. *Long and well-groomed.*

"Never. I say never."

"You are lying, Signor."

"You accused me of that once before, on this very property. If I am a liar, then how could you believe my saying I am no such thing?"

Emily took Phil's empty port glass into the kitchen, and returned with a small brandy from her father's dwindling stock, then more port for herself in one of her mother's ruby glasses. She lit a lamp and he held up his glass to the light.

"The Rhenish was flowing rather freely at supper. I think Sue finds it more palatable than Vinnie's currant wine, although young Ned might disagree after tonight."

"Our currant wine comes straight from the woods, and suits us country folk. Vinnie and I make it in large crocks. We can testify to its potency. And so can Professor Tyler, who once drank three glasses of it and started to quote naughty poems in Latin. I have a sneaky feeling that you have quoted those same poems yourself."

He wondered if Emily knew Catullus's filthy, unforgettable lyrics.

"I stand convicted of racy behavior. But you are more daring than I am. I thought of your May Wine poem tonight. You claim to have a taste unfamiliar to mere mortals, and to drink from shining tankards. Little Tippler!" He folded her arm in his, and held it against him, as he had in the church in Cambridge.

Emily raised her glass to Phil, to thank him for quoting her words. "I'm relieved that poem was published anonymously, sent to Sam Bowles by Sue without my permission. With my name on it, it might have ensured my reputation as a stumbling drunk. Of all the poems to steal from me, I wish they had left that one alone."

"I don't like that word 'steal.' It raises my jurist's hackles. Poems belong to those who made them."

Emily leaned over and kissed his cheek. "Your reward for speaking a truth I have long believed."

Phil hunted for a way to make the conversation safer, before he could be tempted to haul Emily into his lap and disarrange her clothes. "Has the acquaintance with Mr. Higginson done you good? His essays are quite appealing, even if I find his poetry lacks muscle."

"Mr. Higginson saved my life. We have been corresponding since 1862, when I sent him some poems. I am still astonished that a famous man of letters writes to me, but it feels like mail from a kindly planet."

Emily could be dramatic, but she was not play-acting. Her low voice rushed forth in a clear stream. "I trust him, Phil. I did not ask him to make me famous, or to make my verses known. I know that my words create menageries instead of promenades. But, although he gives sound, if conventional, advice, he has never tried to make a project out of me. And he would never have put anything of mine into print without asking me first."

"Years ago you and Sue were close. Am I right? What happened? Even before your father died, I could feel the distance between you, as though a chasm had opened up in the parlor rug, and neither of you could move for fear of falling in."

Emily could not disclose all of her private truths to Phil—there were too many old loves and disappointments—but tonight was different. She wondered whether Father's absence, sad as it was, made disclosures easier.

"Before Sue married Austin, she was everything to me. I found her beautiful and exciting—and the story of her orphanhood and her tavern-keeping father moved me. It must have been hard for her to walk into her home and never know what unhappy scene she might stumble on. Still, she always sang a different melody from us Dickinsons, even Father, who admired her extravagantly. I lived in my imagination, and the family, and cherished friends, and my dear old shaggy Carlo. And she wanted to live in the world. She even traveled to New York by herself before she married Austin, to hear a Jenny Lind concert. I could never have dared to do that."

Phil imagined Emily's small person flitting through the cliffs and canyons of New York, chased by menacing shadows. The thought made him shiver.

"Sue wanted a man's privileges, so she simply took them. Impressive—and risky."

He watched her thumb stroke the stem of her glass, then reached for it and put it aside to hand his glass to her. "Drink a sip of brandy, dear. It is good for easing revelations." Emily tasted the brandy. The color of her eyes, in the subtle light.

"When she kept urging me to join the church, you may imagine the fireworks that leaped from me. Even Father beat a dignified retreat from that campaign. Sending my poems to Sam Bowles's *Republican* was another attempt at control.

A dinner invitation I could refuse, but I could do nothing about—thievery. All the more so because I loved the thief."

Her small bosom rose and fell. She took another sip, just to wet the tip of her tongue. She thought it tasted like amber, if amber had a taste. Sipping from Phil's glass made her feel like a pet of royal pedigree.

"And yet you would be welcome there. I can imagine you dazzling Emerson with your words, or letting some hot air out of Henry Ward Beecher."

Emily laughed, knowing Phil's stringent opinion of Beecher, the great orator with slippery morals.

"When I used to attend large parties at the Evergreens, I felt too small for conversation with strangers. Important men would lean down, cup their ears, and say 'What?' as though I'd just spoken to them in Old Norse. Even the temptation to talk with Ralph Waldo Emerson was not enough to budge me."

She took another sip of brandy. A drop lingered on her lips. Phil touched his little finger to the drop, then tasted it.

They looked at each other for a full minute without speaking. She made a noise somewhere between a sigh and a moan. He arose from the couch and walked back and forth, trying to concentrate on what he would say next. Emily's "liquor never brewed" stirred in his veins. He wanted to urge their talk toward a truth long withheld.

"I have been a judge for many years, yet only recently have I allowed myself to think that Sue may have been the victim of mistreatment, long ago, when she was a child. My worst days in court, as with the Crowe case long ago, confront me with selfish parents and miserable children. The misery can take many forms—verbal, physical, emotional— but always flows from the same dark well. Youngest children dependent on unworthy adults, as Sue was dependent on her hard-drinking father, often endure hard times. On the faces of these victims, I see an expression of confused rage."

Emily reached for his hand. "I have thought the same thing, but I didn't have the right words for it. Sometimes when Sue and Austin are tense with each other, I detect a cloud passing over her face. And it breaks my heart to think the root of Sue's troubles is a distrust that has threatened her capacity to love."

He sat down beside her, his knee touching hers. The closeness was almost unbearable. "When you reach for my hand, Emily, when you wrapped your arms around me in your room, after Edward died, I know that whatever else life has denied you, your capacity to love defines you. Alas, it's a blessing that not everyone has. And its opposite produces more grief. Sue is among that unfortunate company, and Austin suffers the effects." He passed a hand over his forehead, as if to wipe away dark thoughts. "But now let us sit here with each other and rejoice in our friendship."

Emily lifted Phil's hand and kissed it, as lightly as he had kissed hers a few hours before.

"At the moment, dearest jurist, life is denying me nothing."

Twilight overtook the room. The oak tree east of the house disappeared into a flutter of pale leaves.

"I don't want to light another lamp, Phil. Silence with you is a comfort, because you never push me to disclose my private thoughts, you only make disclosure possible. That compact we made long ago still holds. So I'll tell you an old secret about me: in my early twenties I was in love with Sue. I wanted her to be my soul's truest friend and sister. I showed her poems and wrote her passionate letters. One stormy night, we huddled under the covers, creating our own chaos of kisses and shrieks. I have loved thunder ever since."

Phil, who rarely prayed, felt almost prayerful, hearing Emily's intimate disclosure. He also felt a twinge of disappointment that Sue, not he, was the subject of this old secret.

"I am obviously not a woman, and I have never felt for a man what you have felt for her. But I do know you are a passionate person, and I think you always were, even when you were a little girl."

She tucked her hand in his, and kept it there, savoring the tiny electric shock that leaped between their fingers. "I've been struck by lightning more than once. I am a collection of wayward filaments. You must be careful when you get near me." She dropped her eyelids as she made her mischievous smile.

"I'll take all your sparks and filaments, naughty Emily, and one day raise fireworks around your brilliant head." Phil intended to keep his promise.

8.

I died for Beauty
Salem, December 1877

H e watched Elizabeth try to raise her head from the
pillow. Her lips were chapped, her fine dark hair now
completely white, her features strict and diminished. She had
refused food for days, and took only water. With every breath
the world became less real to her.

Remembering his sister Mary's death, Phil thanked
the gods that the months of wracking pain, nausea, and
hallucinations were coming to an end. But every such release
came at a price for those left behind. Life would not be the
same without Elizabeth's gentle talk at the breakfast table
and her patient listening to his courtroom tales as she sat in
her dressing gown and braided her hair.

He had so much to say, to remember and explain. But
there was no more time.

The phantoms of their stillborn twin girls, Eunice and
Susanna, flitted like winter moths across his mind. Not able
to be baptized, they were given their names privately. If
they had lived, they would be thirty-three years old, perhaps
the mothers of his grandchildren. He no longer brooded
on what the twins would have looked like, how their voices
might have skirled through the big house, how he could have

felt their small weight in his lap as he told them stories. He hoped, without much hope, that Elizabeth might find them in her afterlife and scoop them up from their hiding places to nestle against her.

Three years after their death, he and his wife had vowed never to speak of them again. But Elizabeth became pregnant and had a miscarriage, at three months. A boy. Phil blamed himself for his insistent desire. She continued to respond to him with affection, although no longer with the playfulness of their early courtship. After they made love, she would excuse herself and go into her dressing room, she said, to "take care of things." He knew she was trying whatever methods might prevent another pregnancy.

Even as Elizabeth moved past childbearing age, her husband knew she felt like a failure for not giving him children to continue his name and family. Nothing he said brought comfort—not the vast population of Lords in Massachusetts, not the fact that two young cousins had been named for him, not the presence of two Farley nieces in their household, daughters of Elizabeth's widowed sisters. They talked about how different Molly and Abbie were—one cheerful, loud, and athletic, the other small-minded and obsessed with her appearance.

When he and his wife talked about the mystery of family, Elizabeth sometimes brought up the Dickinsons. "They seem to have come from different planets, especially Emily," she said one night. "So why should the Farleys be any different? Or the Lords? Perhaps the human race is trying to give itself a taste of variety."

Over the years, he and Elizabeth found pleasure in their roles as aunt and uncle, givers of birthday gifts, hosts of Thanksgiving feasts. Elizabeth's niece Molly added energy to the household. Mary Farley's daughter, Abbie, took pride in the frequent stories about her "Uncle Lord" in the newspaper. Somewhat to his surprise, he appreciated Abbie's attentiveness to court cases and to honors conferred on him, especially his appointment to the Massachusetts Supreme Court. However difficult Abbie could be, she had a sharp mind and a watchful eye.

"Aunt Elizabeth is having trouble walking," she told her uncle one day toward Christmas, when he returned from a long swing across the state. "You need to pay attention."

"Oh, it's just age, Otis," Elizabeth protested when he observed her pausing on each stair and grasping the banister handrail with white knuckles. "We'll not have the doctor in. He'll just say the obvious."

But the pain grew worse after the New Year, and this time Elizabeth agreed to see Dr. Carlton.

It was not old age, it was cancer. The pain had settled in her lower back, but she had a suspicious mass in her abdomen. A female cancer, they were told. Inoperable. It would take a slow course. For the next few months, the doctor said, much of the time she would feel quite normal.

"*Normal.*" Phil came to despise the word for its false comfort.

Elizabeth was sixty-two—too young to die. His mother had died of cancer at fifty-nine. His sister Mary, dead in her thirties, of typhoid. His brother Nathaniel—elegant, brilliant Nathaniel, who'd shaped his younger brothers into lawyers—dead at sixty-three after years enduring a wasting disease. Phil stopped going to church because he hated the sentimental pap that covered up the truest fact of life, mortality.

By late summer, Elizabeth was bedridden. She took laudanum for the pain, but it brought evil nightmares.

The doctor altered the dosage, but in October the pain surged again.

"Talking and holding your hand helps as much as anything," she told her husband. Her white cap emphasized her spare features and her pale, perfect skin, as if death were cleansing her for the final voyage.

He noticed that her hands had grown thin and spectral. If he held them up to the light, he might see through them to the flickering lamp by her bedside.

Witty conversation, court gossip, family news—all gone.

"I would talk to you until eternity, if possible. I regret each hour I have to spend on court business instead of here with you." He would walk into the house in fear that she had died in his absence, and climbed the stairs slowly, to keep himself calm until he could see her open eyes.

As his sister Mary had done years before, Elizabeth sometimes fell into wistful, dreaming-back moods, turning the pages of her life.

"Sometimes I think about Eunice and Susanna. Which of us they would have resembled. Their eyes, their hair. Their talents. And then the boy. We never gave him a name, he was so—incomplete."

"We could name him now, just for ourselves. It would do no harm, and it might bring you comfort."

She smiled, surprised and grateful. "Another Nathaniel, do you think?"

"That would make, let's see, the fourth. As you know, I'm not keen on dynasties."

"Edward. Let's call him Edward. Edward Dickinson Lord."

Her husband held his forehead against hers until he could speak again, then bent his head into his hands.

By mid-November, her sixty-third birthday, Elizabeth slept most of the time. Dr. Carlton tried various palliatives, but they left her swollen and fretful. Molly and Abbie wandered in and out of the sickroom, and Catherine O'Leary was always nearby, her husband, Tim, alert to the judge's need to hurry to or from court at a moment's notice. Molly would sit for hours by her aunt's bedside, trying to read or knit. Abbie would hurry in, cry a little as if on cue, murmur something, and leave. Elizabeth took little notice of them until one day, at the beginning of December, she struggled to sit up, fixed him with bright, hectic eyes, and asked for pen and paper.

"It has to be pen, doesn't it, Otis?" she asked as he propped her pillows.

"For what purpose?" His voice rose from the bottom of a well.

"Saying something that will last beyond me. Like a will, only different. For your eyes alone."

"Yes, whatever you wish."

A will or a codicil, he knew, always withstood scrutiny better in pen than in pencil. Whatever she declared he would honor if he could. What he heard from Elizabeth's own lips might evade his memory later on. He wrote down her words dutifully, like a court scribe: "I want my husband to be happy again after I am dead."

She lifted a weak hand. "Please do not ask me to repeat this, or explain it. I know what I mean."

"You have always known what you mean, my dear."

He remembered her saying, long ago: "I will marry you. You are the best man I know, and I have known you for all our lives that count. And we'll have many years to make each other happy."

They had known right away, after a sweet August evening in the barn loft, that Elizabeth was pregnant. Only her sister Mary knew, but nobody was surprised that they moved forward the wedding date to early October, since they'd been betrothed for months. Elizabeth wore her best dark blue dress, with a blond lace shawl. Six weeks later, when Mary married her cousin Alfred Farley, Elizabeth wore the same dress, and arranged the shawl carefully over her swelling middle . . . .

"Don't cry, Otis. You look terrible when you cry."

After a moment, he raised his head.

"Emily Dickinson." Her voice, unexpectedly firm. Her gray-green eyes on his. A look both hopeful and admonitory.

"Emily?" He held the pen, paralyzed. He knew why, yet could not fathom her command. Elizabeth seemed to have reached deep into his heart and found a place he could not hide from her or himself.

She pointed to the paper, and he wrote the name. He was used to writing it.

"She has . . . a gift for adoration. But she has learned to temper her hero-worship with common sense. I saw that when we went to Amherst and you helped Emily and her mother write their wills. Her father's loss was terrible, but it added a new force to her character."

Speaking all those words made Elizabeth breathless. Lord put down the pen and held her hand for a few minutes.

Images flickered past him: Emily planting bulbs in the garden. Elizabeth in the drawing room, putting their guests at ease. Emily in Cambridge, hiding her aching eyes as she listened to him read Shakespeare. A tune at midnight in the Homestead garden. Emily at her piano, ardent and shy. What it felt like to hold Emily in his arms as they both wept, on

115

the day of her father's funeral. Elizabeth at her piano after losing the baby boy, trying to coax a Schubert impromptu from the keys.

Elizabeth sank back on the pillow. Her husband did not want to hear what might come next.

"She loves you, and you should marry her. Soon, before it is too late."

"Great God, Elizabeth. What can I say to that? I have not—presumed."

"I know, Otis. You have not. And I also know what she means to you."

He reached for her hand, a little sack of bones, and held it lightly. In her forties, she had become slightly plump, but never lost her elegance. Her body seemed to know how to place the extra weight, as if she had given it the tact and candor of her speech.

She swallowed, coughed, and tried to swallow again. He offered her water, and she gave him all the smile she could.

"Please don't forget that you introduced me to the Dickinsons. Even then you seemed part of that family. If you had met them in court"—she paused for breath—"you would have talked about them for years. About Emily. She is a powerful . . . creature."

"*Creature,*" her husband echoed. Elizabeth always chose the right word. Emily was her own kind of being.

His wife struggled for more words. "I believe you, my love, when you say you have . . . exercised all the restraint you could. Now that I am almost gone, I can say whatever I want, without penalty. Not that you would ever ask for one."

Restraint. Holding back something that would otherwise have leaped across boundaries, if allowed. Yes, Elizabeth read him correctly. He lived in the law, but also in his imagination. Emily had taught him the necessity of living that way, without saying a word of instruction. She called it "Stopless Life."

He and Elizabeth had lost three children whose lives never truly began, yet his love for them was indeed stopless, as was his love for his wife, and for Emily.

A pause, another sip of water. This time she could only whisper. "Men." Another pause. "Men should choose for wives those women who have loved them long and well."

His thoughts resided in Elizabeth's loving, stricken face. "As I chose you, lucky man that I was. But I would contest you about the length of our devotion, even if my memory can't determine when it started."

He sat back in the chair, retrieving a scene he had not revisited in years. "You were with your father. I was fifteen, and you were thirteen. A meeting of the men willing to fund Ipswich Female Seminary. The candidates for the school were parked on hard benches in the back of the room. I resented my father's dragging me along, because I was headed to Amherst College, and I wanted to be up to mischief in the river with my friends. A long, boring meeting. I didn't give a rap about a female seminary. But there you were, in a fawn-colored dress and bonnet. Your big eyes smiling at me from across the room. Our fathers with their famous frowns. You were so perfect. You seemed already complete, even though I was older. And I thought that whoever captured you would be the luckiest man alive."

"Otis. Listen to me." She tried to raise her voice above a whisper. "Marry Emily, if you can persuade her to come out of her shell. You cannot be without a wife. Her kind of love is real, and without end or easy discouragement."

117

He stared at her. "I cannot be without a wife? But one must accept the inevitable."

His wife's words took him across a border into strange territory. Over the years, Emily hovered just beyond his reach, exquisitely near and far. He tried not to ask himself if they preferred hovering to consummation. He was used to holding his desire at a fine, delicate pitch, with consummation an unrealized dream—in the past, now, and possibly forever.

Elizabeth struggled to breathe. He lifted her up, and slipped a glass straw between her lips, to ease her swallowing. "The inevitable is shaped by our will, Otis, not by fate. You have always said so. Besides, think of your father, and my father," she whispered. "They both married again soon after losing your mother and mine. And they were both devoted husbands, like you. And they needed wifely comfort, as you do. As you will."

Phil remembered the day he and his brother Nathaniel had arrived in Ipswich for Sunday dinner, and been introduced to tall, plain-featured Mary Adams. His father looked at Miss Adams as if she were a ripe pear. In spite of his embarrassment, Phil was proud of his father's will to live a full life. He was twenty-five, with enough experience of women to recognize what his father wanted—companionship to ease his loneliness, and balm for his body. Mary Adams now lay beside him in the Ipswich Burying Ground, with his first wife, Eunice, on the other side.

He offered Elizabeth more water. "I can't speak of life without you."

The imaginary bower had shrunk to a pale green pinpoint of light, barely visible in the darkness of his thoughts.

"I know. But think—"

He placed his palm on the white cap and kissed her forehead. He watched by her bedside until she fell asleep. Her breathing had become rough and irregular. The frown-line on her forehead disappeared, appeared, disappeared again.

December 10, 1877

Even when his baby brother, mother, father, sisters, Nathaniel, and then Edward died, Phil had never felt so surrounded by death. If he shut his eyes, he saw a forest of tall, spectral trees. He stood among them, losing his leaves to the winter wind.

Elizabeth had a few hours to live. She had surrendered consciousness to oblivion, and atom by atom, he observed, the long months of pain departed from her face, leaving it serene and full of mysteries. Shadowy figures came into the room and stood as witnesses—Mary, Molly and Abbie, Tim O'Leary and his wife, Catherine. Dr. Carlton would arrive soon.

We are dark angels, he whispered, *whose burden is to lift her up to Heaven, and to hope that there is such a place.*

9.

A Day – at Summer's full
Amherst, Sunderland, April – August 1878

August 1878

S he watches him walk toward the house, and without
waiting for his knock, opens the front door. He sweeps
off his hat, then grasps her hands and kisses each cheek.
Emily has rehearsed several welcoming sentences, but can't
remember any of them.

"You are looking better, Judge Owl."

"Than last April's visit, Emily. I should hope so. In your
company, I expect to look better hour by hour."

His face carries August sun on his high forehead, but
despite his healthy color, Emily notices how Elizabeth's
death has aged him. His eyes wear the bruised look of the
lonely sleeper. Almost three seasons have passed since last
December, but he is still trying to absorb the light, like a
mountain stream bearing coldness beneath its sun-warmed
rocks. For thirty-four years he had Elizabeth by his side, and
now he has memories, and work, and himself.

And he has me, Emily wants to say. Maybe soon she will
pluck up her courage and tell him, in ways he will never forget.

April 1878

When he had visited in April, everybody had felt the strain. In her letters to him over the winter, Emily had struck a plain sorrowful chord, with no references to angels or an afterlife except love and memory. She had written about Father, the life returning to her garden, her belief in Phil's strength, and the long ties of affection between them.

"The worst hours don't come in the middle of the night," he'd said as they sat in the parlor. "They come when I least expect them."

"To me, grief always seems worse at sundown." Emily had tucked her hand in Phil's hand, which felt cold, and tried to rub life back into his fingers. "I've noticed that even animals and plants seem to lose force when evening approaches. I often get distracted, even by simple chores. Four years after Father's death, I still find myself setting a place at the table for him, as I did on the day he died. If I correct myself and gather up the extra silver, I worry that I might attract some kind of curse."

Emily had wrapped herself in her big paisley shawl against the April chill, which always felt to her like winter's final insult. She hoped Phil would return to being the brave, vigorous person she knew, the man who had planted a kiss on her lips in the garden, held her and let her weep, and poured his boundless candor into her ears. Not this heavy-laden figure.

He sighed and put on his hat. "I am expected at Austin's, and I hope there is no grand company this evening. I cannot offer much of my old self. Not that my old self fit in with Sue's glamorous crowds."

The sisters watched him trudge down the leafy path, his shoulders bowed. Late in the evening, when he came back

121

bearing part of a cake decorated with daffodils—a leftover from Austin's birthday—he seemed more cheerful, even a little tipsy. He had ridden over the hump of the day, and tomorrow he would do the same.

August 1878

By his August visit, Phil has regained his customary energy. In addition to a new white linen suit, he sports a fashionable white hat. Emily makes him stand still while she admires his dapper new look. He appears pleased and—oddly for him—shy.

Maggie Maher, who has known the judge for years, clucks over him, to Emily's amusement.

"Never a man alive who didn't like to be made much of by a couple of women—Supremest Judge or no Supremest Judge," Maggie says later. "He's a great sweetheart under that tough hide."

"I would like to take you on a drive to Sunderland," he announces to Emily when they are alone. "Just you. And I promise no wild sport such as Austin likes."

Austin often races his carriage into his own driveway as if it were a Roman chariot, a habit that has become a family joke. Phil's invitation raises the color in her face. A drive into the countryside with him would be perfect bliss. She has not ridden with him since her early twenties, when he would take the young women on wild carriage-rides to Mt. Norwottuck.

"It's a reward for all those beautiful letters. They were a great comfort during the dark days, and I fear I made the most inadequate replies."

If he keeps looking at her so intently, he may see the arteries thrumming in her neck. "I will ride with you on one condition—"

Picnic, he hopes. Wine and cheese, fruit, and her good rye bread.

Emily lowers and raises her eyelids, like one of Vinnie's cats. She can flirt when she wants to, and Phil can stand a bit of flirtation. She wants to remind him that he is a man and she a younger woman, and it is summer, the grass still deep green, the garden teeming with succulent vegetables and a riot of yellow flowers.

"The condition? You are keeping me in suspense."

"That you wear your wonderful hat."

After a quick glance at the house next door, he ushers Emily into her father's carriage. August in Amherst is often a furnace, but today there is a light breeze, and the sky is a deep, uninhibited blue. She speaks little until they have passed the cemetery north of town. Then the landscape's lush beauty takes over, and she begins to relax. The ease of Phil's driving, and of his long graceful fingers on the reins, gives her a physical pleasure.

"Look at the sky—the first of the wild geese are passing." To her astonishment, he emits a perfect imitation of a wild goose.

She lifts her face to the sunshine. *"What is Paradise?"*

He twinkles at her. "Are you asking me, or dropping a hint?"

"A poem I wrote, long ago. Does Paradise have farmers? Today I believe it. The streets are paved with golden grain and at night the houses are lit with rubies."

"Emily, I could listen to your fantasies the livelong day."

"Who says they are fantasies?"

She smiles at him as if she were his own seraph, riding on his shoulder.

At the Montague Road, he turns and drives past Sunderland's handsome farms, until they reach a turning into a meadow. Just below them, the Connecticut River flows, its current bisected by a long narrow island. The noon sun flashes on the water.

"Phil, how did you know about this place? I think Vinnie's suitor Joseph Lyman used to bring her out here, and once we had a family picnic." She remembers Cousin John Graves offering her a lit candle in a cup, to ward off mosquitoes. Vinnie and Joseph disappearing among the trees. Sue taking Father's arm to promenade down to the river. The sweet-starchy smell of lightning bugs. On the ride home, Father reprimanding her sister for her flirtatious ways and her exposure of soft white flesh, and Vinnie shedding tears over Joseph's imminent departure for the South.

Passion then, and passion now—spoken and unspoken.

"Speaking of picnics, I asked Margaret Maher to stow a few things in a basket."

Emily is caught between chagrin that her nerves prevented her from planning the lunch, and delight that Phil has taken care of it, with Maggie's help. She has always considered Maggie a life force.

She looks under Phil's hat and sees his smile.

When they arrive at the picnic spot, he lifts her out of the carriage, pretending to grunt. He loves placing his hands around her waist.

"Have you put on just the merest bit of weight, Emily?"

"Do I feel large to you, Judge Owl?"

"Yes, you are enormous. It is quite shocking. I hardly recognized you when I came into the house. I suppose I should eat everything in the picnic basket. If you are very good, I will allow you a bit of apple."

"How Satanic. I accept the challenge."

Phil aims his apple core between the maple branches and throws it in a long arc, then does the same with Emily's. A boyish grin lights up his face. He turns toward her and settles his hat on the grass, then removes his jacket.

"Tell me about Vinnie and Joseph Lyman."

Emily leans on her elbow and twists a sprig of clover. He has heard about Vinnie and Joseph before, but she indulges his love of a ripe old story.

"So long ago. She loved him to distraction, and thought he had hung the moon on a silver hook. He liked to kiss her, and Vinnie loved so much to be kissed. Father railed at her about propriety. She'd sit on Joseph's lap, right in the parlor, and twine her lovely hair around his neck—and she didn't mind getting caught at it. Poor Father! I do think Vinnie would have eloped with Joseph if he had asked her. She waited and waited. Then he wrote that he was marrying a proper Southern belle named Laura. But there was only one person Joseph ever truly loved."

"Vinnie, I take it?"

"No, himself. Vinnie might have been happy, and children would have given her joy. I ached for her. Other suitors showed up, but no one else ever claimed her heart."

If he likes to hear variations on the theme of love, Emily can supply plenty of her own. Cousin John Graves, who made her an Aeolian harp. Beautiful, shadowy Sue. The mysterious minister Charles Wadsworth of Philadelphia. Witty George Gould, a foot-and-a-half taller than she. Her former neighbor, the glamorous Colonel William Clark— chemistry professor, Civil War veteran, gardener. Sam Bowles, who could tease her almost as well as Phil could. And others who could not give her what she wanted, and

125

thus gave her poems. When she reviews her life so far, she wonders at all her unforgettable loves.

A few infant clouds rise up over the river in the afternoon sun. The west wind trails a smell of dairy farm, loam, and clover. Emily closes her eyes. *A perfect day, just past the full of summer, given by nature to me.*

For a moment, savoring the light and air, she lets him think she is asleep, until she feels his fingers clasping her wrist.

"And what of your own heart, Emily? Who claims it?"

His big voice is quiet, a little creaky, his eyes chips of changeable blue. She takes a deep breath and lets it out slowly. Now, at last, Phil has dared to ask what he wanted to know all these years. After so much *no*, and *not yet, not you*, through the parade of her almost-lovers, why not now, a triumphant *yes?*

She knows that he already knows, of course—he just wants to hear her say it. She, who has teased and provoked him for decades, will not play games with him about the truth. This moment is a sky where clouds part to reveal the sun's bold message.

She looks at him for a long time, then smiles her Etruscan smile, and enters the moment, swimming into its big wave of light. "You, of course. But there is no claim. Only perfect freedom. I have loved you for so long that I can scarcely remember when I first knew it."

Phil starts to speak, but she lays a slim finger on his lips.

"Don't say a word. Let's just watch the river."

He puts his arm around her. Emily fits her bonnet neatly onto the picnic basket, then unfastens her hair and lets it fly free. He lifts up the mass of red from underneath, cooling the back of her neck.

"What a glory." His voice is gruff. "I am not going to ask to kiss you, I am just going to do it."

With one memorable exception, all the kisses Emily has ever experienced—more than others assume she received, and far fewer than she wanted—fly away in a cloud across the river, to be replaced by this one, and the one that follows it, and the one after that.

"We seem to have sailed through the sky on a boat."

One button, then two, then three, she bares her freckled bosom, knowing that Phil has not confirmed until this moment that she wears no corset, only a thin camisole under her light dress.

He lifts her face again. "Any earth with you on it is where I want to be."

Their whispers disappear in the waving grass. He tells her what he feels free to speak, the long history of his tenderness, curiosity, esteem. Her rich, unusual beauty. His desire for her. The joy is a too-bright sun and a soft elusive moon.

"You taste of apples and wine, and I can't have enough of you."

She lifts his hands and fits them onto her hips, then rolls on top of his body, splaying her fingers in his curly hair, as she has long wanted to do. She is a flower, a bee, a shore combed by a wave.

"Emily, your upper lip makes the most fascinating little beak. Right here."

"A perfect fit for an owl's beak. As here. And here."

When she kisses his lips and the tip of his nose, he tells her it is like being kissed by a snapdragon.

He wraps his hands around her back. "I have known you since . . ."

127

How glorious to scoop the years into a sift of bright sand, and fling it into the air. "December 10, 1830. Only you didn't know it was me. But the universe knew, and arranged itself accordingly, so that here we are."

She explores his ear with her tongue, and he moves his hands down her back and below her waist. "All these years, I hadn't fully appreciated your *roundedness*, Miss Dickinson. You have kept your treasures in hiding."

He unbuttons the remaining nine buttons, lifts her camisole, and tastes her. "These are two pink clovers. You are a garden, as I always knew you were." She lightly unties her drawstrings. If a breeze came along now, it could lift off her clothes as if they were milkweed silk.

After a while he eases her beside him and she curls her back against his body.

"Dear, I must say something." He strokes her hair back from her forehead. They have dropped whatever shreds of mask remain, leaving them free and open to each other. "If you would let me, I would take you unto myself, here and now. But you must not let me."

She turns to him, gives him a seraphic smile, and places her finger on his lips. "Nature has claimed us today, and we are free to act according to what she requires of us, obedient only to her laws."

He looks surprised, then nervous, then overjoyed.

As he fits himself against her, she can feel the condition he is in. Knowing how a man is made, she whimpers with joy at seeing how Phil is made. She turns on her back and beckons him to kiss her again. Emily has made her decision about intimacy, and wants to give him what they both desire. I am forty-seven years old, she declares to the gods, and I can offer myself to this long-beloved person.

"I am yours, now and whenever you want. And I intend to claim you, too. The compact between us has not changed, except that it now permits our desire. There are two of us in this magical state of being, and I have developed heartbeats all over my body."

He takes her hand and holds it against himself, as his hand searches for heartbeats, and hers does the same, unbuttoning and freeing him. As they take the time to let nature do her work with them, the sensations are at first almost too much for her, then a series of unexpected pleasures, then all of a sudden perfect and complete.

They rest for a while. Emily licks a stray tear gliding down Phil's temple.

"My dear, I must ask whether it's possible for you to become—"

"With child?" She kisses him heartily, as though awarding him a prize for oratory. "Quite unlikely, Judge Owl. I think you have forgotten how to count. I am forty-seven years old! My body has recently given me the gift of freedom from a certain means of scandal."

"You are young, and dewy, and silken. Forgive me if I forget that you are almost an old lady. And forgive me for—"

"I know what you're about to say, and I want you to be quiet and let your body speak for you, as it has just done so well. Please."

His reply is to grant her wish.

White butterflies decorate the air above them, in company with a bold crow, a breeze bearing a riverine smell, sunlight slanting through the maple branches onto Phil's big shoulders.

She sighs and stretches her arms above her head, then crooks her finger at him and makes a smile so rapturous that it gathers up all the smiles she has ever made. "Look!" She points at two cows standing nearby, chewing in rhythm, long strands of grass disappearing into their mouths, their eyes big dark pools. It is hard to read their expression. Perhaps cows don't have expressions, Emily muses, so she decides they are happy for the couple in the grass, and welcome their merry noise. They hear a farm-boy shout a few ripe country words as he rushes after the cows and flails them home.

She is grateful to be on earth, with Phil and these large benign creatures.

The afternoon stretches before them, a prospect of touch and talk, but there seems little to say, or too much. Emily does not want to think about time, or even believe in it. The year 1878, in the thick of summer, has given birth to a new 1878, a golden being wearing a celestial smile, poised beside a stream in the woodland bower. The river goes on making its self-satisfied hum. Peaceable, with the breeze carrying off the midges, they drift off to sleep.

"Now you must button up my dress and restore me to propriety, if such a thing is possible. And do try to forget the glories you have beheld."

"As if I could!"

He tries the buttons and cannot manage them, because his fingers want to keep unbuttoning them. Emily refastens her dress, pats her bosom, and winks. He sighs, lies back, and laughs as he has not laughed in recent memory.

On the ride back, she leaves her hair down to blow wildly in the breeze, flowing with the exultation of their talk.

Alone in her room, Emily thinks, I want to be with him every moment. But I also want to stand apart, release the pent-up words and receive his reply. When he is in Salem, the writing must suffice, the real and the possible in a stately gavotte.

She will perfect the words and send them flying after him to Salem's crowded courts.

I confess that I love him—I rejoice that I love him—I thank the maker of Heaven and Earth that gave him me to love—the exaltation floods me—I cannot find my channel—The Creek turns Sea at thought of thee . . . .

We went to sleep as if it were a country—let us make it one—...my native Land—my Darling come Oh be a patriot now—Love is a patriot now Gave her life for its country Has it meaning now—Oh nation of the soul thou hast thy freedom now

10.

A neighbor from another world
Amherst, July 1880

"A unt Emily, may I talk to you?"

Ned's voice carries across the garden. Emily puts down her trowel.

"Dear, you have grown so tall, I am having trouble meeting your eyes. Let's go sit among the fruit trees."

There they cannot be seen from the Evergreens. Ned appears pale and anxious. She knows how their conversation is likely to run: first an ordinary question, followed by little worries, then larger ones.

For the past two years, family conversations—except with Vinnie—have given Emily a chance to practice subtle evasions she has never tried, except in poems. When the judge's name comes up, she assumes a pleasant blandness: Yes, he's in Northampton this week and hopes to come for tea. Yes, she believes his sister-in-law and two nieces now occupy his Salem house. No, she doesn't know whether Austin expects him for Commencement.

"Does Judge Lord belong to a church, Aunt Emily?" She's surprised that Ned begins with Phil's church-going habits. Why would he care?

"I believe that Phil—Mr. Lord doesn't do anything ostensible."

"What does 'ostensible' mean? It sounds bad."

"It means that he doesn't do things for appearance's sake."

She hopes Ned takes these words home with him, and repeats them at dinner.

"But what does he believe? Does he believe in God and Jesus?"

Emily suspects that he has heard his mother speculate on the judge's religious credentials. The conversation begins to depress her. The Lords had been frequent guests at the Evergreens, and Sue was proud of her acquaintance with elegant Elizabeth and the important judge. Since Phil started visiting more often, Sue has been markedly cool. Perhaps she or one of the children sees the family carriage rolling away toward the Sunderland road. Or Sue may entertain suspicions about the growing closeness between her sister-in-law and Phil, now an eligible widower. Emily hopes her nephew will ask questions on his own, not because he has been delegated to do so by his mother.

"I think Judge Lord honors all beliefs that people sincerely feel. He couldn't be a worthy judge unless he did so."

"Does that mean Catholics and Jewish people? Arabians and Chinese? And naked people who dance around idols in Fee-Jee?"

Her answer is a smile.

She sees her brother in Ned, but only a hint of Sue. It is tall, witty Mattie who has inherited Sue's edge and brilliance. Before he was born, rumors that Sue had abortions traveled around town, but Emily stopped her ears to them. Then, nine months to the day after Austin's triumphal appearance as Grand Marshal of the Cattle Show horse parade, and five years after his parents' marriage, Ned arrived, a handsome but difficult baby, with mysterious ailments Sue hinted at but never explained.

The summer of his birth had brought thunderstorms and relentless humidity. Late at night, when she wrote at her little table near an open window, she could hear the baby's constant wailing.

The Evergreens must seem like Bedlam, she'd thought, wishing she knew of a gentle sleeping potion she could waft into the air, like a good witch in a fairy tale.

Emily and Sue saw each other rarely until the baby had grown enough to be paraded around Amherst in a wagon, accompanied by Carlo and one of Vinnie's cats, and costumed like the world's youngest Civil War veteran. The Evergreens gradually became a stage for Sue's vivid parties, with exquisite food, plentiful drink, and the light combat of conversation about culture and politics. Every member of the family, even the babies, seemed decked out to be noticed. Austin had acquired a pair of lavender pants, which he wore when presiding at Town Meeting. Vinnie thought they were bizarre and ridiculous, and Emily believed her brother had discovered a talent for clowning. Maggie Maher remarked that the women who attended to laundry and sewing had a rum go of it sometimes.

Now anxiety coils in her nephew's face. He turns his cap around and around. Emily's heart goes out to Ned, but she can do nothing for him except tell him the truth when she can. She has never witnessed his seizures, and prays she would know what to do in such an emergency. Like other family woes—Sue's snobbishness toward neighbors, Mattie's temper—the subject remains taboo.

134

"Ned, look at me. Here, I'll take off my sun-hat to make it easier to see my eyes. And I want you to listen."

She notices that his eyes are wet. She thinks, he is so vulnerable, having to listen to his body for signs of imminent distress. He must be troubled about what will happen to him when he becomes a man. The judge's church-going is only a cover-subject for these private woes.

"People go to church—whatever church they choose—for comfort and peace, and also to see friends and neighbors they know. But some people, like me, prefer to keep the Sabbath staying at home. I suspect Judge Lord does the same. Think about the huge responsibilities he bears. All week he has to make hard decisions—sending people to jail, hearing desperate stories from all over Massachusetts. Forsaken mothers and children. Violence between brothers. Acts of criminal foolishness. Sunday is his day of rest, as it is mine—and your father's."

He seems to accept this explanation, and brightens up. "Father says he has the best legal mind in Massachusetts."

She puts her arm around Ned's shoulders and plants a kiss on his cheek.

"But Mother says that he is too familiar with you, and she is worried that you and he have behaved improperly."

She wants to chuck a rock at the barn wall, but ties her hat strings in a firm knot and leads Ned back to her flower garden, where she resumes digging up the spent annuals. She can't upset him by saying what she thinks of Sue's ungenerous comment. Unlike Mattie, Ned is a peace-loving person. Although easily swayed by his mother's strong personality, he tends to believe the best of people.

"Dear, I think you're old enough to hear me speak plainly about some subjects that may not please your mother.

I'm distressed to hear the word 'improper' from your lips, because it's the last word I could imagine applied to Otis Phillips Lord. Your Aunt Vinnie and I have known him since we were wee girls, and your father has learned much from him. Judge Lord has never done anything improper in our presence."

She thrusts her trowel firmly into the loam, and tries to hide her mischievous smile.

Ned piles the yellowed narcissus stalks into the basket. "You have the oddest expression on your face, Aunt Emily. Are you going to cry or laugh?"

To reassure him, she laughs. "Ned, be patient with me, and one of these days I'll explain to you the mysteries of the universe."

She wonders if she can tell him about love between men and women from a woman's point of view, so that he'll be gratified, not shocked, by the prospect of tenderness, and the pleasures of shared minds and bodies.

"I have a confession to make." The color mounts in his cheeks. "Last time he was here—the judge, I mean—he and Father and I went swimming in the North Amherst pond. We had the pond almost to ourselves. I was happy that three naked men, even two of them Dickinsons, couldn't attract much notice."

"I'm sure that swimming did you good."

The dirt yields up an egg-shaped pebble, and she brushes it clean. What is Ned trying to confess, she wonders. We are country-bred, and have all spent happy times in creeks and ponds, haylofts and mud-holes, on the backs of ponies, and not so long ago, in a fragrant meadow by a river, her freckled bosom and Phil's muscular back exposed to the sunshine.

She won't mention that she, Sue, and their friend Kate, swam in the same pond when they were young women, with nothing on but their shifts. If Phil calls me a garden in my late forties, she thinks, he should have seen us then—Sue a festive peony, Kate a graceful calla lily, and me a happy little daisy. Afterward the three friends lay in the grass with their hair spread all around, and promised never to tell of their boldness.

Emily's head snaps up when Ned goes on talking. "I have seen Father naked, of course. I don't have as much hair on my chest as he does, but otherwise we are quite alike, our legs and hips and feet, and other parts. All of us Dickinsons have fine bodies, as Aunt Vinnie likes to say. But Judge Lord—well, he is an impressive sight."

She amuses herself by thinking of Ned's delivering this news to Sue. "Ned, dear, please remember that you are talking to your so-called maiden aunt."

"Well, if you are, as Mother says, in love with him and planning to marry him, I think you will appreciate—"

"Ned!" She lifts her head to the breeze, to cool her hot face.

"Please don't be put out with me, Aunt Emily. I'm like Aunt Vinnie sometimes. My mouth just opens up and words come out. Sometimes I think I'm a puppet, with Mother's voice or even Father's taking over my brain. I wish your voice would come out of my mouth, but I'm not smart enough for your kind of talk."

She tugs on his pants cuff, and plucks out some new-mown grass. "Let's just sit here for a few minutes and listen to the birds. Then we can talk some more, if you promise me that you'll speak only what you mean to say."

And please no more, she hopes, about the endowments of naked males swimming in the pond. Otherwise she'll be tempted to throw her apron over her head and roll around in the grass.

"Your face is quite pink, Aunt Emily. Shall I get you a glass of water?"

She nods. While Ned fetches the water, she treats herself to a memory of Phil's visit the September she started at Mt. Holyoke, when he also turned pink and she brought him a full cool glass. How could that be so long ago, and still a fountain of happiness?

"Do you love him?" Ned's voice lowers to a whisper. "And would you marry him? He is so much older. . . . Oh, never mind."

She wants to open her heart and tell him that she and Phil Lord are in love, but Ned, excitable and guileless, would only tell his mother. The cool water helps her think what to say next. "Remember that I told you Judge Lord was your grandfather's best friend? And that he has known this family since your father and Vinnie and I were very small? Here's a surprise: when he first visited your grandfather, he was a little younger than you are now. Just starting at Amherst College."

Ned's jaw dropped.

"I—we know him better than anyone else outside the family. Of course we love him, and he loves us, too. It would be a sad thing if we did not have him in our lives. Since your grandfather died, he has been a rock we lean on. And yes, he is my special friend. We speak the same language, and often think the same thoughts."

In every way, including ways she did not expect.

Ned rocks back and forth, struggling with his words. "But you and he—are different together now. We see you laughing in the garden, and he rushes up the steps after his train arrives. He's supposed to be an elderly gentleman, but he has twice the energy Father does. Even Mattie has noticed the way you smile at each other. She says it makes the judge look almost handsome. And Mama worries that you might run away and never see us again."

When Ned wears his bleak Dickinson face, Emily thinks that if she did marry Phil and move to Salem, she would miss him most of all.

"Your grandmother is not well, as you know. I couldn't dream of leaving her and abandoning Vinnie."

How can she talk to Ned about the daily worry of Mother's infirmity, her own need for privacy, Phil's public life, his Farley nieces, and the sweet mischief he and she perform together? One does not heap all that on the head of a fragile, inexperienced nineteen-year-old.

"No, but one day she will die. And then you'll be free, as the judge is now free."

O nation of the soul, thou hast thy freedom now. . . .

Emily sighs. "We can't know what time will do to us, Ned. Or when."

Ned rubs his knees with his hands. "Mother has become quite close to his niece Abbie Farley, you know. I heard them talking about you and Mr. Lord the other day, on the porch. Abbie wanted Mother to read her one of your poems. So she did."

Emily wipes her wet forehead. She has to work to keep from grinding her teeth. "Yes, I know your mother reads my poems to select company. Which one did she choose this time?"

"Something about thunder. It begins, *To pile like Thunder to it's close.*"

Emily finishes the poem for him:

Then crumble grand away
While everything created hid
This – would be Poetry –

Or Love — the two coeval come —
We both and neither prove —
Experience either and consume —
For none see God and live —

He asks her to recite it again, and cocks his head to listen, the way old Carlo did, long ago, sitting beside Emily's writing table as she whispered poems to him at night.

"I like it, Aunt Emily. It makes me shiver, but in a nice way. But Abbie said she didn't understand it, and doesn't like things she can't understand."

That means me, Emily thinks, and her uncle Lord, stripped of his judge's robes and transformed into Phil. Abbie can't comprehend the kind of love that grows like a hidden garden, and bursts forth into paradise. Or the opening and closing of certain doors. Or the raw unhappiness in a glamorous house where a man and wife have tried to please each other and failed.

Lovelessness always takes love as its enemy.
Abbie Farley is a force to be reckoned with. And so is Sister Sue.

*

As she walked through the French doors, Sue wore the same expression on her dark, handsome face that she had worn years ago when she tried and failed to persuade Emily to join the church. Emily sat with her back to the sun slanting into the parlor. Ned had been interrogated after their conversation in the garden, and his mother had mined his words for clues to Emily's secretive behavior.

"You have met Abbie Farley and her mother, Mary, am I right?" She didn't wait for a nod. "So you know how important they are to Otis, especially now that he is without

Elizabeth in that huge house. I wish that you would be more hospitable to them when they visit."

"I am as hospitable as I can be. But they are not here to visit me. And I have other work to attend to, as you know." She chose words as if picking perfect cherries from a bowl.

Sue pulled her embroidery out of her workbasket. Emily chewed at the inside of her lower lip. Sue's elaborate skill could keep her eyes on her work while she talked, and her visit would be longer than Emily wished.

"I have noticed—or should I say we have noticed—Austin, Mattie, Ned, and I—that when Otis is here, you and he spend hours together. Mattie says she has seen the two of you drive off in the carriage, not to return until much later. I would hate to think that there is a whiff of scandal about these activities."

Waspish, Emily thought—the perfect word for her tone of voice.

"He is sixty-eight years old, Sue. And a widower. And if you're suggesting that this Virgin Recluse, as I have been called, is capable of causing scandal, then you are paying me a compliment I never thought to receive." She tried to keep her tone even.

"It was dear Sam Bowles who called you a Virgin Recluse. And was he right?"

Sue's smile wore a hook.

Emily said nothing.

"You are still a virgin, dear, I take it. At least you dress like one."

"Do virgins wear a uniform? Pity, I never knew."

She thought of asking, who would mind if a woman in her late forties who hadn't taken holy orders seized a joy long overdue?

Sue made one of her performance-sighs. "We used to be such confidantes, in our twenties. I told you things I never told another soul, and you kept my secrets. About my assignation with Austin in the Revere Hotel, when we became secretly engaged. How he wanted me to give myself to him then, and I could not. About my fears of childbirth, and my seeking advice to prevent pregnancy. Did you benefit from that advice yourself?"

Emily tried out a witch-laugh. "I have shared with you a great deal of my own history. But there is no need for you to hold it against me. And no need for you to paint it in lurid colors, unless for your own entertainment."

She paced around the parlor. She longed to hear Vinnie's footsteps hurrying up the stairs to Mother's room, or the whistle of a teakettle in the kitchen—a signal that she was needed elsewhere. The estrangement between her and Sue weighed her down.

"I don't hold your history against you!" Sue wrapped the silk threads around the needles and thrust them into her basket. She might be thrusting them into my chest, Emily thought, as tears pooled in her eyes.

"Yes, my pseudo-sister, you do." She stood before Sue and let her see the tears on her cheeks. "I am sorry that you can't wish me well, when I have wished you well from the beginning. And Austin, too."

"You were jealous of us, I think," Sue's words sounded harsh and flat.

"Yes, I was, at the beginning. I wanted someone to love me the way Austin was obsessed with you. I wanted the whole of love—you know what I mean—and I didn't expect to have it without paying a price. But that didn't keep me from wanting it."

"What has your judge told you of his arrangements with Abbie and Mary Farley?"

Emily faced her, aware of the light dying behind her back. Her stomach jumped. For a moment, she thought she might be sick. "Do you have something to say that you think I should know?"

"Abbie and Mary are the judge's heirs, did you know that? And naturally, Abbie is concerned that he might marry again, and she and her mother would be cast out into the cold."

Indignation took away the sick feeling and set its claws into Emily's heart. "Of all the people you and I have ever known, including Father and Austin and Sam Bowles, Otis Phillips Lord is the most bounteous. Of course he would provide for everyone in his household, including his servants, the O'Learys." She came as close to shouting as she had since the day long before when Father slapped his horse and she screamed and cried. "You know his reputation for integrity, as do thousands of others across Massachusetts. Can you believe that he would leave Elizabeth's relatives in financial distress?"

"Of course not. But his family should come first." Apparently satisfied to have delivered her preachments, Sue flung a quick kiss at the air near Emily's cheek, and left the house.

Watching her make her way along the path, Emily felt relief to see the back of her. She hated the way her blood felt thick, as though loaded with bird-shot.

Later, lying in bed awake, Emily conjured up the muscles below Phil's shoulder-blades, his long elegant feet, the sensuous asymmetry of his upper lip, the clear passion in his blue eyes. But it did no good. She saw Mary Farley's face, so like her sister Elizabeth's, and Abbie Farley's crimped curls and precise little features. Sue's eyes, dark with judgment.

The owl on the amber sill settled his feathers and went to sleep.

For a long time, before she finally drifted off, she pictured Austin and Ned riding off into a gray forest, where they would wander for hours until given up for lost.

11.

A Shining Secret
Crawford Notch, New Hampshire,
Amherst, August 1880

Crawford Notch

O n the lawn of the Crawford House Hotel, Phil exchanged a thick-nibbed ink pen for a fine one, and sketched the thin slanting lines of a rainstorm moving northeast toward Crawford Notch. He was pleased with his rendering of the White Mountains landscape he loved, its knobby rocks and bristling evergreens. He'd finish the drawing in half an hour, if—

"It's Judge Lord, isn't it?"

"We don't mean to interrupt. Please do continue your work. We like watching."

He glanced up and saw two well-dressed middle-aged women.

"Good afternoon, Mrs.—"

"Lynde, Eustacia Lynde. And this is Mrs. Helen Shaw. We heard the talk you gave on *Hamlet* last Sunday, for the Shakespeare Reading Group. We are sisters, from Peabody."

"It was a fine talk, Judge Lord, and you read the quotations so movingly. You are truly a bardologist, I believe.

145

And apparently a fine artist, too." Mrs. Shaw clearly took pride in her appreciative sensibility.

He glanced at the lowering sky. Perhaps—he sighed— the sketch was destined to remain one of his unfinished masterpieces. He tipped his hat to Mrs. Lynde and Mrs. Shaw, arrayed in purple, with black shawls. Widows in half-mourning, he assumed.

"I believe we met here a few years ago, quite briefly," Mrs. Lynde said. "That was when my husband Frank was still alive. And Helen's husband Gerald. And—your wife. We're so sorry to hear she passed away."

Her sister nodded mournfully.

"Thank you." He hoped his brevity would put an end to that conversation.

Mrs. Shaw, who had round cheeks and a capacious frontage, bobbled her curls. "Her name was Elizabeth—am I right? She was so elegant and well-spoken. I am sorry for your loss."

He didn't remember the women or their husbands, but Elizabeth had been able to charm perfect strangers, in her quiet way.

They chatted about the attractions of Crawford Notch. Mrs. Lynde, the more refined of the two, had a pleasant contralto and almond-shaped dark eyes. When he felt a few raindrops, he covered the drawing with oilcloth, packed up his things, and offered to walk the ladies to the Crawford House reception room, in time for the sherry hour. It seemed impolite to do otherwise, even though he wanted to return to his room and write Emily an answer to her latest distressing letter about Sue.

He hastened into the lobby to give his gear to Tim O'Leary, to take to his room. The concierge, a small man with a small mustache and a twitchy expression, handed him a letter, bowed, and hurried off. Phil knew his type, the kind that wore a confidential air barely disguising the desire to pry. He waved away the tray of sherry glasses. The waiter, who knew the judge's taste, promised to bring him a large whiskey-and-soda.

He quickly read Emily's letter—a short one that managed to be ardent, effusive, and worrying all at once, as it told him more about recent conversations. Sue had stepped across a line, even for her, in trying to warn off Emily from her friendship with the judge, even to suggest what his priorities should be. The business about his financial arrangements for the Farleys raised the heat in his neck. He pondered writing Sue to suggest that she tend to her own family, but it would be like poking a stick into a hornet's nest.

What contrivances simple jealousy could make.

The waiter hovered nearby with the welcome whiskey-and-soda. Phil folded up the letter, took a sip of his drink, and rose to join the ladies.

The next day, he was able to finish his sketch without interruption. He planned to have it framed, and send it to Emily.

Crawford Notch, NH
4 August, 1880

Darling Emily,

Your last letter gave me pain. You have become my life's unexpected blessing, and I loathe the thought of anyone hurting you.

I don't know what to advise about Sue's hostilities. Abbie has always been anxious about money. Her father's manufacturing business teetered on the brink. I wish I could find her suitable employment, perhaps doing light duties in a fashionable ladies' shop.

Sue might be able to help Abbie, as they have similar interests. I remember the early days of hospitality in the Evergreens, when Austin seemed eager to start a family. The long delay before Ned's arrival wore him out, and I heard him speak bitterly about the prospect of children.

I wish I could help.

Especially do I wish you were here with me, among the mountains. We could wake up to see the mountains staring at your brilliant hair and eyes, and laugh at what that great stone face would say, when he peers in our window at our snow-peaks among the bed-sheets.

One day, I promise you, this will not be a fantasy, but a joyous excursion, to a place that refreshes my health and spirit.

He described the hotel's social life, the promenades around the hotel porch followed by rich meals—a routine he knew Emily would dislike. On his White Mountains excursions, Phil had always preferred to walk outdoors, or to ride a patient, strong-backed mule and explore the countryside.

Although he was tempted to tell her about Mrs. Lynde and Mrs. Shaw, he wanted to do so when he had Emily in his lap and could kiss her neck.

Phil had experienced this kind of attention before. If he let it develop, there would follow the prolonged handclasp, the seductive look. He would be polite to the women, but he wasn't interested in being seduced.

In the lobby, he'd happened to hear the widows discussing him, as he stood near a large fern.

"He is still good-looking, Helen, don't you think? I prefer big men."

"Yes, and rich, I'm told. A prominent judge."

"His family is ancient. But he is not. I suspect he can still get up to mischief."

"Helen! Mind what you're saying. We don't want to be thought of as fortune hunters. Or worse."

Phil eased around the fern toward the gentlemen's bar. He grinned, not without satisfaction. He knew colleagues who visited grand hotels as if they were sporting-houses. A nice sum, placed in the hands of the concierge, guaranteed sexual diversions for prosperous men. Whenever he recognized someone accompanied by a likely-looking woman, he turned away, unwilling to judge anyone who stepped outside propriety. If Mrs. Lynde and Mrs. Shaw were in fact fortune hunters, or aging chorus girls in disguise, he wished them luck.

Returning to his letter, he asked Emily what she was doing at six p.m. on a mild afternoon, and reminded her of a happy picnic or two in the nearby hills. He rejoiced in his memory of their shared pleasures.

This morning I took an odd, nearly vertical trip up the little cog railway that snakes up the flank of Mt. Washington, past trees that seem to be leaning over, preparing to crash down the steep grade, except that—as our nattily dressed brakeman told us—they are perfectly upright, and the passengers were the ones leaning as if crazed by the wind.

I took Tim along, and the ride delighted him. But I wanted you next to me as we climbed up, to emerge at the base of the Summit House. Whipped by the breeze, we linked arms in a chain to walk from the terminus to the stone hut.

Two women fastened themselves to me, one on each side like limpets. Limpets don't have your sumptuous hair, magical heartbeats, clover-blossoms, and snapdragon-lips.

Dear Emily, my niece Abbie does not matter, never mind her supposed friendship with Sue. Only you and I matter, but I know you have a generous heart, and that you still feel connected to Sue, because having loved once, you never forget.

The Truth is sometimes difficult, but our Truth can be a force for health and happiness.

Talk with Vinnie, when and where you can. She loves and knows us. My warmest regards to Maggie Maher, the all-knowing counterpart to my manservant and friend Tim O'Leary. He will make sure that this letter reaches you.

When you stand at the window tonight, in your ivory nightgown, please listen to the echoes from the Northeast, my own loud and loving voice. And write to me of your dreams.

Your Ancient Swain,
Phil

Amherst

8 August, 1880

Dearest Phil,

Last night I dreamed that you and I rode in a balloon, swift as a Chariot, past the mortal noise of the Population below. The balloon carried a basket shaped like a Canoe that rocked back and forth as we climbed upward. We were as entranced as two children, although we did not behave like children.

The World dropped away, and soon there were just the two of us, with a bright strand of River shining below. We slept for a while, then woke up and turned to each other, careful in our movements so that we wouldn't tumble to Earth. Then the Stars came out, one by one, as we passed among the mountains, until Sunrise witnessed our soft return to the ground. Invisible

Presences gathered around—Vinnie, and Maggie, and your trusted Tim—and tied our craft to some Hemlocks, just as the Sun showed its face.

Your letter rests my harried heart. Vinnie and I have asked Maggie to tend to Mother, while we talk in the barn, surrounded by Hay and Hens.

Think of me tomorrow, and heap your blessings on me.

Your Everlasting Emily

*

"Maggie knows. I know. Mother knows." Vinnie puts an arm around her sister's small waist and kisses her on the cheek. "No reproaches from any of us. And of course, our lips are sealed."

Emily's eyes brim. "Even Mother?"

Vinnie hands her a somewhat dusty handkerchief, and starts to laugh.

"What's so funny?"

"You are, Em. You guard your privacy so well—it's one of your fine arts—and our judge has long been able to keep his face taciturn, as a good judge must. But you and he are more like two butterflies, or springtime puppies, than you realize. I just hope that something will come of it. You know what I mean." Vinnie dug her elbow into Emily's side, and winked.

"Mother, too?"

"Despite her weakness and confusion, there are bright patches in Mother's mind. I believe she pretends to nap, so that she can listen to the house. After all, it's her house. And remember how she loved Father, body and soul."

"Yet Father was a lonely man, Vin."

"Sometimes he was, and maybe she was lonely too, imprisoned in those headaches. Maybe you saw him that way because you wanted to be his chief comfort."

The comment stings, as Vinnie sometimes can.

"You're right. Possessive older daughter. Father and I were more alike than Mother and I were, although I'm glad I didn't inherit his bushy eyebrows. And we were alike in other ways, deep inside ourselves. But I believe he loved Mother."

She remembers Father's dream on the train from Boston, his tender sleepy muttering.

Vinnie reminds her of their being awakened by laughter coming from their parents' bedroom, and once, on a rainy Sunday afternoon, noises that sounded like a pillow fight.

If she mentioned that memory, they would not be able to stop laughing, and soon their shrieks would bring Dennis or Maggie running to see if there had been an accident.

"'Love and a cold cannot be hid.' I think she must have said that to me long ago, when I was enthralled by George Gould, or Cousin John, or someone else. Or maybe it was about you and Joseph Lyman. A dreamy look would come over Mother's face. And once—think of my remembering it now—she said that Father was a handsome man *in every way.*"

Emily and Vinnie giggle softly. Below the loft, hens in the coop trill and squeak.

"Mother thinks you and Phil are betrothed, or soon will be. That's why she isn't upset that you and he have crossed the Great Divide."

"What do you think, Vin?" She plucks two pieces of hay and twists them around each other. "About everything. You can tell me."

"About your intimacy, do you mean? Hang on to that hay bale, because I think that, by the time women reach forty, they should be able to do whatever they like, and if that means joyously coupling, then the courts should issue them a free pass saying, 'Love as you please.'"

"Wouldn't Phil have fun issuing those free passes! Well-dressed ladies would be lined up outside his courtroom, to make private appointments with him in his chambers." She imagines the two limpets he'd written about, clinging to him on Mt. Washington. Attractive limpets, she guessed, grateful to anchor themselves to the distinguished Judge Lord.

There are some conversations only sisters can have, and she knows this is one of them.

"You ask me whether I'd approve of my sister's marrying, at nearly fifty, a man eighteen years older, and moving all the way to noisy, dusty Salem?"

"Go ahead and finish that thought. You omitted the part about my leaving you and Mother in Amherst, and living with strangers, one of whom I don't like."

"Abbie Farley. I catch her narrowing her eyes when she looks at you, like a ferret at a rat-hole. You and Phil are always careful and polite, but remember what you just said about love and a cold. He can't stop those blue eyes from flashing at you now and then. You don't have to tell me that you looked up to him, and not just literally, for years and years. In some way, your loving him makes everything all right, even though I would be sad to see you move to Salem. You'd be like a pioneer woman, only going in the wrong direction." Vinnie's lower lip trembles.

"Oh, Vinnie. Me as a pioneer woman. Filthy shoes and a poke bonnet, and having to smack an ox's backside to keep the wagon train going." She ties the twist of hay into a knot, to make a corn-dolly for Gib.

153

"I don't know what to do about Abbie. Or for that matter, myself. I need quiet, and my garden, and you and Austin. I can't think of not seeing you every day, as we have all our lives. And I need to care for Mother. She and I weren't close when I was a child, but now I cherish her. And I need Phil, too. I wrote him once that he had taken my will away and I didn't know where he had laid it."

Emily lies back in the hay and stretches her arms. Images of Phil in the meadow leap behind her eyes. She remembers what Ned said about swimming in the pond, and feels a warm heaviness below her middle.

"Sue's unfriendliness toward Phil and me is worse than anything else. I carry rocks in my heart, and write him, receive his bounteous wisdom, and the rocks tumble away."

"I can feel the rocks, too. She's jealous of your finding love, or rediscovering it, when she herself has run dry. Or maybe she always was jealous. She resents your happiness because she and Austin have not been happy for years. I can see the misery in his face. Our Phil is not going to disclose your shining secret—it's against his code of honor. He's protective of Austin. And Ned."

Emily twists the corn dolly until her fingers ache.

"Ned's attacks are horribly real, but also a metaphor for the tumult in his parents' marriage. We should pity Sue, if we are kind. And Phil has always been part of our landscape. Certainly part of mine."

"Could you and he marry and live here in Amherst? That would solve everything."

She has been over this problem again and again, and it always comes out the same way. "No, it wouldn't. Phil can't give up working any more than Father could have. It would kill him. And he can't transform himself into a country

154

lawyer from being a Massachusetts Supreme Court justice. I thought I had found a solution when we had a magic afternoon in Sunderland and became lovers—"

Below them, the barn door opens and shuts, letting in a blade of dusty sunlight. Emily sits up. "Maggie? Is that you?" She gets up and peers over the edge of the loft. "I had better check. It might have been Dennis or Tom." Emily springs down the ladder as fast as she dares, then hurries out of the barn.

Running away down the path, shrieking, her hair flipping back and forth, is Mattie.

12.

To Rock a Fretting Truth to Sleep
Amherst, September 1880

"Reckless, selfish, insolent." Austin slammed his hands on his knees. "My only daughter!"

Emily knew that father and daughter had frequent tiffs. "Mattie is a true Dickinson, full of restless vitality and talent. But she's also Sue's daughter, and prone to fits of anger that seem unnatural in a girl her age."

Austin plucked a little cigar from his pocket and rolled it around between thumb and finger, gave Emily an inquiring glance, and put it back.

"I know it relaxes you, but I can't stand the smell in my room. Forgive me."

"Talking about my daughter puts my nerves on edge. Sneaking around and listening to conversations! She has paid a high price for overhearing some of my bitter words to her mother about the wretched excess of constant entertaining. My pleas about having peace and quiet bounce off her, and then things get worse, because Sue always takes her side. I'm angry with myself for not being able to settle the conflicts in my own house. A man should—"

"Austin, *A Man Should* could be the title of a book you and hundreds of grown men read as their daily Bible. Put it down and give yourself a rest." She sat on her bed, sorting through a pile of scrap paper to select pieces for her pocket, in case poems came to her ear in the kitchen or garden.

"Mattie is trying to figure out the mysteries of men and women, social life, and her own family. You have fascinated her forever because you're a poet who refuses to participate in the kind of life Sue wants her daughter to have."

Guilt about what Mattie had overheard in the barn made Emily feel nervous and brittle. She saw no way to offer explanations. The girl would have to learn about love, in her own time—if she could.

"We must give up this subject and hope that Mattie finds other diversions."

She set aside a months-old telegram, an old envelope, and a chocolate wrapper, and opened her dressing-room door to hear sounds from Mother's room. Her mother snored when she slept, a light musical snore, like a cat's purr.

"Maybe I'm the one who has been reckless and selfish. If it's a crime to lay hands on a Supreme Court Justice, then I am guilty. Don't blush, Austin—you are a grown-up, as I pretend to be. I wrote Phil that he was my church, and we had a little hymn that no one knew but us. How naïve that was. I thought my life was a book I could write myself. Now it's sitting open for any wind to turn the pages."

He smiled—a smile so like Father's, she felt a lump in her throat. Whatever way the wind blew, she sensed the deep connection between Austin and Vinnie and herself. They would always protect each other.

"I want to ask about you and Otis, but you are the most private person I know. I said so to Sue a few weeks ago, when she came into the library and kicked up a fuss. She always conducts her scenes in her best clothes, as if she could still stir

157

my longing, although her harangue chilled my every nerve. I adopted my best lawyer-language and told her that she had no right to invade your privacy or pass judgment on you."

Emily almost wished she wore a corset, so that she could excuse herself and loosen it. Her chest felt hot and tight. "She has kept away from me, lately, I suppose because she fears her own volcanic storms. It's upsetting to know that someone I have loved for decades begrudges me happiness. I wonder what kind of a life she expected me to have—and Phil, too. We do have some good years left."

From the window, she saw Ned hurrying along the path to the Homestead, followed by Mattie, wearing a face her aunts called the Determined Dickinson—pursed lips, a frown. The look always made Emily nervous. She hoped her niece was not planning to climb trees today. Mattie was an expert tree-climber, at least on the way up. Her father often had to fetch a ladder and talk her down from a huge hemlock. Then she'd repeat the same trick a few days later. Ned and Gib could be loud and obstreperous, but Mattie occupied a category by herself. Emily believed her niece didn't enjoy her rebellions. What a pity—all that energy wasted on anger at the world.

Austin interrupted her thoughts. "When Sue began to talk about Father, she railed about what he would think of you and his best friend having a love affair, and about Father's worry, when you were younger and going riding with George Gould and Vaughn Emmons and God knows whom else, about your keeping your virtue intact. And she accused you of intriguing with the judge at midnight in the garden, many years ago."

He dropped his head into his hands. She noticed their prominent veins and paleness.

"Being a Dickinson is like belonging to some baronial family, with elaborate codes and punishments, and carefully guarded women. Yet you and Vinnie enjoyed freedoms that Sue and her sisters did not. Mattie as well, perhaps too much so. She rides the whirlwind."

Emily reached out and patted her brother's handsome side-whiskers. "I have known from the time Sue met our family that she felt an attachment to Father, and he to her. He visited her twice in Baltimore, when she was teaching there. I missed her terribly, and became lonely and jealous, especially when Father came back from Baltimore with no letter from Sue for me. I think he believed she would bring a new vitality to this family, with her exotic appearance and brilliant wit."

When Father met Sue, she was in her late teens, and he a handsome man in his mid-forties, married to a sweet, nervous woman who suffered headaches and depression. She could scarcely bear to think that Edward Dickinson, of all people, had forbidden feelings—as Phil had felt for her.

"Did Father ever sense what was wrong between you? You had all the normal hopes and dreams about Sue, and possibly she did too. In the early days, she and I had many sisterly conversations about you, but she was always evasive, even about your interlude in the Revere Hotel."

A shaky sigh came from Austin. He fiddled with the cigar in his pocket, releasing a faint acrid smell. "The less said about that, the better. I thought everything was all right, but a few days later Sue wrote me a letter that tore my hide off for being forward, and accused me of thinking that because she was an orphan, her virtue was mine to seize."

Emily grasped her brother's hand. "Sue carries around a long list of our iniquities. But the intriguing in the garden, as she put it, is one of the happiest memories of my life. Commencement, 1862, I asked Phil to sing a tune at midnight, and then demanded a kiss from him, a real kiss."

Austin's jaw dropped. "You demanded a kiss from the judge when Elizabeth was still alive? Emily, you are a bold project. I always thought Vinnie was the flirt in the family. Now I imagine a steady stream of men visiting those naughty Dickinson girls when Father and I were away. What's a brother to do now?"

"As a lawyer, you know that if law exists, so does lawlessness. It's a habit of the universe, as far as I can tell, and I think you know where my own truant heart belongs. But sometimes propriety and lawlessness tangle up, the way a vine will take over a wall. Sue's powerful appeal may have worked on Father's protective instinct, as it did on yours and mine."

He looked shocked. "Do you think Father wanted Sue for himself?"

Emily took a few deep breaths. "What Father wanted, and what Sue wanted, or fancied she did, are unknown subjects. Both of them desired affection and attention, and she needed a family, her own being such a disaster. I've spent years wandering among these briars and trying to tend to the bruises and scratches. I wish I could tend to yours, too."

Austin's mouth wore his customary bitterness, and when tears filled his eyes, he looked ashamed. "I did love her then. She could crawl right into my veins with her mixture of charm and mockery. I foolishly supposed that marrying her would right the imbalance between us and take away my jealousy of you and Father—so brilliant, so capable—with me a distant third in a race I didn't know I was running. On our wedding night, she was nervous, and I did my tender best. She turned aside. The rest of the honeymoon was the same." He got out his handkerchief and blew his nose.

They heard a child's footsteps rushing up the stairs. Gib flung open Emily's door. He had bits of straw in his hair and sawdust on his pants. "Ned and Mattie are fighting in the barn! You have to make them stop!"

Mattie tried to land a punch on her brother, who kept ducking her flying fist. Emily feared that Ned would get the worst of it, because his sister was physically stronger. They shouted Judge Lord's and Emily's names like war-cries. Mattie rounded on Emily and accused her aunt of preparing to betray the family, while Ned yelled that Mattie was in the grip of demons. A howling Gib ran away down the path. Austin tried to grab his daughter's wrist, and she delivered a sharp kick to his shin.

Emily hurried to the well and fetched a bucket of water. Surprised by her own strength, she hurled the water at Mattie and stood with her arms folded and her eyes burning. Her wet skirt steamed. In their coop, the hens flapped and shrieked.

"There is more where that came from, and I am prepared to cool you off by any means necessary. If you won't apologize to me, then at least tell your father and your brother that you are sorry for this Vesuvian outbreak of rage! This is Amherst, Massachusetts—not southern Italy!"

Mattie stood, panting, her wet hair stuck to her head. "*You* are the one who has brought disgrace on our family!" Like a witness at a witch-trial, she pointed her finger at her aunt, then burst into tears and ran out of the barn.

Ned sank down on a hay bale and looked as though he might be sick. Austin put his arm around his son's shoulders. "Try to calm down, and then we'll go inside and have some tea. Maybe Emily has some beer in the house."

She thought she would like a beer herself, maybe laced with brandy. When she opened the barn door, she saw a sight she would never forget: Vinnie, Mother, and Maggie Maher stood in the window of the blue room, looking down at the barnyard, their hands over their mouths in identical gestures of shock, as though the Homestead had become a gladiators' arena.

She trudged upstairs, wondering what in the world she would say to her mother.

*

Later, she sat at her table and tried to think of how to write Phil about the day's events without distorting any detail. She tried for a light tone. He would read straight through it.

Darling,

> *This day has been so full of shock and surprise, I hardly know how to continue the story. If I were someone else writing it, it would sound almost comical. We have scarcely had such noise on this property since Dennis Scannell was caught waltzing with the cow.*
>
> *All is quiet, it being midnight, my favorite hour, when I imagine hearing you outside my window singing like an Owl-Troubadour. No emissaries have come from Next Door. I won't open my Pandora's box and let forth further troubles. Austin, Vinnie, Ned, and Maggie know about you and me. Ned will pay a price for being my champion in the lists.*
>
> *The oddest thing I have to tell you about is Mother. She is frail and sometimes fretful. But today, when I walked into the blue room, she embraced me, then talked with me alone while Vinnie and Maggie tended to Austin and Ned. For a few*

moments, she was mistress of this house, not an aging invalid. She made a wobbly smile and said that she had sometimes felt herself to have been a distant and inadequate mother. That she had long known I was in love with you. She said, "You call him Phil? Well, never mind. You can call him Mr. Blue Eyes, or Lord Longshanks, or whatever you fancy." What a joy to hear that!

I'll never forget what she said next, or the serene look on her face.

"You have never been a child to ask permission, Emily. You're forty-nine years old, think of it! You don't look much older than you did when you and Carlo would make your neighborhood pilgrimages. Should you wish to spend your life with Phil, you have my blessing. You both deserve to be happy."

Lord Blue Eyes, I'll leave out what she said about the joy of physical embraces, because my hand is trembling. She told me not to worry about what Sue and Mattie might say about me, and said she had always resisted an air of command from a daughter-in-law or a granddaughter. It's true, Phil—you yourself know how perfectly she kept this house. Then she spoke up for herself: "Sue has no reason to look down her nose at me. I tried to win her over, but eventually, I gave up, as if I'd let a large moth fly off my finger." I felt like cheering.

Then she put her head to one side, like a songbird, and said that I may have gotten my stubbornness from her, after all.

I helped her walk to the window, to show her the barnyard, restored to normalcy. Dennis carrying the rakes into the tool-shed, Maggie bringing in a basket of fresh eggs. It might have been any peaceable homestead anywhere in New England. Then Mother and I spied a big proud cardinal and his mate on the tree west of the barn. We stood there admiring them, Mother clapping her hands softly, as though they were her special visitors. Maggie came in with tea and, God love her, a glass of beer for my parched throat—but by then Mother needed rest. She grasped my hand and said "The future will take care of itself, if you take care of each other."

Honorable and beloved Owl, you spoke of "Hope" surpassing "Home"—I thought that Hope was Home, but if I knew the future, I would be the wrong sort of Sorceress for you. Think of the Cardinals, when you think of us.

Your Abiding Emily

13.

These Fevered Days
Salem, Amherst, March – April 1881

Salem, March 1881

P hil swam in dark waters as he pursued a large serpent
that stretched across the Ipswich River channel. From
the shore, his father shouted at him to swim back, before the
tide turned. He gulped air and attempted a frog-kick that sent
him backwards toward the beast's jaws, with double row of
spiked teeth and a long green tongue. He gave a thick shout.

As the nightmare spiraled away, Phil felt a hand and
heard a voice. Tim O'Leary grasped his shoulder until his
eyelids fluttered open. Opening his consciousness to daylight,
he guessed that the hour was somewhere between six and
seven, that he was alive, and that a pot of brisk Earl Grey,
its bergamot perfume curling toward his pillow, stood on the
tray, with a letter from Emily.

30 March, 1881

Dearest Jurist,

*Mr. Timothy O'Leary wrote to tell me you were sick with
flu and could not write. I think of you every waking minute,
and send you imagined Cordials and Caresses.*

165

Today I had Tom Kelley put a box of flowers on the train to Salem. The hyacinths are still in bud, but when they open, I hope they chase the fever from your handsome arteries, so that your Blood rises in appropriate parts of your Self.

A small dark stream has appeared between here and Next Door. Sue does not cross it. Ned roams around the barn. I have seen a letter sticking from his pocket. Anyone who adds to his burdens is my sworn Enemy.

I await any Mail from you, even a single scribbled word.

Austin is wrestling with the Faculty about a new astronomer he wishes to appoint. I think we could all benefit from star-gazing. When you are better, ask Tim to take you up to your roof walk, and try to sight the stars that hang over both our houses. We know what they mean to us, in all seasons. They are old enough to remember the night I arrived in my life—and yours.

My Seraphic Naughty, I expect that you would benefit from another kind of wrestling. But all in good time. I send flights of wishes, and phantom Kisses.

Your Emily

Emily's letters gave him joy, but his eyes burned and throbbed. Mary Farley, her daughter Abbie, and Abbie's cousin Molly took turns bathing his forehead with a cool rag. Molly had a gentle touch, but when Abbie kept dripping water on the carpet, her mother told her to make herself useful elsewhere. The judge's fever spiked, sank, and spiked again. Tim O'Leary retrieved pieces of paper strewn across Mr. Lord's bed and tucked them under his pillow. One morning, Tim found the bed sheets soaked, the fever broken, and Mr. Lord sitting up, hungry and asking for his mail.

He wrote Emily that his skin now wore a healthy flush. Their code—words like flesh or blood, veins, or arteries— inscribed their longing. He read her letters aloud.

My little devices to live till Monday would darken all your glee for you have a good deal of glee in your nature's corners the most lurking—and never to be trusted . . . without ones prayers. Full of works and plots and little happinesses the thought of you protracts them all and makes them sham and cold.

Works and plots and little happinesses. Emily knew the sweet secrets of daily life, his sensual way of teasing her, as he took her tentative, blushing "no" and turned it into "yes," the game they played with each other.

Phil relaxed on his pillows and treated himself to a spicy daydream about buying a railroad car, or a balloon, or a small country inn with a room kept ready for his private use. Why should he not spend the fortune he had earned—working for decades as a jurist, buying and selling property all over Essex County—if not for his own happiness? As he inhaled the lavender scent of Emily's letter, pleasure and frustration twined around each other. He needed to get up and take some exercise.

When Tim O'Leary walked with the judge on his morning constitutional, Lord told him stories of drunks, murderers, gangs of thugs, frauds and cheats, abusers of wives and children, brothel-keepers, slimy lawyers, and corrupt state officials. He loved telling Tim about the Dickinsons. Sometimes he quoted Emily's poetry.

There is no Frigate like a Book
To take us Lands away
Nor any Coursers like a Page

167

Of prancing Poetry –
This Traverse may the poorest take
Without oppress of Toll –
How frugal is the Chariot
That bears the Human Soul –

"What do you make of that, Tim?"

Phil enjoyed his sidewalk theatrics. A few passersby, recognizing the judge's stately figure, slowed down to listen. He loved to command an audience—often with the help of Shakespeare. Occasionally he sneaked in a poem Emily had sent him.

"It sounds like a hymn, sir, but a different kind of hymn. What is 'oppress of toll'? Does it mean that we can all read without paying a tax on books? If so, I agree with this poem, sir. Reading is a great freedom."

Phil grasped Tim's hand and shook it. "Got it in a second, Tim, as expected. My brother Nathaniel would agree with us if he were here. You were good to him. Hard work to tend a sick man all those years."

"Mr. Nathaniel never complained, and he loved having company. He could quote Shakespeare from morn till night, and I never tired of hearing him."

The memory of crippled Nathaniel, bearing his suffering with an uncanny grace, eased into Phil's heart. The two men slowed down and fell silent, as the sun rose above Salem's chilly streets. Smoke spiraled up from the handsome chimneys around Washington Square. He felt the chill, but didn't want to retreat home. He willed himself to grow stronger day by day, and wished he could will himself to grow younger.

"I like the way Miss Dickinson starts on a ship and ends in a chariot. That's very fine."

He would write Emily what Tim had said about her poem.

"I hope to meet her one day, sir. Perhaps she and her family might visit?"

Phil placed his walking-stick carefully in the melting snow. His breath came harder in the cold Atlantic air.

"Miss Dickinson's mother is not well, and she and her sister have the care of her. I wish the lady well, but fervently wish things were otherwise."

Tim nodded, but said nothing. Lord knew that he listened and understood.

Tim caught the flu just as Lord resumed his duties in the Northampton court. The spring brought dozens of cases, along with reporters from the *Republican* who had heard that the ailing Judge Lord was expected to resign any day. Determined to challenge this rumor with an energetic performance, he was pleased not to disappoint the crowd. When he gave one slimy defense attorney a tongue-lashing, the man keeled over in a faint.

In fleeting moments, he worried that in the rush to catch his train to Northampton, he had not been careful enough with the locked box in the bureau where he kept Emily's letters.

*

Amherst, April 1881

Ned watched Emily at work in her conservatory, and she let him observe without trying to tutor him, unless he asked. She shook the dirt from a purple heliotrope, plucked away a few of its matted roots, and put it into a fresh pot.

"Why do you rip the roots away?"

"Only a few of them, so that the others will have a chance to grow."

He sniffed the plant. "It's an odd smell. Like vanilla."

"Some people find it too much, but I like it, especially outside. It's Phil—Judge Lord's—favorite plant. I once teased him that he'd probably eaten heliotrope when he was a boy in knee-pants."

"I have trouble imagining the judge in knee-pants."

She smiled. There was nothing wrong with the judge's knees.

"Aunt Emily, two letters have arrived at home from Salem. From Abbie Farley."

Having received a bounteous letter from Phil the day before, Emily wondered what was bothering Ned. He seemed anxious, and kept reaching to check his back pocket.

"Is there a problem, dear? You know you can tell me."

"Abbie—well, I'm not sure I like her. She never wants to go rambling, and she said that the dinosaur footprints at the College bored her to death. I guess she'd rather go shopping in Springfield. She and Mother have become great pals, which I find odd, since Mother's so much older."

Emily regarded her nephew, morose and uncomfortable. This wasn't about Abbie's shopping. "Ned, speak."

"It means having to confess something I did that I wish I hadn't done, and now I have to think about it all the time."

She heard his plain-spoken misery. "Let me make sure that we are safe for confidences. Would you rather go upstairs?"

She washed her hands at the kitchen pump and led her nephew up the back stairs to her room.

"I overheard Mother and Father talking about you and Judge Lord. I've heard him before, getting angry at her about invading your privacy, but this time Mother said something about a letter she had received."

"From Abbie Farley, I take it."

Ned gulped and rushed out the words. "Aunt Emily, this is something Abbie sent Mother that you wrote to Mr. Lord. Or maybe she'd copied it."

Emily sat down hard in her writing-chair. Phil kept her letters and poems locked up. Of the hundreds of letters she'd written in her life, those to him were especially rich, intimate, and daring.

As he would advise, she tried to make her thoughts follow careful footsteps. If Abbie had raided her uncle's box of letters, she must have been alone in the house, or his servants were busy. She remembered that Tim O'Leary had caught his flu. Seeing that Ned watched her with alarm, she tried to keep her breathing under control, but suspicions kindled in her brain. Tim supervised the household, but if he was sick in bed, Abbie might have found a way into her uncle's bureau and opened his private box. She wouldn't think twice about reading a love letter from Emily.

Ned knelt beside her chair and put his hand on her knee. "It gets worse, Aunt Emily. Father snatched the letter out of Mother's hand, and then drove her out of the room. I thought he would strike her, or that she would strike him. She had a letter-opener in her hand and at first I thought it was a knife. I tiptoed into the parlor and hid next to the piano. Then I heard him leave the library and thunder out the door. I sneaked into the library and found the letter in his desk. I thought of burning it, but I think it belongs to you. I didn't read it, I swear. I just recognized Abbie's spiky writing and saw that the envelope was thick." He handed it to Emily.

. . . To lie so near your longing—to touch it as I passed, for I am but a restive sleeper and often should journey from your Arms through the happy night, but you will lift me back, wont you, for

only there I ask to be. I say, if I felt the longing nearer—than in our dear past, perhaps I would not resist to bless it, because it would be right.

Of course she knew the words by heart. Accompanying the copy of her letter was Abbie's note to Sue:

They had a 'dear past,' did they? Does this mean they intrigued before Aunt Elizabeth died? Or that she wished to intrigue with him, but he was too honorable to do so? I shudder to think what the 'longing' means, but I am not entirely ignorant. One thing is for sure: my uncle is still strong enough to lift that little red-headed hussy and carry her around. Imagine! And what is 'it,' pray tell, the longing, or the 'dear past,' and what 'it' does she not resist blessing, the longing or the dear past, or something else? And what does she imagine 'would be right,'? Well, these are no longer mysteries to me: she means to have him, and that portends ill for my mother and cousin Molly and me. Emily will have his considerable fortune, and his fine house, and the piano, and Elizabeth's furs and jewels. And the three of us REAL family will have to move back to Ipswich and live in a wretched little cottage. It is not to be borne. Sue, you must help!

Trying to keep her teeth from chattering, Emily folded the letters carefully and replaced them in the envelope. She took her nephew's face in her hands.

"Ned, as you honor this family and the memory of your grandfather, who was Judge Lord's closest friend, please take this envelope straight back to where you found it, and don't let your mother see you doing it. And promise me that you won't read it."

She held his eyes in hers until he made the promise.

"But what is so bad about it?"

"Abbie's words distort the truth. You are almost twenty, and I am almost fifty, but part of my business on this planet is to love, and to tell the truth. About Abbie, I will say only that she is upset that her uncle and I have become close. I suspect she is quite unhappy, in spite of having been taken in by the Lords and given a life of privilege in Salem."

Even with her tremulous voice and chilly hands, Emily was proud of demonstrating a lawyer's logic. Ned, trying to work things out, spoke slowly. "I think she had a young man, during the War, who has a lot of money but spends it all on travel and doesn't go with her any longer."

"That would be difficult, so we must try to think charitable thoughts."

She wanted Ned to slip off home before his mother came looking for him. Emily kissed her nephew on each cheek, and hurried him down the back stairs.

When Maggie knocked at her door, Emily was hanging over the commode, throwing up. Maggie knelt beside her and held her head. After a minute Emily wiped her lips and sat back against the dressing-room door.

"I saw Ned rushing down the stairs, Miss Emily. Did he upset you?"

"Yes, but it's not his fault." Her voice was a choked whisper.

As her fluttering insides calmed down, she tried not to think of Phil's learning about his niece's treachery. How could she tell him, and how would he treat the matter in his own house? She knew he was careful to leave his judge's robes and demeanor in the courthouse.

Maggie covered the commode and helped Emily to her reading chair. She bathed Emily's face with a cool cloth and helped her change into a fresh nightgown.

"We should keep you in quarantine from that lot next door. They seem to walk into this house trailing storm-clouds. We can't have you getting the tummies every time one of them shows up. You'll be down to a rag, a bone, and a hank of hair in no time. Think what your judge would say, now."

Emily gave her a wan smile, and Maggie ordered her to rest in bed and take a little tea and toast. She fell into a weary sleep.

Later, she heard a rap on her door and jumped to hide Phil's latest letter. Mattie walked in without asking permission, as she often did, and handed her a note. Her face showed evidence of tears. She looked more like Ned than ever.

I, Martha Gilbert Dickinson, hereby do formally apologize for my conduct toward my Aunt Emily Elizabeth Dickinson and my brother Ned, and for any distress suffered by those who witnessed my display of temper. I am heartily sorry and wish to state that such will never happen again.

"Thank you, Mattie," Emily said with a trace of formality. She folded the note and slipped it under the covers. As she tried to think of some harmless subject of conversation, her mind felt like a streambed of dry sand aching for water. If she told her niece to leave, the girl would be hurt, and a hurt Mattie, in the strained household, might cause more trouble. Emily imagined the confusions in her young mind: her parents' sour marriage, her older brother's doubtful health, her aunt's intimacy with a man she found odd and old.

"You look quite pale, Aunt Emily. Are you well?"

"I'm not sick, and not exactly well either. But I will be."

She rose from her bed, put her arm around her niece's shoulders, and allowed her to help her into her robe. "Let's go prowl in the library and see if there's some music you might like to take home. Sometimes the old songs still have their charms."

Mattie gave her a wobbly smile.

That smile is all the reward I can expect, for the moment. Hope's wings are too thin to lift me.

She prayed that Ned had done as she had asked.

14.

There Comes A Warning like a Spy
Salem, October 1881

"A bbie, I would like to have you accompany me on a walk around Salem. It's a fine Sunday afternoon, and you are dressed quite becomingly. If you'll pardon your old uncle for saying so, you deserve to be shown off."

Phil put on his hat as Tim O'Leary opened the front door for him, and Abbie pulled on her gloves.

His niece frequently wore new dresses and hats, while her cousin Molly didn't seem to care what she wore as long as it was clean and comfortable. Abbie liked to cinch in her plump waist and wear bonnets with elaborate, ticklish feathers and fronds. It was mostly her uncle's money she was spending. He wished his sister-in-law would teach her daughter how to sew her own clothes, or hire a seamstress to refashion some of Elizabeth's old gowns that he had offered her.

Abbie wore a new topaz-colored silk dress with lace trim and a bustle over her large backside. She gave her uncle a suspicious look, but he assumed a smile of innocent blandness as she fixed her bonnet in the hall mirror.

He rarely walked with his niece, who tended to chatter about superficial things and pause at length in front of shop windows. He preferred to set his own brisk pace for his daily

176

three miles, down to the waterfront, around Washington Square Park, then to Lemon Street, where Tim O'Leary lived, and back through the historic district, then past the courthouse. Observing the diverse people and architecture of Salem stimulated his curiosity. His niece stimulated it in a more worrisome way. Her attempts to manipulate others, including him, were galling to behold. Reluctant to mention Abbie's treacheries to her mother, he intended to manage their conversation in his own way, and to hint that he knew what she was up to. He looked forward to the challenge.

"That is a new frock you're wearing, am I right? It looks too good for Salem. You must have purchased it in Boston."

"Yes, I went by myself on the train. Women can do that these days, you know, without raising an eyebrow. Ten years ago I would have been thought quite forward."

Ten years ago, he thought, Elizabeth would have taken you to Boston, and held your elbow so that you didn't make a fool of yourself in the shops and streets.

"I think you're brave to venture into noisy Boston on your own. Parts of downtown teem with all manner of people you would want to pass by quickly. And 'forward' is not a word that should apply to you. There's no need for forwardness if you come from the pedigrees of the Farleys and the Lords."

He winced inwardly at his uttering such pretentious nonsense. The Farleys and the Lords, like the Dickinsons, had had the good luck to arrive in the Colonies, make their fortune, and produce healthy children. None of them, thank God, had a drop of royal blood. He stepped aside to let two women pass them on the narrow sidewalk. He lowered his voice so that the women would not catch his words.

"See how much more fashionably dressed you are than those plain women. I'm betting that one of them will find a way to inspect you."

Sure enough, the older of the pair turned around, raked her glance up and down Abbie's dress, and whispered to the other one. The judge lifted his hat, and the women scurried down an alley toward Derby Street. He chuckled, although he wanted to guffaw.

"I hope you're not too bored living with Molly and your mother in my lonely echoing house. My court duties restrict my leisure to take you to the theatre or concerts. It's not for lack of interest, believe me."

"In us, or in concerts and theatre?" Her voice had an edge.

"It's been a long time since I heard a concert. I'm afraid my hearing is not as sharp as it was. But I've heard some memorable performances, and should you learn of one that appeals to you—"

"Which one was the most memorable?" Abbie demanded.

They walked on toward Washington Square, the judge deliberately slowing his pace. "My brother George lives right there, on that beautiful corner. It's a pity that we live so close and hardly see each other. Families are odd, aren't they? I think his snobbish wife has always found me uncouth."

That was true. Elizabeth had tried and failed to win over the haughty Mary Marshall Lord—but he and George sometimes found a few hours to sneak down to a gentlemen's pub for a pint or two, and talk law and politics.

"The concert, Uncle Lord?"

"Let's see—it could have been Bach's *Christmas Oratorio*, in the years when Elizabeth sang in the Oratorio Society. Or Haydn's *Creation*, in Boston." He hummed a bit of "On Mighty Pens." Abbie was embarrassed at his sonorous baritone.

"But in my long life I've never heard anything like Anton Rubinstein, years ago in Boston, with Elizabeth and the Dickinsons."

"I didn't think that Mrs. Dickinson went out, much less traveled. Even less her daughter. Like mother, like daughter, I suppose."

"Let's sit on a bench and let the sun warm our faces." He chose a bench that faced George's house. The windows were shut tight. One of George's daughters suffered from mental illness, and was kept upstairs with an attendant. People said that she had broken down after a revival meeting, but Lord suspected the daughter had fallen in love with a suitor her mother found unacceptable, as she did all her children's suitors.

"The concert was my gift in honor of my friend Edward's seventieth birthday. Elizabeth and I, Edward, and—" He paused and made a light cough, a judge's way to create suspense before giving a bench verdict. "And Emily—junior, not her mother."

"Emily!" Abbie's lips twisted. "I thought she never went out or saw anybody. She actually came to Boston? Wearing a white dress, I suppose? Oh Uncle, you're making it up."

"I assure you I am not. It was a special occasion, and she and her father enjoyed it, despite his becoming fatigued. I had invited them to Salem, but a winter storm intervened. It was too bad—you might have met Emily and her father while Elizabeth was still alive."

Lord watched various emotions—surprise, curiosity, disgust—play across Abbie's face.

"What on earth did she wear, for Heaven's sake?"

He adjusted his hat to conceal his eyes. "I am a member of the male species, and you know how ill-suited men are to talk of fashion. I can only describe it as quite attractive." He remembered the green silk dress with the pleated ruffles and delicate scooped neckline, Emily's charming bustle, the hint of freckled bosom, and the careful kiss she planted on his cheek. "But you were asking about Rubinstein. Did you like him when you heard him?"

"Oh—why yes, of course. He flung his hair back and forth. I suppose that's some kind of Russian gesture."

"You were taking piano lessons from Elizabeth then. Hearing Rubinstein must have been instructive. What did he play?" He recalled the painful sound of Abbie practicing Clementi in a browbeating manner, as though to punish him for writing such dull stuff.

Abbie removed a glove, inspected it, and refitted it on her hand. "Actually, I—think it was Beethoven." A good, safe answer, he observed, since the Russian pianist always played Beethoven. "Shall we get up and walk down past the Seven Gables?"

She placed her hand in the crook of his elbow. Her footsteps were more of the trudging than the gliding variety, perhaps because of heavy thoughts. "Does Emily allow herself to leave Amherst? Or was that only once?"

He could guess her worry: could it happen again?

"She has her mother to take care of, a duty she and Vinnie take quite seriously. But I think under the right circumstances, she might leave Amherst. What they are, I couldn't possibly surmise." He hoped she would hear his formal tone.

"Sue says she refuses to come to parties next door, even though she might have met famous people like Frederick Law Olmsted and even Ralph Waldo Emerson."

"Whom she elects to meet or not is entirely her business, don't you think? She chooses her company with care. Affection trumps—how should I put it—fashion."

"You have read her poems, I presume." This said in a frosty tone, as though reading poems was a misdemeanor.

"You *presume* correctly. As I *presume* that Sue Dickinson has shown you some of them. I don't imagine poetry is quite the thing with you, Abbie, am I right? A volume of *letters*—now that might be more interesting." He knew how to drop the hook of the right word.

"Yes, letters. They give away so much more than poetry, don't they? Letters are never a waste of time. One can always find something between the lines."

Clearly, Abbie was trying to set a trap for him.

"I have never considered any time spent with Emily, in person or paper, to be wasted. After all my years on the bench, I know what wasted time is. To answer your unasked question, I admire her poems and her letters, full of surprises. Giving things away lies in the hands of reader and writer. Even a determined investigator can't always crack the code."

He gave his niece a judge's sharp glance. He would not give away what he had learned of Abbie's turn as a spy. Power lay in keeping the secret at hand, like a well-oiled pistol.

She turned her attention to a shop window: bonnets, hair-ribbons, and other fripperies. Thank God it was Sunday, he thought, and the shops closed.

He could almost hear the words banging around in Abbie's head. *Affection, usefulness, wasted time, investigator, crack the code.*

They turned their backs to the park and walked down Orange Street toward Derby. The judge paused on the corner to admire the Custom House.

"What a handsome town we live in, don't we? One architectural marvel after another. Perhaps one day we'll be able to show Emily and Vinnie the wonders of Salem."

"Would you take them out in that big schooner named after you? Sue told me that Emily has never seen the sea—imagine!"

"Oh dear, the *Otis P. Lord*. What an ungainly boat, although I hear it brings in tons of cod. The prospect sounds rather smelly, and I, at least, would much rather be swimming than sailing. I've never been able to return the graciousness I've been offered at the Homestead, and it makes me feel guilty." He wondered if Emily had ever learned to swim, and tacked away from his imaginings.

Abbie sniffed, as he knew she would do. "You can feel guilty if you like, Uncle, but there's no budging Emily, even if her invalid mother turns into an angel."

"Nicely put, my dear." His voice mixed the moist with the dry. He almost marveled at how Abbie could insert a drop of poison into a mild metaphor.

They turned north, up Summer Street. He'd planned the walk carefully, having observed who was likely to emerge from a certain door at a certain time of day, to visit his banker. Even on a Sunday, bankers had appointments with prosperous clients. Abbie tried to press her uncle to walk faster, but he stopped to admire a freshly painted wrought-iron fence.

Emerging from a handsome doorway near Essex Street was a dapper fortyish gentleman, wearing a dark gray suit and carrying a Malacca cane.

"Mr. William West, good day to you." The judge held out his hand, and the dapper gentleman shook it lightly, then blinked at Abbie. Mr. West bowed and raised his fashionable hat, just a little.

"Hello, Will West. It has been ages since I've seen you." Abbie's blush reached to her lower eyelids. "I hope you're well."

Will West, it appeared, had a stammer, or had just developed one. "I–I am g-glad to see you, M-Miss Farley. I have b-been travelling."

"Where did you go this time?" Her tone was aggrieved. Phil felt sorry for her, and for Will West.

"Oh, England again. I l-like England. I'd like to l-live there, if p-possible."

Take her with you, Will West, Phil wanted to say. I'll pay the freight.

Pleading tardiness for his appointment, West scooted up Essex Street, as the judge and his niece walked up North Street. Abbie wore an unhappy face.

"Oh, uncle, I'm sorry we encountered him. My old almost-beau."

"Perhaps he'll call on you one of these days, since he knows you're in town, and not stuck in the country."

"No, he won't. And I'll sit home and be miserable. I almost wish I were stuck in the country town of Amherst, as you put it. At least there's Sue, and sometimes Ned, if he's not being too much of a boy. And you don't seem to mind the place too much!"

He would not parry this thrust.

They stepped up from the bright street into the shadows of his house. He gave Abbie another strict appraising glance and turned down the temperature of his voice a few degrees, a practice he found effective in chastening wayward lawyers. "Can you think of a reason why an old widower would mind a few refreshing days among cherished friends, my dear niece?"

She would not meet his eyes. They entered the hallway and allowed Tim O'Leary to take their hats and gloves. Tim's raised eyebrow was the signal he expected, about mail waiting for the judge.

Phil looked down at Abbie. "If you can think of one, you must tell me what it is. And if you can't, then let me hear no more vain talk from you about my closest friends."

*

October 1881

My Dearest Emily,

I have tried to do the hardest thing a person can do without supernatural help, and that is to move a hard heart. I did not succeed. On my walk with Abbie, I was so clever that I almost made myself sick. Laughter and a hearty sense of the absurd can only hide so much. Twice I came close to declaring how things are between you and me, but I remembered your request to trust only those who truly love us. In the meantime, I have begun to think of our future together. I'll begin by paying off my mortgage on Tim O'Leary's house, and soon divest myself of some coastal properties.

Be patient with me, my dear, and by springtime we'll see a clearer path. Only a month ago! It feels like six months since we stole out to the barn and gave the chickens a night they could long remember, if they weren't chickens.

Little Phil

October 1881

Little Phil of loved Philology—

Who else could wrap my wrist in love and wit? "Little Phil" engraved inside the clasp, the bracelet placed close to my pulse. I let Mother examine it, and she clapped her hands with delight. She loved the little tassel with the dainty beads. Touching your name makes heartbeats rise up again.

How you can be so naughty and provoking at a distance is only one of the Miracles, wrought by your flowing hand. I would like to do the same thing to you.

Next Door, especially Sue, are distracted by the new arrivals, Prof. David Todd, the astronomer, and his wife Mabel. Ned is infatuated with her. I glimpse her from my window as she takes Ned's arm and walks past the house. She is pretty and well dressed, and will soon, I predict, enthrall every male under the age of eighty.

Vinnie, having heard the young woman perform on the piano, has invited her to entertain Mother. I shall contrive a way to hear from upstairs.

I am no prophet, but if I sneak outside and press my ear to the Grass, I can sense the tremors of a new Volcano, arising from our Earthquake. The fact of our love has changed the weather and warmed up the dirt under our feet.

In return for the handsome bracelet, here is a poem:

How fleet – how indiscreet an one –
How always wrong is Love –
The joyful little Deity
We are not scourged to serve –

Thank God you and I are beyond religion, except for Ourselves.

Your Artery and Vein

185

15.

Before He comes We weigh the Time
Amherst, February – April 1882

E mily tested the gingerbread with her finger and sliced it into generous pieces for Gib and his friends. Maggie tucked a warm dishcloth around the fragrant plate. Making treats for the neighborhood children gave sweetness to every day and a rich smell to the house. Emily would often take a basket of gingerbread upstairs, tie a rope to the handle, and wait for the little band of pirates, led by Gib, to sneak around the house and stand under a back window, demanding treasure in their piping voices.

At that moment, Sue walked into the kitchen. Maggie gave a brief curtsey and hurried out. Emily had scarcely seen Sue since September. In December she'd received some out-of-season roses and a note, with a thorn in its hint that Emily avoided her. The word *"Love"* was spelled *LVOE*. Written hastily, Emily thought, or in a code she declined to decipher.

A few weeks before, Sue had rapped vainly at the bolted kitchen door. To her aggrieved note, Emily replied that she should have knocked "with a trumpet." The permissions previously granted by unlocked doors had evolved into silent refusals, achieved by turns of a key. Emily now ruled the household in her quiet way.

186

When Sue patted the tortoiseshell comb in her hair, Emily wondered if the gesture signaled that the comb was a gift from Austin, who had given Sue many handsome presents. More and more she felt her heart to be a castle guarded by a stream thick with bulrushes. Safe inside her battlements, she was a queen of a tiny realm made of paper, pencil, needles and thread, hyacinth bulbs in the window, and Phil's bold letters secreted in their ebony box.

Sue swished around the room on a tour of inspection, lifting the lid on the sugar bowl, peering into the breadbox, sniffing the air. Emily had almost finished making another cake, and was glad for the diversion.

"Have you met young Mabel Todd, dear? She is quite interesting, and interested in you, too. I have taken the liberty of reading some of your poems to her. We have entertained her and her charming husband, David. They are quite the most worthwhile people to arrive in Amherst lately. I wish that you could pry yourself from your room and receive them—at least Mabel. We have become great friends. She plays the piano quite beautifully, with a trained touch, and also sings. I'm thinking of persuading her to give Mattie a few lessons."

Emily wondered whether her sister-in-law had suffered a lapse of memory. Surely she had not forgotten her distaste for tea parties and receptions, or her view of professors as "manikins." She concentrated on her cake and its sugar and almond frosting. *I own every crumb of this cake, but nobody owns a crumb of me.*

"I have heard from Ned that Mrs. Todd is not to be missed, but as you know, I make no exceptions to my general rule about people I have never met."

187

She kept her voice even. Surely Sue knew better than to argue to her firm, straight back.

"Oh, Emily." Sorrow replaced her customary reproach at Emily's refusal. "I have missed you so much." She sank into the chair near the stove. "I seem to have done something to put you at a distance from me, and whatever it is, I am sorry."

Whatever it is raised the hairs on the back of Emily's neck. She regarded her sister-in-law with mixed pity and skepticism. Underneath the bright veneer of politeness, Sue dealt in harsh judgments and jealousy, and abetted Abbie's thieving and spying. These were simple, undeniable facts. In a few weeks, when Phil came to Amherst with the Farley troupe, he and Emily would have to be especially watchful.

Clearing her throat, Sue moved toward the impregnable fortress. "I miss our telling secrets to each other, as we did long ago. Do you remember? When Cousin John stayed with us and you played the piano and we were up all night shrieking from a thunderstorm?"

How could I forget the wild nights—Cousin John's holding us each on his lap, in turn, letting us sip wine from the same glass. In the middle of the night, with my soul-mate Sue in the same bed, the pleasure of sharing the noise and the lightning.

Emily assumed a neutral expression. Mistrust had done its work. Their ample secrets had starved themselves into ghosts. Her love of privacy generated its own kind of wildness.

"You have always stood for storms to me, Sue. Remember, I said that you front on the Gulf Stream. But now I find it necessary—oh, *blazes!*"

"Blazes" was Phil's favorite epithet. Sue was shocked to hear it.

She scooted a pan out of the oven. The top of the cake was slightly burnt.

"But now?"

Delicately, Emily began to pick off the burnt bits. "I take my own power in my hand, even if I don't go against the world."

"Whatever could you mean? Enigmatic Emily."

As Sue laughed her dry little laugh, Emily folded her secrets into herself. *You cannot possibly know what I mean, unless you wrest it from Phil, and you never will.*

"I hope Ned's shaking spells have proved temporary, but Austin doesn't say much about them to me and Vinnie."

Sue went to the sideboard and helped herself to cider. Her hand shook and she spilled a little. "Austin is almost too tired to talk. Whenever Ned has a seizure, he leaps out of bed, still half-asleep, to run upstairs and tend to him. I'm afraid I am not a good nurse. All I can do is try to help his headaches the next morning, but when he asks why his jaw hurts and why he is so tired, I have no answer. We are worn out, I can tell you. This has gone on for years, and no doctor has explained it properly. If it weren't for Gib, I think Austin would take ship on a freighter bound for Brisbane or Tierra del Fuego. Except, as Mattie says, he would have to be dynamited to leave Amherst."

Emily took note of the strain and self-pity. But she could see only Ned's sad face and long thin arms, and hear the frustrated longing in his voice when he mentioned Mrs. Todd—an echo of Austin's long-ago infatuation with Sue.

Love's stricken "why."

"Please," Sue almost begged—a new tone for her—"Let me request that you see Mrs. Todd. She is attractive and witty. I think Ned has almost fallen in love with her. She's only a few years older than our dear afflicted boy. He's always hastening to her house to see if he can do some little thing for

189

her, which she graciously accepts. Perhaps she could play the piano for Mother?"

Wiping her hands on her apron, Emily faced Sue, wondering if she could smell the burnt almonds—a few molecules removed from cyanide's fatal breath. "Anything Mrs. Todd does for Mother will be quite welcome."

Emily would decline to meet Mrs. Todd face to face if the young woman had become one of Sue's social projects. Of course Sue would try to put her friend forward in this community—a far more sophisticated place than when she had vowed to establish the Evergreens as Amherst's social center. Sue kissed Emily on the cheek and hurried out of the house, leaving her to repair the burnt cake.

When Mabel Todd came to play the piano for Mother, Emily sat in the blue room at the top of the stairs and held her mother's hand. Mabel played and sang some Beethoven songs. Emily noticed that her sense of drama prevailed over her attention to musical detail, but the performance appealed to Mother's love of songs. When Austin came in to greet Mother, she signaled him to remain quiet and listen to some Chopin. As the music climbed the stairs, she noticed her brother's face wearing an unaccustomed smile.

*

April

Then the spring of 1882 turned deadly.

In late March, when Austin and the president, Julius Seelye, were in Boston, the college's main building burned to the ground. A fire-expert declared that Walker Hall, a handsome neo-Romanesque structure, acted like "a chimney" to the flames. Classrooms, offices, books, records—all destroyed.

A few days later, Emily learned of her friend Charles Wadsworth's sudden death in Philadelphia. She confided her grief to Vinnie, who had sat beside her when the sisters heard the mighty preacher on their trip to Washington in 1855. His remarkable voice made thunder in the pulpit, and after the sermon, like a kind of magus, the minister disappeared down a trap door. Wadsworth had stirred Emily's heart and soul. He was more poet than preacher.

"You mustn't mind my tears, Vin. Waiting for Phil's visit makes my emotions run just beneath my skin."

Vinnie kissed Emily's pale cheek. "Come and talk to me."

With their mother asleep upstairs as Maggie sewed in a nearby chair, the sisters sat in the dining room. Emily's appetite flagged, but she accepted tea and a slice of toast.

"Were you in love with the minister?" Vinnie plucked at her sleeve.

"When I heard him on that Philadelphia visit—were we ever so young?—I thought I'd been accidentally shot in the woods by a deer hunter."

"Allow me to find my way out of that deer-hunting metaphor. I do remember the voice: rich and dark, like strong coffee."

"You have a way with metaphor yourself. I should tell you, I think God is an Unmoved Mover, but Jesus stands for truth and light. Wadsworth spoke of Jesus as though he were a real man, with parents and friends, and rough, carpenter's hands. A new voice in my life, which I have scarcely heard since."

Vinnie fetched a bottle of currant wine from the sideboard and two of Mother's ruby glasses.

"I wrote to Wadsworth afterwards, but it probably didn't make much sense to him, since it didn't make much sense to me. Mother had retreated into despair, and I thought a curse had fallen upon the family. Father wrapped himself in sadness and guilt. Over the years, my need to talk about Mother and Father, and then myself, became the basis of my friendship with Wadsworth. I only saw him twice after Philadelphia, but we exchanged many letters."

She sipped her wine and leaned her head on Vinnie's shoulder. "Was I in love with Charles Wadsworth? He held little physical attraction for me, except for those compelling eyes, and that earth-shaking baritone. I suppose I respond to eyes and voice more than any other feature—at least at first. He once said his life held many dark secrets, and that gave me something to ponder day and night. Maybe we come to love that way, by constant thinking, and not by bolts of lightning or rapturous kisses."

"And Phil? Did constant thinking make you love him?"

Emily ran her little finger around her glass rim, making a tiny musical squeal.

Phil was too mighty to explain, unless she talked about a time before she could read or write.

"My heart has many doors. I loved Wadsworth, I adored Sam Bowles—who could resist his celestial eyes and his teasing ways? At first I wanted simply to have Phil near me, like a kindly domestic sun, warm and reliable. But later, his physical presence added power to everything he did and said. He looked at me as few men have, and I rode toward him on that sunbeam. I began to notice his eyes, and shoulders, the way his hair curls, his sidelong mischievous smile. I found excuses to touch his hand or kiss him on the cheek."

"Look at that blush, now—you appear to have gone on a wild ride on an untamed horse. Phil is a powerful man. I wish you could see your face when he walks into the house and you help him off with his cloak. I half expect you to climb on him and start biting his ears." Vinnie laughed, amused at the picture she'd described.

"My outrageous sister, let's go out in the garden and plan where we'll put the tomatoes. And I'll tell you a secret." She wiped her eyes. Wadsworth had moved to the next world, and she would bury him in her memory, as best she could.

On this April afternoon, Emily imagined the sky's frothy clouds borne across the state to Salem, where Phil would see them in a few hours. He would be here soon, his hands around her waist, picking her up and calling her pet names—Daisy, Jumbo, Siren, Sylph—as they whispered their secret plans.

After they surveyed the vegetable patch and picked a sunny spot, the sisters wandered down to the flower garden. The soil smelled cold, fresh, and expectant. Phoebes and nuthatches danced around in the air, noisy and busy with love, food, and territory.

"The secret, Emily? Stand and deliver. I wish I could sketch like Phil, with you as my subject. The look on your face is a scandal."

She told Vinnie the story of Commencement, 1862, the owl poem, and the kiss she demanded from the judge as midnight rang in his fiftieth birthday.

"I asked for one kiss, and assumed it would have to stand for all the others I had no right to hope for. I had no place in his life except as his good friend's daughter. But he had known me by then for over thirty years, think of it! And I had long observed he needed more glee in his life. Like Father."

"Glee!" Vinnie hooted. "You can call it that if you want!"

"If Father had known of my daring act—especially using his own description of the owl-judge in that poem—he would have whaled me with a hairbrush."

She noticed that the place in the garden where the kiss had happened now sprouted some *Narcissus poeticus,* with their white corollas and dainty coral centers. Reaching into the flowerbed to snap off some long-dead stalks of sedum, she remembered waiting on the garden bench until midnight, in delicious worry and hope.

"Welcome to midnight, Judge Lord. It is my best hour," she murmured.

"Phil once told me that you reminded him of Cleopatra! 'A law unto herself,' those were his exact words. And he smiled when he said them."

"What an odd April this has been, and it's not even half over. Walker Hall burning, Wadsworth dying, and Phil having to bring the troupe with him. . . ."

"I wish the circus were coming to town this week." Vinnie executed one of her frequent conversational leaps.

"The circus! Why? Gib would enjoy it. At three in the morning, I've watched Jumbo the Elephant lumber down Main Street."

"I'm not thinking of Gib. I'm thinking of some brown-skinned man kidnapping Abbie and taking her to Ethiopia, or wherever circus elephants come from."

The sisters treated themselves to a rich laugh.

They watched Austin approaching the house across the path, his head bent and shoulders slumped. The Walker Hall fire seemed to have left ash in Austin's eyebrows and side-whiskers. His normally well-groomed fingernails wore thin gray half-moons, and thick bags hung under his eyes. Emily wanted to speak sternly to him about taking time off, but her brother had Father's devotion to his work, and nothing could change it. As his father had been, he was married to Amherst and its college. Emily could tell that he didn't want to talk about the fire.

"Has Mrs. Todd played again for Mother? David told me that she might. In such a short time, she has become the talk of Amherst. She attributes it to me—and Sue, of course, who manages what passes for society around here."

Emily noticed that color rose in Austin's face as he talked about the handsome young Todds. She squeezed her brother's hand. "Yes, it was just lovely. Mother fell asleep, as she often does, with a smile on her lips."

She hoped this accomplished young woman, so different from the proper dames of Amherst, would bring a freshness to the Evergreens' elaborate social scene, and be a force for good in that house.

16.

The Thrill came slowly like a Boon
Amherst, April 1882

"The lightning bolt suits you." Emily traces its shape on his backside. "Warm and electric."

It is late afternoon, her favorite time of day—a nest of quietness and pleasure in the big house. Vinnie is napping with her two favorite cats, Mother sleeping, Maggie enjoying her afternoon off.

"You are making me warmer."

Phil flinches and relaxes. Emily has discovered another ticklish spot. She tells him to turn over again, so that he can submit to her inspection and caresses.

"When, and how, and why? You kept this secret tattoo from me, and now comes the little punishment."

She pinches the warm place on his left hip.

"Remember, we have kept our assignations mostly in the dark, making virtue—ha, ha—from necessity. I assumed you would notice this interesting feature sooner or later. Should I have mentioned it when I held you on my knee long ago? When you were five, and you used to blow 'Whig!' in my ear?" Phil chuckles at the memory of Emily, age five, at the breakfast table. Fastening her lips on his ear, she'd left a trail of strawberry jam. "You have always been an outlaw, but now you have to explain yourself—ouch!—to your judge."

"I'm waiting for enlightenment. 'Ha, ha' will only go so far."

"Aren't we all eager for enlightenment! But first, I claim some warmth for my very own." He plucks the sheet from Emily's waist. "I wonder how many hours I could spend discovering all of your freckles. You sport them in the most interesting parts of yourself."

"I used to hate them, but I've gotten used to them. But please don't tell me they are angels' kisses, or any such nonsense."

"More like devil's kisses."

He shifts and she nestles against him. The light in the back bedroom overlooking the garden makes a glowing pool. Emily says they are like two young trout, enjoying the spring waters before the hooks and lines appear. She splays her fingers among the hairs on his chest.

"I will tickle the bottoms of your feet until you tell me how that tattoo came to occupy your flesh."

Phil pretends to sigh. "All right, have your way. I had just turned twenty in July '32, I was about to graduate, and my brother Nathaniel took me to a jolly event, with cake and champagne, aboard a steamship in Boston Harbor. Luckily the ship wasn't moving, although after a time I thought we were headed toward Bermuda. I woke up the next day with a head like the Rock of Gibraltar, and the lightning bolt where you have found it."

Emily inspects the tattoo again, tracing it on his rump with her finger. "Did it hurt? The little needle? The ink or dye or whatever was rubbed in?"

"I don't remember. I was vaguely aware of it, but as I wasn't precisely sitting on it—" She smiles at his lawyer-talk.

"But almost, you are. Suppose the courtiers knew that their jurist wore such a thing, on his—"

He covers her lips with his hand. Her brown eyes shine.

"Now I am jealous," she teases. "I'd like a tattoo of my own, maybe in the same place."

"If anyone should touch your pretty body with a needle, I'll have his guts for garters."

"Shiver me timbers! I love your pirate talk. Take me captive, please. Incarcerate me in your deep red arteries. I want to be in the place itself, as you are in mine. Love is a bloody business, don't you think?"

He has become accustomed to Emily's wild metaphors, her volcanoes, maelstroms, explosions, train wrecks, burglaries, and something she calls the "prowling booger."

"You, Miss Dickinson, a privileged and protected resident of a college town, have known more violence and crime than your old judge. I shudder to think what you could do if you were trained in small-arms fire, especially with these lovely slender arms." He holds up her left arm and strokes it from her braceleted wrist to her shoulder.

"Do you know that I have played pirate games with the neighborhood children?"

"More of your infinite variety, you wench. Did you run up the skull and bones from the barn roof?"

"I captured the little pirates and made them walk the plank. Several of them are now walking about the neighborhood on peg-legs. I lowered gingerbread in a basket from a window while they waved their wooden swords. Their mothers didn't always like their supper spoiled, but I wanted to make them happy. I've never had such a grateful audience."

"Let us leave off speaking for a few moments, while I scout out a proper place for a tattoo of a daisy."

She offers him her laziest smile. If the smile had arms and legs, it would be lying indolent in the grass. "I think it is time that I told you about how I lost my virginity."

Various emotions take turns on his face—shock, worry, confusion, curiosity. "Our earlier lives are our business, don't you think? If you'd ask for a story in equal trade, I don't know that I could bring myself to tell it."

She rests her chin on his chest and fixes him with her eyes. Was it Elizabeth, she wonders. Or did he visit a sporting house in Boston or, God help us, Amherst? She had long pondered the rituals of young manhood, and the women who assisted in them. As far as she knew, she had never met one. No doubt many such women wore disguises as proper matrons. And why should they not?

Phil's upper lip breaks out in a film of sweat. Plump cousin Lucy was now a grandmother, praise God. "Oh, you don't have to tell your story. In fact, please don't." He waits for the revelation.

"I lost it to Folly."

"Folly? Do you mean that you deliberately arranged this occasion?"

"In a manner of speaking. It was the day you came to visit before your court appearance in Northampton. Decades ago. We spent some time in the garden, and you knelt beside me on the quilt and asked me to call you Phil, and then you and Father went riding."

199

"I remember that day vividly, but I am completely mystified about the folly, Emily. Had you hidden someone in the barn?"

"No, she lived in the barn."

"She?!"

"Our pony, Folly. When you and Father took off on those handsome black horses, I was in a fit of envy and several other Seven Deadlies besides. I wanted to ride, too, but not on that ridiculous sidesaddle. So I rode Folly astride, the way you and Father rode, and by the time I got back home, the deed had been done."

He notices no shame or pride, just a willful happiness.

"Did it—hurt?" Phil strokes her hair.

"No, it was inconvenient, but I made myself respectable before you sat down to dinner. Father was angry with me for taking my truant ride, so I missed the meal. And all the time you were spooning up my excellent berry tart, I was out in the barn plying the curry comb on Folly and Father's horses, and laughing, because I had a secret I couldn't reveal, even to my mother or sister. Later, when I caught a curious look on Father's face, or for that matter, yours, I nearly lost my composure. My virtue, such as it was, remained intact, even though I had managed to lose the evidence of it on a pony."

Phil makes the face he always makes when Emily pushes him over a leap of surprise.

"Are you offended?" She wears a look of sneaky triumph.

"Of course not." He kisses her in several tender places. *"Folly!"* He starts to laugh, and can't stop.

Their ardor gradually subsides with the afternoon light, and yields to wistfulness. Tomorrow he has to go to court in Springfield, and they don't know when they'll see each other again.

She fingers a silver curl. "You know what my home means to me, but just when I'd concluded it was everything, you came to visit and took me on a picnic to Sunderland. And nothing has been the same since that golden afternoon."

It is a troublesome subject: where to live, how to manage. They agree to leave it alone until the Springfield trial is over.

He folds his hands under his head, and Emily reaches her arm around his middle.

"Dearest sylph, this has been another golden day, after a long gray time. We've come into the spring again. When I was ill with the flu, and the rumors about my resignation started flying, I thought we were doomed. But as I once told you, we profane our dearest pleasures if we seize them too greedily. I am talking mostly about myself. You are not at all greedy, except in a way I love."

If she proposed to abandon her mother and Vinnie for a runaway life with him, he would refuse her, despite his profound desire. And if she made such a proposal and he accepted it, she would not be Emily Dickinson, or he Phil Lord.

The bower he imagined for so many years has become their own corner of Paradise.

The past recedes into a benign white fog obscuring the vista of his long marriage. With her happy body lying against his own, he tells himself that the present is always best, even when it sometimes has the contours of a dream. He folds himself around her, as though he has wings and commands a nest, and she sleeps like his own shining mate.

17.

Oh Shadow on the Grass
Amherst, Salem, April – June 1882

In the Springfield *Republican:*

> *Wednesday, May 3: Judge Lord of the supreme court, sick at Salem, was delirious last night, his mind dwelling on cases in court, and his condition gave little hope of recovery.*

> *Monday, May 8: Judge Lord has passed the crisis at Salem, and there is hope that he will soon be about again.*

> *Sunday, May 14: It is rumored that should he recover he will resign his position on the bench. . . .*

Amherst, May 1882

In the Homestead kitchen, Emily banged a nutmeg to powder. Vinnie and Maggie watched over her for the slightest tremor. She could feel her loss of weight and color. Her white dress floated above her waistline, and the collar stood out from her thin neck. Every morning, Vinnie insisted on bringing up a breakfast tray with toast and a fresh poached egg.

"Every egg you eat is a new dawn, Em. Even the hens are cheering you on, in their comical way."

She thought of her joyful dalliance in the barn with Phil, and picking straw out of his hair. *Put them on the stand and let them cackle.*

After a couple of weeks, news of Phil's remarkable improvement restored her appetite and energy. As her spirits lightened, everyone in the household took heart.

Emily received daily messages from neighbors inquiring about her friend Judge Lord. Austin came over twice a day until she began to tire of being inspected for her latest mood. She wanted to guard her hope alone, a damaged plant she vowed to bring back to life.

She preferred to hear Maggie and Vinnie talk of the judge as if he had just spent a few days with them and planned to visit soon, instead of some day in the indefinite future.

"Tom will not soon forget that day, Miss Emily." Maggie dabbed at her face with her apron. "He is too shy to ask you how you are keeping, but I always tell him."

Vinnie squeezed her sister's hand until she flinched. "It's still in my mind—Austin bringing in the paper with the news, and Prof. Chickering ringing the doorbell, and Tom holding you against his blue jacket and telling you that the judge would be better."

The memory of that terrible morning made her feel that she had barely escaped from drowning. For several days, her daily schedule consisted of tears, writing, and prayers—all hopeless, until she had reason to hope otherwise.

"He's a strong man to get better so fast—and I think I know why." Maggie set a cup of tea in front of Emily, and patted her shoulder.

Vinnie teased, "You're a little sweet on the judge yourself, I do believe."

Maggie shook her head, having lost the power of speech.

Emily sat at her desk and re-read the copies she'd made of letters she wrote Phil after his visit. Hurrying back to Salem after the Springfield trial, he'd written her about trying to fight off a cold. She imagined herself in two places at once.

30 April 1882

. . . I am told it is only a pair of Sundays since you went from me. I feel it many years. Today is April's last—it has been an April of meaning to me. I have been in your Bosom. My Philadelphia has passed from Earth, and Ralph Waldo Emerson . . . has touched the secret Spring. Which Earth are we in? Heaven, a Sunday or two ago—but that also has ceased—

Momentousness is ripening. I hope that all is firm. Could we yield each other to the impregnable chances till we had met once more?

Monday

I'm glad you are "at Home." Please think it with a codicil. My own were homeless if you were. Was my sweet "Phil" proud? What Hour? Could you tell me?

. . . Our Life together was long forgiveness on your part toward me. The trespass of my rustic Love upon your Realms of Ermine, only a Sovereign could forgive—I never knelt to other— The Spirit never twice alike, but every time another—that other more divine. Oh, had I found it sooner! Yet Tenderness has not a Date—it comes—and overwhelms. . . .

She worried about whether he was able to read and write. After the initial reassuring telegram—MR LORD BETTER. RECEIVING BEST CARE—Abbie had sent no more news. Appointing herself the bearer of official bulletins from the Lord household, Abbie seemed to take pleasure in her power to give or withhold. The rest of the week passed with only a general note in the *Republican* about the judge's improvement. Writing Abbie, Emily felt humiliated and frantic. This time, she snipped out the newspaper story and pinned it to her letter.

Is he able to speak or to hear voices or to say 'Come in,' when his Amherst knocks? Fill his Hand with Love as sweet as Orchard Blossoms, which he will share with each of you—I know his boundless ways—

Her message was clear: "I am his Amherst, he my Salem, and I know him better than you do. My gift of apple blossoms expresses Love, not ownership. And you, Abbie, do not own him, not now or ever."

Salem, May – June 1882

By the first of June, the judge was up and moving about. Tim took him on walks, and limited his visitors to three a day, including Dr. Carlton. He retired early but slept in fits. He wanted his old life back, with the sweet green paradises of his visits to Amherst. Emily sent a box of fresh flowers every other day. Tim O'Leary had been given command of the mail, so that Abbie could not steal a letter.

On their last day together in Amherst, Phil had told Emily that he would soon announce his intention to retire from the bench. He would tell his family that they would marry as soon as he could procure a suitable house for the Farleys. If necessary, he would live in Amherst for the next year or so while securing additional care for Emily's mother.

"Momentousness is ripening." It was time, at last, to seize the life before them.

But when Phil returned to Salem, he was tired and sick. The month of court hearings in western Massachusetts had worn him out. A sodden buzzing filled his head. He felt old and past any hope of self-renewal. He'd made it through the last day of a murder trial only because the jury needed to rest overnight. Emily wrote, *"I thought them the loveliest Jury I had ever met."*

His second day home, he roused himself and dressed for dinner, and complimented Catherine's hearty veal stew. After the table was cleared, he asked for a few moments with the family to make his announcement.

"I have done with guises." Emily's words meshed with his. How joyful to speak in her language. "I believe that lucky and devoted marriages give hope for future happiness. It was true of my father, and is true of me. My father held my mother in the highest regard, and mourned her sincerely, as I have mourned Elizabeth. But he needed an earthly happiness with a compatible mate, and he found it with Mary Adams. Now I hope for the same with Emily. I hardly expected this turn of events at my age, but I have known the Dickinsons for decades, and since my friend Edward's untimely death, we have become especially . . . close. Luckily I have enough resources to care for all of you." He raised his wineglass and looked around the table.

Mary, his sister-in-law, nodded and smiled. Molly clapped her hands and chattered about moving to Newburyport or Gloucester. A strange choking snarl came from Abbie. Her face livid, she slammed down her wineglass, rose and strode over to her uncle's chair, to confront him with her angry face. "How dare you play havoc with our lives!" she shouted. Spittle flew from her mouth and sprayed his forehead. He had anticipated her displeasure, but not such outright ugliness.

Shocked by her daughter's behavior, Mary Farley arose. Abbie raved on. "We have stayed in this huge house and cared for you, and endured the disrespect of your servants, who spy on us and mean us harm! And now you intend to insult the memory of your dead wife by planning to marry a completely unsuitable woman, who brings nothing to this family but her strange reputation, her unfashionable ways, her immorality! Truly, Uncle Lord, you have been bewitched. Why are you telling us, rather than asking our permission, to do this unconscionable thing?"

He sat, rigid and horrified, unable to speak. Mary Farley took her daughter by the elbow and led her away to propel her, shrieking and crying, up the stairs. Molly sat with her head in her hands, then approached her uncle and kissed him on the cheek. Her round blue eyes swam with tears.

"Uncle Otis, please ignore what Abbie says. I wish I could wipe her words away. You are the head of our household, and it's plain idiotic for her to think you need to ask our permission to do anything, especially whatever makes you happy. I don't know Emily Dickinson, and I'm not very smart, but I can tell that she has lifted your spirits. May I do something for you now? Fetch you coffee, or a whiskey? You look awful."

"Thank you for offering, Molly. If you would call Tim . . ."

He could scarcely wrap his mind around Abbie's villainous rudeness, but he saw that now, defeated of a career as a spy, she wanted to punish him. He wished he could declare that love had triumphed over selfishness, and would do so again. He wiped his hot forehead and blew his nose. The dining room tilted to one side, and pain traveled to his scalp from the back of his neck. Observing her uncle with alarm, Molly drew back the curtains and opened the window wider. The candles guttered in their sticks, sending gouts of wax onto the tablecloth. He could hear shouting from upstairs.

"Conflagration. Blazes."

Molly blew out the candles, and rang for Tim.

"Sir, I shall take you up and bring you a restorative."

For a moment, Phil wondered who this kind, tall Irishman could be. "Ah, Tim O'Leary. I am grateful, but sorry that you heard that upsetting business."

He had trouble with the words: grateful, upsetting, business. Too many t's and s's. His tongue felt thick.

"It is a thing of the moment, sir, and it will pass."

Tim leaned over him. The judge's eyes moved back and forth, and his mouth pulled down on one side. He felt himself making odd flapping movements with his right hand. There was a roaring in his ears, and he couldn't see.

He struggled to his feet and collapsed, as Tim caught him.

*

3 June 1882

Dear Miss Dickinson,

> *I write on behalf of Mr. Lord, whose manservant I am.*
> *He has entrusted me to keep you informed of his Health. I received your kind letter this morning. Dr. Carlton gives a good Report of him. I am pleased to say that his Speech has been fully restored. He uses a cane when he walks, and I am always at his Side.*

He speaks of You often, and asks permission for me to read any Poems you send. He has quoted some of them to me, and they are very fine and make me Think. They have a Music that touches my Irish soul.

I would convey more personal Messages from Mr. Lord, but he says that you will know what he means by "Sweet Pirate," and "Elysium," and "Ransacked Closets," and "my Amherst."

I trust that with practice, he will soon have his bold Hand back, with which to write You.

We are quite busy in his Household, and I am doing my best to perform my Guard Duty with the mail.

If you wish to send letters under Cover to me here, I am plain Tim O'Leary, and I wish you well.

18.

"Emily Jumbo!"
Amherst, Salem, December 1882

Amherst, December 2

"Vinnie, I need your help. Next week, I'm going to Salem. My birthday present to myself. Only you and Maggie and Tom must know. It's a lot to ask, and I hope you'll forgive me for whatever weight lands on your shoulders."

Vinnie sits down as if pulled from below. Her curls fly around her flour-streaked face. She sniffs and fumbles in her apron pocket, blinks rapidly and clears her throat.

"Don't worry, my floury sister, it is only a visit. But now that Phil is well again, it's time I roused myself from my stubborn torpor. I have promised nothing, except to be in Salem for a few days. I have been wild to see him in his own home, to touch things that belong to him, sleep under his roof, hear the sounds he hears every day."

"Could you live in Salem? Be his wife? You are already so close. I love Phil too, you know, although not as you do. That laughter from the bedroom! That sly look on his face when he slings you into the carriage and drives off, as if you were a captured princess!"

Emily hugs her sister and brushes the flour from her hair. "I don't know the answer to that, dear. But Mother has been gone almost a month. Think of it, Vin, we're orphans, and also grown-ups. I am tired of denying Phil. But Amherst is my home. I am rooted here, and I fear being torn up and repotted."

Vinnie dabs her nose, and counts on her fingers. "Train schedule. Money. Fresh clothes. Winter underthings. Stockings. Lace-trimmed nightgown. Your nice ivory robe, with the embroidery. Black shawl. Hair pins, combs, face cream, chemises, drawers, veil, veil, veil. I think you should take Maggie with you. Think of it, Em. All those strangers, the dark, the jostling. What if you get lost and end up in the Great North Woods?"

"You are funny, Vin. I do speak English, in my own way, and I can ask for directions, unless it is from bears or elks." Emily is relieved to hear her sister laugh.

Although Emily feels nervous about traveling alone in the December dark, she will be safely seen off and safely met. Maggie is needed at home to turn away unwelcome inquiries. No one next door is to know, even Austin. Her refusal to attend parties at the Evergreens has prepared the way for her rebellion.

"I guess I'll have to trust Phil to take care of you."

"For the sake of privacy, he will send Tim O'Leary to meet me at the station. I will travel through the dark and take my courage in my hand. Nobody will notice me, as I learned at the Rubinstein concert. I'll be just another small woman in a black dress."

After her sister rushes off to attend to the list, Emily sits on her bed and surveys her room—the four large bright windows, the bureau, the reading chair, the nightstand, the little table where she writes. She hears the factory whistle from down the street, the chuffing noise of a train pulling into the station, wagons and carriages, horses and children. Even on a dull December day, Amherst is alive in all her senses.

She and Phil have a history in this room. They held each other and wept together on the day of Father's funeral, a day of grief and tenderness. She has written to him at her little table, listened for his arriving train, read his powerful, adoring letters. She wonders if her room will miss her in her absence, and whether she will feel homesick or strange in Phil's house. Phil knows about her fear of intrusions, a nervousness she can't control, but she trusts they will be safe together. The thought of Abbie Farley flaps like a winter crow past her window, and she tries to conjure up a raptor to drive it away.

December 8

As the train bumps over the tracks, Emily relaxes into the seat, and remembers her trip from Boston on the train with Father, when he treated her to the story of two little girls chasing Mr. Lord around the garden. Vinnie's generous joy in helping her pack for her visit brings tears of gratitude. She sighs, wondering whether she could bear to leave Vinnie on her own in the Homestead, if she and Phil did marry. The thought is too weighty to bear. She and Phil will have to reason out the future together, somehow.

Putting aside Elizabeth Barrett Browning's poems, she peers at the ocher-and-white villages tucked among the hills above Worcester and the clouds above the factories. Now and then, light from a solitary house gleams like a penny. She imagines the family in the house, the mother preparing dinner, the children scuttling underfoot, the father—if they have one—soaping his arms and face after a hard day of labor. She envisions their hands clasped around the table, asking a blessing. Lives she doesn't know, and couldn't have known. But these lives surround her life, like acres of invisible trees around the sanctuary of her writing table.

Last night's snowfall scarcely reaches the top of the grass. The big engine chuffs along, spilling cold flakes from its sharp nose. Emily cracks open the top window to see the smoke blowing backward over the cars, like the tail of a running horse.

The train's wheels carry her words:

All that I do
Is in review
To his enamored mind
I know his eye
Where e'er I ply
Is pushing close behind

Not any Port
Not any flight
But he doth there preside
What omnipresence lies in wait
For her to be a Bride

What a world of sensuous images lies in "omnipresence." Phil's arms folded behind his head, his eyes on her, waiting for a kiss, and all that follows, his fingers and lips tracing her desire to its source, her own fingers and lips doing the same for him.

"Aunt Emily!"

"Ned!" She hurries between trains at Lowell Station, trying to ignore the crowds and keep her skirts from being trampled by rude boots. Why, of all times and trains, did her train and Ned's train have to arrive there together?

"You are on a train trip! Where are you going?"

Emily eludes his question. Ned is sweet but not quick. He lacks a lawyer's mind, bless him. She lifts her veil to greet her tall nephew. "Where have you come from?"

"Salem. I was visiting Judge Lord." His voice has a dull edge, and his eyes are evasive. Phil had not mentioned that Ned was going to visit him.

"Why, Ned? I never thought you liked Salem."

"It was Mother's idea. She's tired of me and my problems. And Father is preoccupied with the college, and some other matter I can't talk about now. So she sent me east for a few days, to see friends in Boston and then accept the judge's standing invitation to visit him. I didn't want to be a bother to Mr. Lord, but Mother insisted. Well, never mind. I am astonished to see you, Aunt Emily. And all by yourself! Please let me help you."

Emily gently refuses. By now Ned knows about her closeness to the judge, and is one of the few who knows his nickname, "Little Phil." She considers telling him the truth about her visit, but thinks it had better wait. They have just a minute before their trains depart, although she does not say where she's going. She wants to keep Ned talking about himself until she boards her train to Salem.

"Ned, I'm disturbed by what you say of your mother's command to you. Promise we will talk soon, in confidence."

She suspects what the "other matter" is. Mabel Todd's name is often on Austin's lips. This is no passing fancy—her brother has fallen in love. Ned has seemed vulnerable and heart-sore lately, and Emily thinks she knows why.

"Aunt Emily—where—?" The steam rolls over them, as train whistles come from different directions. "Are your eyes troubling you? Is a friend ill? Can I help you?"

Ned's voice disappears as Emily waves and hurries away, grateful for the steam-cloud and the noise.

On the train she unfolds the letter Phil wrote shortly after her mother died, inviting her to Salem, and the answer she copied. Her reply was populated with rhymes:

> . . . *You said with loved timidity in asking me to your dear Home, you would "try not to make it unpleasant." So delicate a diffidence, how beautiful to see! I do not think a Girl extant has so divine a modesty. You even call me to your Breast with apology! Of what must my poor Heart be made? . . . The tender Priest of Hope need not . . . allure his Offering—'tis on his altar ere he asks. . . .*

The train chugs past the backs of brick factories, shuttered in the December dark. So many people, living close together! She could never live in such a place, but others have no choice. Northeast Massachusetts is not a pretty corner of the state—except that Phil Lord lives there, and Salem is famous for its beautiful architecture, as well as a history of heartless crimes and worldly trade.

Over her book, Emily sneaks glimpses at people she will never see again. The faces of her fellow passengers appear tired from daily burdens—harried businessmen, mothers with fretting children, women in black. She, who rarely leaves home, rides in the fitful light of wonder and chill.

Beneath these sensations is the warm ripe throb—anticipation, the pendent fruit that will soon drop into her lap. Emily shuts her eyes and sees Phil's beautiful hands, gray curls, strong arms, and sneaky smile. In her heart and head lie the compliments he has bestowed on her, cordials to make her blood caper in her veins. She shifts in her seat. One never knows what wildness lurks beneath a respectable woman's dark clothes.

When the train arrives an hour later at Salem's neo-Gothic terminal, a man in his late forties approaches Emily to help her down the carriage steps. He immediately knows who she is. He tips his hat. She gives him her hand.

"I am Tim O'Leary, ma'am. The judge sent me to meet you. He is guarding the castle for your arrival."

Tim has astonishing red hair that stands up straight from his forehead in a brush. His limbs seem fashioned of wires and knobs, and his wide, long-toothed smile is charming.

"I am glad to see you, Mr. O'Leary." Here is someone she instantly trusts. Phil has told her that Tim has many talents, not the least of them discretion.

The huge house has a light in every window. No castle, but a passenger ship waiting for her to glide up the gangplank and be saluted by the captain.

Phil comes toward her, helps her remove her dark cloak, muff and bonnet, and kisses her. He is dressed formally, his white silk stock in place, his hair freshly trimmed.

"I can hardly believe——" they both say at once.

Ned and Mattie had described the judge's house as "a tomb," dark and filled with ancient furniture from colonial days. "It's so different from our Evergreens," Mattie opined at age six, "Not nearly as bright and stylish." Emily understands why Phil's house, on a busy street near the courthouse, would appear forbidding to her nephew and niece. It lacks the outward charm of the Homestead and the Dickinsons' meadow and gardens. Yet its rooms glow with a comfortable beauty: bird's-eye maple highboys, thick Turkish carpets, oil paintings gleaming in the light, and the dining table with elaborate turned legs, set for two people with silver and crystal. As much of a jewel-box as it is, the Evergreens cannot match this.

As her eyes grow accustomed to the light, Emily notices the balance and simplicity in the décor. The palette looks dark at first, but gradually she discerns the deep reds and greens, with intricate gold patterns woven in carpets and wall-coverings. Phil takes her arm and leads her through the rooms. Every object—the paintings, one by John Kensett, a painter whose work hangs in the Evergreens, the bronze statuettes of horses—appears long-cherished. Several unsigned pen-and-ink sketches of the White Mountains decorate the walls: looming rock faces, waterfalls, chasms, with tiny human figures tucked into the landscape. One sketch of an approaching storm has a card inserted in the frame: *To Emily Jumbo From Little Phil.*

The guest-room sleigh bed wears a blue and white quilt, the windows light-blue silk tasseled curtains. The armoire's long mirror almost scares her, and she avoids looking at it. The modern bathroom across the hall has a water closet and a marble sink with fresh towels and a bottle of rosewater. Alone, she unfastens her hair, brushes it clean, and coils it at the back of her head. Then she washes up and changes into a dark blue silk dress borrowed from Vinnie, with one of her mother's lace shawls. It doesn't matter that shawls, and the cameo at her throat, are no longer fashionable. She teases two strands of hair into graceful waves in front of her ears, as she used to do when she was twenty. The mirror offers her a soft smile.

Emily tastes the squash soup flavored with ginger, but manages only a cup of it, and a few bites of guinea fowl braised in sage and wine. Under their conversation, her mind re-creates her impressions, one by one: *I am here at his*

217

*table, watching Phil put food into his mouth and chew and swallow it,
as I have seen him do many times. Here is his house, a glass of claret
from his cellar, his beaming face, his eyes on me.*

Catherine O'Leary, a pretty, plump woman with bright
pink cheeks, brings a bowl of fruit, some utensils, and two
small Chinese plates. Emily lifts up a red pear to admire it,
and deftly removes an ivory crescent with a pink navel and
three winking seeds.

"I saw Ned when I changed trains. His face was full of
acrobatics. He said he'd been here, exiled by his mother.
Tell me."

"Poor Ned. He arrived with little notice, and I fear I
bored him terribly, distracted by your impending arrival. I
was out of sorts, to tell you the truth, worried that he might
ask to stay over and interfere with our plans." He reaches for
her hand. "It still seems to me a dream that you are with me
in this house, sitting at my table in the candlelight."

"I could say the same thing. I seem to have emerged from
a kind of fog, and I'm not talking about my winter journey.
But I wish I hadn't run into Ned, who is not a happy young
man. There will be awkward questions at home."

"How could he be happy? He is still struggling with his
illness, and the conflict at home is bound to oppress him. But
we needn't answer any question, awkward or not. We have
earned the right to our happiness. Have some more wine. I
can tell that you love it."

She relaxes her spine against the chair's elegant curved
back, and sips the Bordeaux, wondering how she will ever
return to the homemade red currant variety.

When she smiles, he tells her she appears twenty years
younger. He leans forward and touches the wavy strands of
hair, smiling approval.

"How is it that I'm so at ease? I've scarcely ventured from home in nine years, as you know. But dreams kept me happy during the train ride, staring out the window, gathering up the sights."

"Yes, that is like you."

He holds out his hand for hers—their old gesture of friendship from her girlhood, now a sign of a new promise between them.

"Is it all right that I am sitting here, at Elizabeth's table? I must be bold, Phil, or all is lost."

He folds his napkin and sets it beside the fruit plate. "Sometime I will tell you what Elizabeth said to me toward the end, before the last crisis came upon her and she couldn't speak. You will feel honored, I think."

Their eyes take refuge in the candlelight. She sees no sign of Abbie this evening, only Tim and Catherine O'Leary. Phil has planned as he promised.

"The Farley troupe has gone to Boston for a week, to do some Christmas shopping. I sweetened the time with theater and opera tickets, although I fear opera is wasted on Molly. Abbie will enjoy surveying the crowds and pronouncing upon their fashions. And, of course, spending what she believes is her own money."

She sends a silent prayer of relief into the night.

He pushes a small box in front of her plate. "For your birthday, and in honor of this visit."

She holds the square coral ring up to the candlelight and asks him to fit it onto her left ring finger. It harmonizes with the "Little Phil" bracelet she now wears all the time.

"How did you know I would love this? The color, the shape. The engravings on the band look almost like dinosaur footprints!"

"I think they are supposed to be tulips, but I like your description better. The ring belonged to my sister Mary. I have kept it all these years for reasons I didn't even know. Its brightness suits you. It seems right to me that you wear something from the vasty deep."

At important moments, he slips into Shakespeare.

"You would make a fine Prospero. You can always summon spirits, especially mine."

He fills her glass from the carafe. "To that end, here's more nectar for your blushing lips."

When Emily wakes the next morning, alone in a huge bed with two rumpled pillows, she thinks that her life has both changed and not changed. She hears carriage wheels and horses' hooves muffled by snow, and somewhere, a train horn. A small bell tinkles downstairs. Her head is filled with poetry and wonder.

Oh, honey of an hour, I never knew thy power. She sits up quickly in the big bed, and sees Phil seated in his chair, wearing his mulberry dressing gown. He has a sketchpad on his knee.

"Good morning, Emily. You make a picture, and I can't resist."

Phil has always loved to sketch, to feel the ink flowing boldly across paper. There before him on the page is a sleeping face draped with a fall of hair, a white uncovered shoulder, a faint swell of a breast. The drawing stirs him.

"I hope it is not one of your usual caricatures. I am not dressed for caricature."

"Emily Jumbo, you are not dressed at all. But I promise not to make you into something that would hang in a saloon."

The idea is so preposterous that she starts to laugh, and hides her face in the pillow. He cannot remember how long it has been since his stately house entertained such a merry noise.

"Phil, you are full of surprises. The Crawford Notch sketch, the ring—all of it."

"And so are you, which makes me very happy. Would you like tea?"

"Tea, and thee."

"Which first?" He comes over to behold her and peels back the sheet.

"Guess." She pulls at the tie of his dressing gown.

*

When Phil remembers his old friend Edward's protective ways with Emily, the judge in him rebels against the lover in him, and wonders if he has become one of the nasty old men he has tried in court, flinging the weight of the law against their venial acts. He remains mystified at how the quiet brook of affection gradually became a sea. Their long habit of teasing and provoking takes on fresh meanings with every intimate occasion, bodies and minds playing together. Her gold-brown eyes watch him caress her slowly, and his blue eyes watch her graceful hands at work.

Long ago, an obscure journalist had written of Lord that he would have made a good sea captain. The metaphor rings true. If he has become a mariner of a strong craft, Emily is a pretty spider, stowed away and alert to every movement in the air.

Her ring gleams in the nest of white linen. He whispers in her sleeping ear, *Let Rome in Tiber melt, here is my space.*

But no empire looms outside the window—only wintry Salem, a dull morning sky with white flakes sifting and, inside, a small hearth with a winking flame.

On Sunday, Emily's birthday, Phil asks her if she would like to view the sea.

"I propose to take you up to the roof walk. I had Tim rebuild the ladder and it's quite strong."

A smiling Catherine fetches their winter wraps.

She climbs the narrow stairs after Phil. He opens the trap door and pulls her up into the light. The sharp cold air feels sweet in her lungs, clearing away the muzziness in her head from two nights and a day spent indoors. The pink-gold sky accents Salem's tall red brick houses and snow-covered cobblestones.

He holds her close and points out the sights: the Courthouse, a red brick neo-Romanesque pile; the slate-colored Witch House; the Common, a large white trapezoid criss-crossed with narrow paths. In the distance, barely visible, is the House of the Seven Gables, so long imagined. She spies the blunt shapes of several fishing boats, muscling their way into the harbor. Beyond the masts of steamships and schooners, the dark gray Atlantic.

She has dreamed of the Atlantic Ocean for what seems her whole life. In her poems, she has sailed on it, traveled beneath it, glimpsed shipwrecks, fishermen, even mermaids. She has imagined walking on the beach with Carlo. Mighty waves curl toward her, asking her to follow them, giving her indecipherable messages.

So this is Salem, at last. Elegant houses, painted colors she has never seen in Amherst: gold, rose, delicious shades of green. Ships swaying in the harbor. Chinese sailors, Lascars, Italians, a daily sight on the crowded streets. From Phil's roof, the old town looks like the stage of an opera.

"Does the sea change? Is it always gray?

He pulls back her shawl and kisses her neck. "It changes every minute, and yet it looks changeless. Not one color, but all colors. I love to look at the sea, which I have done all my life, but I'm glad not to know it better. I'm a mountain-and-lake man."

Emily shuts her eyes, and speaks a poem:

As if the Sea should part
And show a further Sea –
And that – a further – and the Three
But a Presumption be –

Of Periods of Seas –
Unvisited of Shores –
Themselves the Verge of Seas to be –
Eternity – is Those –

"Dear, you know everything important to know. You were a sibyl in another life, I'm sure. Compared to you, I am just a fly crawling on a statue's blind face."

"What utter nonsense. I shall stop your lips."

She kisses him. His lips are chapped, in the winter air.

They turn around to watch the light descend over Federal Street, the North River, and the cemetery beyond.

"That is Harmony Grove, where Elizabeth is buried. She died five years ago today. When you wrote that your mother slipped away like a snowflake, you could have been describing Elizabeth's death, on your forty-seventh birthday."

Emily leans against him. So much she still has to learn about Phil Lord.

"You will lie there too, one day?"

"Yes."

223

"Forgive me, but I have to ask whether, if you die before me, there is anything I can do for you in your immortal state."

"Just remember me." His voice is deep and gentle. "I think Elizabeth would be relieved and glad that we are here together. I promised to tell you what she said shortly before she died. She told me that she wanted me to be happy again. And to marry you, if I could persuade you. She said that men should always marry those who love them well."

The cold breeze picks up, and Emily holds her heavy shawl up to her face. She has not known until now that Elizabeth's generosity touches her own future as well as Phil's.

"Your wife knew long ago that I loved you. She told me so, in Cambridge, and I admitted it, because I couldn't lie. I have rarely felt such kindness and dignity from anyone. I was humbled by her wisdom then, and I'm humbled now." She runs her fingers over the coral ring's warm shape, and burrows against his chest.

"You are here, and I am here. Our earth is moving along, with both of us balanced on its rim."

They watch the street lamps, and the salmon-colored sky growing brighter behind Chestnut Street, just before descending into darkness.

Emily peers down at North Street. Near the Witch House, a man and a woman are walking south. The woman wears a handsome fur hat and coat with fur on the sleeves. Emily recognizes her, and ducks behind Phil's shoulder, even though the pair can't see them.

It is Abbie Farley, arm in arm with Will West.

19.

Ashes denote that Fire was
Salem, December 10; Amherst,
late December 1882

When she spied Abbie from the roof walk, Emily panicked and nearly fell down the ladder. She rushed to the blue-and-white guest room and began to grab her things from the wardrobe and roll them into her traveling bag. She feared that the next few minutes would bring a peremptory knock on the door, followed by exposure, anger, and embarrassment. Phil hurried after her. It took him several minutes and a glass of port wine to calm her down.

"Hold my hand and breathe quietly, and sip these rubies. This is my house. I own it, I live in it, and you have nothing to fear. Please believe me. I have seen you upset, but not in this frantic state, and I'll do anything to reassure you that your fears are groundless."

Phil took off his gloves and fur coat and removed her shawl. She swallowed more wine as he stroked her shoulders. Her hands had turned icy and her teeth were chattering.

"My anxieties are an embarrassment to me, as Mother's nervous episodes were to her, but right now I can't seem to control them."

"Listen to me, and look at me. You're in a state of shock, and it will pass."

He did not ring for Catherine, but fetched a basin of warm water, a washcloth and soft towel.

She lifted her face, and he kissed her eyelids. He ran the cloth over her cheeks and patted them dry, unpinned her hair, and brushed it, as he had on the day of her father's funeral. Then he wiped each finger, taking special care with the coral ring. In a few minutes, she breathed easily. He thought, part of my task as her protector is to protect her from herself.

"I arranged for Abbie and Molly and Mary to stay at the Parker House in Boston. But I couldn't send spies to dog their footsteps into shops and restaurants. Mary was to let me know by telegraph of any change of plan, and I didn't need to explain why. She was Elizabeth's chief confidante, and has long known my feelings for you."

Emily regretted that she hadn't spent time alone with Mary when the troupe visited Amherst.

"I suspect Abbie secretly arranged to return to Salem and meet Will West, her sometime suitor. She may have succeeded in reviving his interest in her, although he seems a rather pale and passionless man. If he is courting her, so much the better. Time—and money—will tell. I'm a judge, but I'm also a good detective."

Detectives were among Emily's favorite employees of the law. She sat up straight and fastened her eyes on his.

"Abbie is quite recognizable in Salem, not only for being my niece, but for being the most elaborately fashionable woman in town, in all seasons and styles. Her displays invite critical comment. Mr. West also comes from a prominent family. So she is apparently open about this alliance, whatever it is."

He plied the washcloth gently around Emily's almond-shaped fingernails.

"I expect that Abbie will soon rejoin her mother and Molly. I arranged a sumptuous meal for them this evening at Locke-Ober, one of Boston's finest restaurants. Abbie would not want to miss a chance to see and be seen in their typical elegant crowd of gourmands. And remember, Tim O'Leary is our friend and protector."

She took a few deep breaths. Attacks of anxiety always made her brain roil with little earthquakes she found bewildering.

"She is still your niece, and this is her home. I have no reason to like her, nor she to like me. We seem to be such opposites. But I couldn't bear to think she felt displaced in any way, especially after that wretched scene here at your dining table last spring. You've told me only the bare minimum of that story."

He kissed her forehead. "My memory of that evening is somewhat impaired because of my illness, and it would do you no good to hear more details, even if I could retrieve them. And here I am, fully recovered and in your company, as you're in mine."

Her emotions rode up and down like a balloon in a whipping wind. "Would it be easier for you to put me on the next train immediately?"

He held her face in his hands. "Do you want me to?"

"No. But I had to ask."

The prospect of cutting short their happy interlude was unbearable to both of them.

"Has anything about the past two days disappointed you, dear? Do you ache for Amherst, and your familiar ground? I know how much home means to you, but this is what I have, and I offer it to you."

His words made her feel ashamed. He had done everything possible to protect their time together, but she couldn't expect him to weave a magical net around them. He was a man of the world, urbane, wise, and powerful. And she was, first and always, a poet. She belonged in Amherst. But she belonged with Phil, too.

"I am Emily Jumbo. And I am yours, as you are mine."

*

Three days later, Emily discovered that, despite Vinnie's and Maggie's precautions, Sue, ever-suspicious of unexplained absences, had engaged in her own detective work. When Ned came home, his mother sat him down in the library and pointed to the railway timetables, then let fly a volley of questions. Unable to lie, he admitted that he had seen his aunt at Lowell Station.

Without knocking, Sue walked into Emily's bedroom. Emily arose from her little table and pulled a sheet of paper over the letter she was writing.

"It has been too long since we talked." Sue's voice was frosty.

What a pity to contort such a lovely mouth into a hard, cold grimace.

She pulled off her gloves, which looked new, as did her handsome red and black shawl. Emily thought the Napoleonic colors suited her.

"The drawing room, if you will." She liked to employ a voice of command against Sue's aggressive gestures.

Emily took her time lighting the fire already laid in the fireplace. The December dusk coiled up Main Street. Orange and purple ribbons wavered behind the curtains.

"Ned saw you when you changed trains. What, pray tell, were you doing there? Were you going to Salem? And if so, why?"

When Emily laughed her special laugh for ridiculous things, Sue's dark eyes flashed as they picked up her shawl's red highlights. "Don't mock me. I was not born yesterday. We were born nine days apart. You do remember when I walked into this house months ago and found you reclining in his arms." Sue's upper lip curled.

"If you walk into a house unbidden, you may see what you don't want to see. This is my house, and Vinnie's. Anyone may visit here, with permission. At the moment, since you don't have permission, you are an intruder."

Sue's hostility had once brought her to tears. Now she willed herself to remain steady as an oak tree.

"And does your invitation also welcome immorality?"

"What do you call immorality? Please describe it so that I can learn my lesson." Sue liked to teach lessons, and considered herself the family's moral authority.

The parlor fire threw whiplash patterns against the wallpaper.

"*Vesuvius at home,*" Emily said simply. A line Sue would recognize. Austin's attraction to Mabel Todd, and Emily's love affair with the judge, had brought Sue's jealousies to a fever pitch. If her brother was in love with someone else, then his wife had to ask herself how she could have prevented it. If she couldn't shame Mabel Todd into submission, then Emily might do for a stand-in.

"You—and Judge Lord—on the sofa, entwined. You crouching above him, kissing! His hands on your backside, your clothing disarranged. Anyone might have seen you!"

"Anyone who invaded the house, you mean. Peddlers and the butcher's boy come to the kitchen door, and knock."

229

Emily thought of asking whether Sue had let Austin unfasten her clothes in their early days, baring her breasts to kisses and caresses. "How did you know the man I was kissing was Phil Lord? I've called him Phil, for years, at his request. Let me sketch the picture you describe."

Sue looked horrified and distraught.

"I was, as you say, leaning above this man. And my hair was—covering his face? What features were visible? Could you identify the sounds you heard as particular kisses, and is your ear for kisses as expert as a true musician's ear? Can you identify the key of F when Mattie plays it on the piano? This kind of testimony would not light a match in court, much less a lamp. I'm the daughter and sister of a lawyer, so I should know." She sensed the volcano rumbling, far beneath its fire-streaked earth.

"Have you forgotten who you are? You are the aunt of my children. They seek you out, to tell them the truth."

"I don't lie to children or anyone else." Emily felt her father's presence, his dark eyes on hers, his talent for strict argument in her voice.

"Ned was aghast at the thought of your traveling alone. How could you do it? And what would people think about your alliance with a powerful and esteemed jurist?"

"Point one: didn't you travel to New York all by yourself, to hear Jenny Lind, before you married my brother? And to Michigan and Vermont, and Boston? Point two: Phil Lord bore witness to the night I was born. We've known each other for fifty-two years." Home, and her own history, stoked her strength. "A third point: the judge is a widower, as you know, as I am a spinster." Emily didn't like either of those words, but their accuracy was incontestable.

Outside, the tallest evergreens carried remnants of sun in their top branches. Light withdrew from the edges of afternoon like a tide from a shingle. She watched Sue's face start to crumple, then reassume its hard mask. Her heart aching, she remembered her conversation with Phil about the mistreatment of children. Their confused rage, the mistrust bred from cruelty. How can I ask about this, she wondered, and then thought: how can I not?

"Do you imagine that I never loved you? I did, Sue, and I remember. Loving a person doesn't close the door to loving another one."

Sue looked down at the carpet, her shoulders shaking. "Certain doors, as you put it, were closed to me from the beginning. I can't explain why. When I was young, I was too young to understand my own life. But I became good at hiding the hurt of seeing what I shouldn't have seen, in the home with my feeble mother and inebriated father, where I tried to grow up as fast as I could."

Emily took a step toward her. "Do you mean—?" *What word should she choose? Cruelty? Violence?*

Sue's raised hand warned her off. "For the sake of this family, and our reputation in this town, I beg you not to ask. You have an imagination, and you know enough of my story to follow me into the maze of my childhood. But I will not speak of it again. It is too late for confidences."

Emily wondered how long it had been too late. A moment went by, carrying two lifetimes, and the wreckage of her love for Sue, her memories of the excitement, disclosures, shared pleasures. If these memories required grieving, she would grieve. She was used to it.

Emily's white dress glowed spectral in the firelight. Her chosen color gave her power.

My strength is as the strength of ten, because I am no longer pure.

231

20.

Sumptuous Destitution
Amherst, September 1883

Phil sways toward her, leaning on his cane. At first they can only stand and smile at each other, unable to speak after months apart. When Emily wraps her arms around him, she imagines herself a flowering vine whose strong tendrils hold him up.

She leads him out into the sunny autumn afternoon.

The same light, the same hour, as in the garden long ago, when he asked me to call him the name I have cherished all these years.

"I am sorry—" His voice is rough. She fingers his curls, works her way down his shoulders, then reaches under his coat to encircle him. She kisses him as he kissed her long ago, gathering his lips in hers. He smells of wool and bay rum and himself.

"You are here now, and we shall have no nonsense. You admire common sense, and we need it more than ever."

I shall carry you if necessary, she wants to say. His retirement from the bench and his physical weakness have burgled his pride. His letters scarcely mention Abbie, and Emily hopes his niece has retreated into irrelevance.

Three in the afternoon: time for wine and gingerbread, and whatever diversions he would enjoy. "Shall we sit in the garden? Or would you rather be where I can grab you and kiss you whenever I like?"

His answer is to take her hand and lead her back into the house.

His eyes are the same, his hands, his lips, his voice, his tenderness. At last he is back in Amherst. Emily blinks away tears even as she smiles in wonder at how he fills the house with his presence, as he always has.

She has missed him beyond measure. In her letters, she has tried to keep her misery from him, but she often succumbs to the vacant spaces around her—Father, Sam Bowles, Mother. Time is supposed to be a healer, she thinks, but it is also a tormentor. It's not Phil's fault for having to cancel visits, on his doctor's orders. Nor hers for suffering from a badly sprained ankle and occasional bouts of dizziness. Yet her desire for Phil persists. The frailty and the cane don't matter. She wants him next to her in the garden bedroom, their hands all over each other.

"I think it might rain." She makes the sentence tuneful. "I saw a spray of rain, from the kitchen window. The skies are going to fall any minute."

Phil joins her on the sofa in the south parlor, where the shades are drawn. "My growls are turning into purrs."

She takes a gray-white curl between her fingers. "Noble Lord, your scalp is kingly. Beware of the natives, who would seize a lock for a prize. As you once seized one of mine."

She remembers a morning in Salem, when he clipped a russet lock and placed it with the strands he had unwound from a sleeve button, on the day of Father's funeral, and kept all these years. When he told her this, her heart felt so full she couldn't speak. There seemed no end to the stories they disclosed, long hidden in their lives. Now she has the key to the bower, warm from its long seclusion.

But time has taken the measure of him. They will not pretend otherwise. She wishes she knew a spell to restore him to the Phil of five years ago, but the only spells she knows are her own loving words.

"I will not inflict my self-pity on you. But I'm not making sufficient progress. I sleep fitfully and take exercise too little. If only I could throw away this infernal cane. The fact is, I am old. I don't know what's worse, being seventy-one or being retired. I've been thinking of resuming a bit of court work next spring. I would give a tooth or a toe to be useful again." He sighs. "Enough about my creaky old self. Tell me about Austin. How is he managing the difficulties with Ned?"

Emily gets up and roams about the parlor, then sits beside Phil and takes his hand. She notices that his circulation has cooled. "I'm afraid the situation has recently become more tangled. I'm not the only one in this family to have been surprised by love, although my joy, as you know, did not come lately. Austin is in love with Mabel Todd. My brother has become transformed. You've met her, I think."

She tells him that Austin has told his sisters the story about the September evening, a year ago, when he and Mabel stood in the rain and confessed their love. She and Vinnie have noticed a difference in his demeanor, even his posture. Emily has met her little daughter, the shy and winsome Millicent, but she has steered clear of Mabel, by pure instinct. About Sue, she says nothing.

He shakes his head, neither frowning nor smiling.

"Think of it, Phil—Austin and his half-cracked sister in love at the same time with people they are not married to. Our parents are flailing about in their alabaster chambers."

"My years on the bench taught me how men and women in love can do stupid things. Of course I don't consider our behavior stupid. But we are free and he is tied. I hope he exercises restraint."

"So do I. But who am I to advise him to remain strait-laced?"

He kisses the blue veins of her wrist, above the gold mesh bracelet. "Austin has been so miserable, I am glad for him, as well as afraid. Sue isn't likely to tolerate humiliation. She dominates Amherst's social scene, and Mrs. Todd is a generation younger than her husband. I met her only once, and she is indeed charming and intelligent. Also fond of being the center of attention. I hope she's not playing him for an old fool. Younger women carry their own brand of danger."

Her wide brows lifted, she gives Phil a long candid look. "Coming from the land of witchcraft, you know the dangers of younger women." Her tone is studied and dry.

He winces at what he has just said. "You chasten me, and rightly so."

"Now you are going to say that you didn't mean *me*."

"Of course I didn't. Come here, please, and try to forgive me." He draws her to him and rests his head on her bosom. "Your heart sounds like a squirrel's heart. Please tell me of your own health, Emily."

"Today, my concern is only you. If my heart beats a bit fast, it is entirely your fault."

Being apart has weighed on them. In the spring, when he was ill, Emily sent him flowers so often that Abbie was compelled to write Ned about the "humbug" of elderly romance. Brief confusions and weaknesses have made him unable to write as often as he wants to. He knows this makes her suffer. Their December idyll has been devoured by time.

"Lately I have become clumsy in speech as well as gait. I don't deserve you, although I love you with all my heart."

He doesn't mention the fainting spells, the night sweats, and the feeling of dread that sometimes grips him when he awakes before dawn and can't return to sleep. Nor his recurring dream of Emily, decked in white feathers and perched on the rail of his roof walk, preparing to fly back to Amherst.

She wraps her arms around his back in longing and mourning, and rocks him gently.

"I should have persuaded you to marry me, in December, before it was too late." His voice is muffled. He lifts her left hand and kisses the mesh bracelet and the coral ring.

"It's not too late for us to go on loving each other, is it, dear? And being close?" She has thought about all the possibilities too often, and nearly wrung them dry. "Emily Jumbo Lord" is now a phantom.

"My heart is the same, and my brain. But my body. . . ."

"If you still have strength in your arms to hold me, then that is enough. " Emily marvels at how the years drop away when he smiles. "I have recently been called a witch, but I would like to ride up on a broomstick and land on your roof walk in the city of witches. If Abbie happened to look up, she'd get the fright of her life. In any case, witchcraft is wiser than we are."

Uncannily, she has burrowed into the book of his dreams. His eyes flash. "Who called you a witch?"

"Abbie. In a letter to Ned, poor guileless boy, who didn't keep it to himself. I suspect he thought it was both funny and true. I should remind him that witches wear black, not white, and keep cats as familiars, something I wouldn't do for diamonds."

Phil starts to rise until Emily pushes him back onto the sofa. "I should like to clap my niece in the stocks for a day or two, or have her sew the letter A on her dress, for avarice. When I learned she had sent you that dreadful photograph of me, looking as though I had an appointment with a taxidermist, I wanted to put her out to sea in an open boat."

She'd received the photograph in late July—a full view of Phil, sitting in his garden in his frock coat, his eyelids heavy and sleepy. He appeared half-dead, and she assumed that Abbie had sent it to warn her that her uncle had little time left on earth.

He sighs, but with a touch of humor. "You know you are truly old when people tell you that you look dignified."

"I have never seen you *not* look dignified."

He raises his heroic eyebrows. "I should like a chance to prove you wrong. And—" He puts a finger on her parted lips. "Do not, on pain of your life, ask me if I can make it up the stairs."

*

In the big bedroom above the garden, he turns on his side, after letting Emily massage his back with lavender oil, so comforting that he doesn't mind smelling like a woman.

"Ah, Emily, I am more tired than I thought. All is not firm."

She rests on one elbow and plays with the hairs on his chest. "Hold me close, and do nothing with your lips other than kiss me. Napping is also allowed."

But he can't sleep, or even doze. Something is bothering him.

"I feel the waves in your mind. Show me their freight, please."

"Your 'Philadelphia.' Reverend Wadsworth. You said over a year ago that he had died. Are you in mourning for him?"

She props her back with a pillow, then moves his hand between her breasts. Her heart is right there, under his touch. She has no reason to avoid his question, although she doesn't like it. "I do mourn Charles Wadsworth, yes."

"And did you love him?"

"Yes."

"And were you intimate?"

She, who has answered so many of Phil's questions and asked so many, feels a surge of resistance, and moves his hand away. The waiting, for each of us, she thinks, has been almost too much. Yet what choice do we have? *I will not give up*, her heart shouts. "How would you respond if you heard a lawyer ask that question to a woman on the stand?"

"It depends on the crime being charged."

He is still a judge and always will be, as she will always be a truant and a reprobate. "And what crime am I charged with?"

"None, my dear. You call me your Salem, and yourself my Amherst. And you had a Philadelphia. Is there also a Chicago and a San Francisco?"

"Yes, and a Worcester and a Milwaukee and a Springfield. And let's not forget Elysium and the River Styx."

He winces, and she draws the sheet up to her neck. Her voice is sharp and unapologetic. She thinks, so let it be. "Why are you interrogating me about the history of my heart? I have never asked you about yours, and I assume there is one. Don't think I haven't wondered about your earlier life. But you are its owner, and I am the owner of the love I felt for others. If you want me to name them, as you name your former sweethearts, we'll have an unforgettable afternoon, and it won't do us any good." She will not abandon the strength of her language. It is who she is.

"This is all about Little Phil and his failures."

Emily sits up and faces him. When he grasps a lock of her hair, she extricates it from his fingers and shakes her head. "No, it is about distance and time, family and health. Over a year ago you came back from the undiscovered country, and found me waiting for you. For many weeks I sang to use that waiting, and I will go on doing so forever. But you have no reason to ask me these questions."

His face is guilty and mournful. "I am still jealous as a schoolboy, poor old coot that I am. The closer we become, the more I realize how much of you there is. I think you are Emily Jumbo after all." He dislodges the sheet and gives her two precise kisses. She cannot help but smile.

She bends to rub his forehead with her own. They stay quiet, wrapped around each other. His blue eyes light up and stay on hers. The many poems she has written about him gather in her mind like a rich autumn garden, touched by frost, as gently as he touches her.

Please reach out your hand to me, and snap the spider's web, she wants to say.

"Will you stay with me, and take the chance of paradise?"

Her head on Phil's chest, Emily listens to his breathing until it grows deep and steady. When the world is still, she dresses, tiptoes down the hall to her room, and resumes her work by lamplight.

It is a beginning. It is always a beginning.

21.

Image of Light, Adieu
Amherst, Salem, October 1883

A wraith appears in the dining room doorway: Emily, her hair down, carrying paper and pen. She makes a scratchy noise, like a weeper run dry. Vinnie leads her to the sofa.

Eight-year-old Gib's sudden death from typhoid fever has made a wreck of the family. Five days of desperate illness, raving, hallucinations. Hurrying into a bedroom filled with acrid smells, Emily heard Gib cry out for his friends, for the door to be opened, for release. Nauseated, she stumbled home, and was helped to bed. A few hours later, he was gone.

"Please, Vinnie. I can't even hold a pencil. Phil doesn't know. Somebody must write him." Her voice holds the high notes of panic.

"Knowing you couldn't, I wrote him yesterday. Not much, just the bare news. But he may know already from the *Republican*. You'll be hearing soon. " She strokes Emily's hair, which needs washing, as does her own. Her fingers leave tracks. They both smell like ammonia and bark. Yellow stains under their arms, gray rings around their necks.

"Oh, Vinnie, look at us. We are a mess. I haven't the strength to keep myself."

240

For the first time in weeks, Emily notices that her sister's hair, usually a lush reddish-brown, is flat and dull, plastered to her head. Vinnie's lively deep blue eyes are red-rimmed, her round pink cheeks sickroom-pale.

Maggie closes the kitchen door against any intruders, family or friend. Austin is in the garden, she tells Emily and Vinnie. For hours, she says, their brother has been digging trenches for bulbs, a specter in his thin black jacket, at work on his own grave. He won't speak to any of the men, not Dennis Scannell, or even Tom Kelley. When they approach him, their hats in their hands, he waves them away.

"I am going to take charge of the two of you, because that is my responsibility in this sad house. Miss Emily and Miss Vinnie, I am going to send for Meg, and we will draw the blinds in the kitchen and give you each a nice warm bath. Sisters taking care of sisters, as is only right. Saints alive, you both need it, and you'll feel better." Maggie crosses her arms over her chest and stands against the door like a sentry.

Two tin tubs, gallons of warm water, lavender oil, mild soap, and two large drying cloths later, Emily and Vinnie emerge clean and grateful. Meg dries their hair, then rubs lotion into their arms and across their shoulders. They sit in their shifts near the stove while Maggie and Meg comb the tangles from their hair. The tenderness makes them all weep, but gently, with no fitful sobbing. When their hair is dry, Maggie takes a cool cloth to their faces.

"Now both of you, to bed," she orders. "I've refreshed the sheets, so you won't be crawling back into the foxholes you emerged from, if you don't mind my saying so."

Emily tries a weak smile, Vinnie's head is falling over with exhaustion. Before she is tucked in, Emily grasps Maggie's hand. "If someone could go for Mrs. Todd, it would be a mercy. Austin needs her."

Maggie unties her apron, slams on her bonnet, and hurries out.

*

Phil receives Vinnie's brief letter within minutes after Tim O'Leary brings the *Republican* carrying the story of Gib's death and funeral. He shuts the door to the library and gives way to tears, as he remembers Gib in Emily's conservatory, the little boy's bright head leaning against his arm as they gazed at an ant crawling around in the throat of a red lily. Vinnie has written what she can, and he must guess the rest.

Dear Phil,

We have lost our Gilbert to typhoid. He was taken the late afternoon of October 5 after only a few days. You may imagine how we are. Emily saw the child the night before and has not been the same since. The Doctor has visited, and said that she suffers from nervous exhaustion. No sleep since the ordeal began, nor for me. Maggie helps with the care of us. What healing, for this loss? Em is too sick to write, but she talks of you with love and will write when she can hold a pencil. Austin is in despair and says he wants to follow Gib. I don't know what is to become of our brother, but we will pray and try to keep strong. Stay well, Phil. I know you will write Em when you can.

In sorrow,
Vinnie

He rings for Tim and a cup of tea. Seeing the judge's red eyes and tear-stained face, Tim asks Catherine to put extra sugar on the tea-tray, and a small flask of brandy.

When Tim comes back later, the judge is sorting through scraps of paper covered with a tatter of illegible writing. "I'm distracted, Tim, and I need your help once again, to write to my dear friends. I wouldn't ask you to do this, but at the moment my hand seems to have deserted me." His right hand hangs from his sleeve.

The judge explains the tragedy in the Dickinson household. Tim, father of five, bows his head and crosses himself.

"Would you be so kind as to write what I dictate to you? I can't live with myself if I don't get some word to Miss Dickinson, and her brother and sister."

"Of course, sir." He nods toward the cup of tea. Phil pours in a bit of brandy, then drinks it, although he can't touch Catherine's gingerbread. He starts with Vinnie, then Austin. When he buries his eyes in his handkerchief, Tim goes off to have his wife refresh the teapot.

Emily's letter is hard to manage. She will be reading Tim's script, and will have to trust the depth of Phil's response.

My dearest Emily,

> *The unspeakable news came today, and I am as deep in grief for you as in love I have long borne for you and your family. Gilbert shone with a light that also emanates from you, however dimmed it may be at present.*
>
> *I ask you to put your hand in mine over the miles between us, and imagine yourself held close in our family feeling.*
>
> *I will write in my own writing when I can. You know that Tim is a trustworthy carrier of messages, now as in the past.*
>
> *My thoughts and my love are with you constantly. Phil*

When the judge hands Tim the letter to be sealed and mailed, he can see, reflected in his manservant's face, how old and miserable he looks. He feels gray inside, as if his heart were sitting in a swamp. He has to keep his strength, for the sake of whatever hope remains to him and Emily.

Tomorrow, rain or shine, he will ask Tim to take him for a walk and see that he does not stumble.

Upon his return to Salem from his visit to Amherst, he had received a letter full of her spirited metaphors meant to boost his flagging strength, and to convey her hope that they could still give each other joy.

The withdrawal of the Fuel of Rapture does not withdraw the Rapture itself.

Like Powder in a Drawer, we pass it with a Prayer, it's Thunders only dormant.

*

In their bower, the September light easing through the north window across their bodies, they had brought each other to life again. As he struggled with his inconstant health, Phil drew upon the memories of that afternoon. Now he sat in his reading-chair, put his head back, and conjured up an image of Emily in bed, the sheet falling off her shoulder, her chestnut hair, her full lips open slightly in sleep—an image that brought back last December in Salem. Comforting, lovely, unbearable. His recent visit was just a few weeks ago. He could hardly believe it. When mortality came to call, it gave no warning.

He fetched the box from his bureau and took out a letter she had written to him in August, anticipating his visit to

244

Amherst. The family had endured a difficult summer. As always, Emily put her whole mind into understanding the pattern of words and days:

> *The oddest things in this world are Death and Life, although their feet touch the Tides that flow toward us from the World beyond. Mother is more real to me in some ways than she was when alive. She slept so often and made such little Noise.*
>
> *Now comes an Entente between the houses—a Rose here, a Cake there, some Cookies baked by Mattie—imperfect but accepted with pleasure—and comforting balm for my clumsy sprained Ankle. These are a language I can understand, when words from Next Door seem thin and hollow.*
>
> *Another is the care of the sick. Austin suffered another bout of malaria, but has now begun to creep out from its shadow. Ned's affliction continues, made worse by the tension in his house. If you could send him a kind word, it would give him hope. He still regrets having disclosed my unlikely appearance at the train station, but I tell him that there is nothing to forgive.*
>
> *I try to believe the same of Sue, and 'almost' has to be enough, until she dares to sail the great waters of understanding. I hope she will, for the sake of the long history between us.*
>
> *Love has eluded her, now that Mabel has captured Austin's long-suffering heart. Sue wears the jewels that Austin decked her in, as if they could revive his indulgent ways.*
>
> *She eluded his love as well, although it came to call sincerely and humbly, when she was practicing to be a Siren. What replaces that love is a Mystery to me.*
>
> *My Love for you, like yours for me, sweeps around me, hour by hour. The coral ring and the bracelet are signs of You, the singular gift of my Life.*
>
> *Your Mermaid*

When he hears the knock at his door, Phil folds the letter and tucks it away.

"It's Mary. Could you bear to see me?"

His sister-in-law comes in, bringing a dish of ice cream. He takes a few spoonfuls. "I didn't know I wanted this, but apparently I did."

She sits beside his chair. "I would gladly accompany you to Amherst, if you wish to go. Or arrange things so Miss Dickinson can visit here without impediment, if she is well enough to travel."

His hand is trembling, and Mary takes the dish. "I'm grateful to you for recognizing my closeness to Emily. As you know, I had hoped that . . . She is bedridden and her brother is desperately sad. About Sue Dickinson I can only guess. She has always been an enigma to me. Gilbert was the child of her middle age, and he seemed to have given her a joy she otherwise lacked. Emily and Vinnie are struggling with Austin's despair. I think a visit will have to wait."

He takes his handkerchief and wipes his eyes. "How does one prevent a dear friend from taking his life?"

Her shocked face tells him the answer she would choose. "God does not give us any burden we cannot bear, if we trust in him."

Phil can't bring himself to challenge this premise. Is she saying that a child's untimely death lies in God's hands as in the scales of justice, or that the human soul has a vaster capacity than it can possibly know? The first he cannot believe—nor has never believed. The second Emily had captured in a poem so wise and unpredictable he hardly dared to quote it, but as Mary listened, he did:

Heaven is so far of the Mind
That were the Mind dissolved –

The Site – of it – by Architect
Could not again be proved –

'Tis Vast – as our Capacity –
As fair – as our idea –
To Him of adequate desire
No further 'tis, than Here –

"I do wish you the love of God. It may be easier to bear than you think. And I wish the same for the Dickinsons, especially the one you love most."

"As you know by now, I prefer difficult things to easy ones."

She smiles at him, a smile so like Elizabeth's that he falls speechless. "I am sorry that Abbie begrudges you the happiness you have found with Emily Dickinson. I have long since given up expecting my daughter to be generous, or wondering how she became so selfish. Lately I had high hopes of a new accord between Abbie and Will West, but he has sailed away to Europe again, more's the pity. I don't think he is the man for her, or perhaps for anyone."

He waits for her to go on.

"You have provided generously for us, and I am grateful beyond measure. Abbie takes that bounty for granted. I don't know how to make her realize her luck, although I live in hope."

"My sharing my fortune is wholly my decision, and I am firm in it.

"It is best to be frank, rather than to leave harmful mysteries behind. I don't know how much longer I am going to live—now don't say anything—but I ask you that all my letters be burnt immediately without reading. When the time comes. By you alone. Do you understand?"

247

"Of course. And I will do that for you." Her face is sad and solemn.

"If a child of eight can die, then an old man had better be prepared."

Mary opens the curtains on a bright view of the garden. "Otis, was it hard for you to make the will, last summer?"

"Experience taught me long ago that making a will is always hard. I have only regretted not being able to mention explicitly people important to me."

He needn't name Emily. She already knew. "I think I understand. Of course there are always private arrangements you can make?"

Phil has already planned what he has set in motion—an arrangement not included in his will. He has instructed his lawyer to sell a Lord property in Ipswich, a year after his death. It is a handsome house, and will do well in the market, whenever that may be. The money will go into an account for Emily and Vinnie.

"Yes, and there are brilliant days, even in the dying of the year. And there is Shakespeare, and ice cream."

She hands him his Shakespeare book, kisses his forehead, and takes away the dishes.

*

"I wish you would let Mabel see you," Austin tells Emily, who is confined to bed with headaches and nausea.

"I can't. Not now. That Mabel sees and comforts you is a comfort to me, dear. But I can't help but think of Sue's loss."

She winces at the bitter look on Austin's face. How is it possible both to rejoice in his illicit love, and to regret that it had happened? Because of Phil, and the loss of her beloved Gib, she feels closer to Austin than ever. If Mabel

Todd helps him survive, neither Vinnie nor Emily will pass judgment on them.

"How she could allow our child to play in dirty water up in Shutesbury I cannot and will not understand. She has done such damage! I am in a blaming state of mind, and you know what that does to me."

Emily reaches out her hand and unfurls his fist. "Surely she did not want Gib to die, any more than you did. And little boys will always play in the mud. You and I did as children. You can't bind yourself to such a wheel of wrath. It won't bring Gib back, and it will hurt you."

"I would follow him, if it weren't for you and Vinnie, and Mabel."

Emily feels a spasm of sickness, and asks Austin to fetch Maggie quickly.

When he comes back a few hours later, accompanied by Vinnie, he carries *The Amherst Record's* obituary of Gib, "Death of a Promising Boy." Emily can scarcely sit up, but insists that Austin read the piece to her.

He starts to read, and breaks down. Vinnie takes the paper:

When he stopped an older person on the street to see him ride his velocipede, it was because of a common interest he supposed people had in each other. The richest kind of democracy had taken possession of that little heart.

"He gathered hearts, not flowers," Emily murmurs, as Vinnie wipes her face. "He especially loved the red lilies, but he wouldn't pick them." She remembers seeing Gib's blond head resting against Phil's arm, his delight in his Uncle Lord's gentle teasing. He should have had a living son, she thinks.

She wonders what he would have looked like, and whether he would have his father's sense of humor.

The sound of the piano reaches them through the half-open door.

"Bach. What a comfort. It must be Mabel. I have told her to let herself in."

"Please leave the door open, so that I can listen. It is so refreshing, like being in a boat on the sea at night."

"Em, you have never been in a boat on the sea at night or any other time," Vinnie points out. "But if you can imagine it, then that's all you need."

They leave her in peace, or as much peace as sleep will give her.

To Susan Gilbert Dickinson early October 1883
The Vision of Immortal Life has been fulfilled – …
Gilbert rejoiced in Secrets – His Life was panting with them – With what menace of Light he cried "Don't tell, Aunt Emily"! Now my ascended Playmate must instruct me. Show us, prattling Preceptor, but the way to thee!….
I see him in the Star, and meet his sweet velocity in everything that flies –
His Life was like the Bugle,
which winds itself away,
his Elegy an Echo –
his Requiem ecstasy –
Dawn and Meridian in one, wherefore would he wait, wronged only of Night, which he left for us –
Emily –

22.

The going from a world we know
Salem, Amherst, March – July 1884

Salem, March 1884

Mary Farley adjusts her reading glasses and unfolds the letter from Amherst.

The letter carries a light scent of crocus and early narcissus. Sometimes it is roses, or evergreens, or hellebore. Two weeks ago, jasmine, at the end of winter. On her visits to Amherst, Mary had glimpsed Emily's conservatory and inhaled its paradisal scents. A few soft petals drift from the bottom of the page. Phil opens his hand, and she drops them into his palm. He knows who sent them.

"Read me, please."

There is no salutation or closing, just a paragraph.

That Love is all there is
Is all we know of Love. . . .
How much would I not have known, but for you?
I see by your departing light all I need to see.
You asked me to remember you. That will take another lifetime,
and more besides. Until then, memory will carry me, on its owl
wings. Then we shall see what we can make of devotion.

251

Mary tells her brother-in-law that Elizabeth had a worthy successor, all the more because she could write like this.

"I wish I had been brave enough to know her better." By then he can't hear her.

Dr. Carlton is holding his wrist. Phil has had another stroke, and is unconscious.

*

Emily sits at her table, the sounds of returning birds coming through the southwest windows. Mary Farley has written that Otis Phillips Lord died at noon yesterday, March 13.

After he came back into consciousness yesterday morning I read him your beautiful letter and he asked me to put it near his hand. Then I read him, at his request, a letter you had written years ago, including a funny story from the local paper. He tried to speak, but all I heard was "Emily" and "Jumbo," then a barely audible chuckle. I turned away for a moment, and when I turned back, he was gone. There was no pain, and he was smiling.

What was I doing at noon yesterday, she asks herself. A Thursday, sun contending with clouds, a jurist's kind of weather. I was in the conservatory, among the hyacinths and heliotrope. He was still my Salem, smiling at me.

She sees nothing more to do but wait for death, but hasn't she always been waiting? Months and miles made such small footsteps. When she hears the late afternoon train horn, she remembers her impatient waiting for Phil to arrive and the joy of seeing the magisterial figure walk into the hall and remove his hat. Many years before, when he swept up the two tiny girls Emily and Vinnie and kissed their blooming cheeks, could she have known what he would come to mean to her?

Phil might say that even when the stars of her birth-night watched over them, their love came to be rather than was meant to be. If she loved to explore their shared past for the roots of their autumnal garden, he would bless her mind for its inventiveness.

She had sent him many poems, but only one seemed to encompass all the time she had known Phil Lord.

I live with Him – I see His face –
I go no more away
For Visitor – or Sundown –
Death's single privacy

The Only One – forestalling Mine –
And that – by Right that He
Presents a Claim invisible –
No Wedlock – granted Me –

I live with Him – I hear his Voice –
I stand alive – Today –
To witness to the Certainty
Of Immortality –

Taught Me – by Time – the lower Way –
Conviction, every day –
That Life like This – is stopless –
Be Judgment – what it may –

23.

Each that we lose takes part of us
Amherst, July 1884

N oon is the fatal hour—when Father was stricken in the State House, when Phil died, when death came to call on her a month ago in the kitchen, when she was making a cake, and went away without a crumb. Emily can scarcely believe she is alive, and her parents and Gib and Phil are gone. Phil was the cup from which she learned to drink ecstasy, she wrote Loo and Fanny Norcross. Now the cup is empty.

> *So give me back to Death –*
> *The Death I never feared*
> *Except that it deprived of thee –*
> *And now, by Life deprived,*
> *In my own Grave I breathe*
> *And estimate it's size –*
> *It's size is all that Hell can guess –*
> *And all that Heaven was –*

Vinnie had found the poem on Emily's little table the day she had blacked out, and told her later that reading it nearly killed her.

"You're not done with poetry, yet, Em, and it's not done with you." Vinnie's eyes are wet, but she speaks in a voice

254

of command, the first remark in months that makes her sister smile.

"We are of the sky, dear, and we shall see what the sky makes of us. Perhaps the angel of darkness didn't like the cake I was making when I collapsed."

Vinnie places daylilies in a vase and sets them on a windowsill. The color will remind her sister that the earth still produces beautiful gifts, even on painful days. Today is July 11, 1884, the date of Phil's seventy-second birthday. He is in the bosom of Eternity, that visitor he inscribed in his last letter to Emily. He had written: *A Caller comes*, and mentioned seeing a snowdrop and a crocus on his daily walk. The early spring flowers gave him hope that as each day brought another minute of sunshine, he could conquer the winter that persisted in his body.

"I still feel shaky when I think of you lying on the kitchen floor, with Dr. Fish hovering and Maggie sobbing with her apron over her head."

She sits up and raises her arms so that Vinnie can remove her nightgown and bathe her. Emily notices that her sister is thinner than she has ever been. Vinnie's hair, faithfully washed by Maggie every other week, is still scooped into a wayward bun, and she fits their mother's old blue gown. Her pale Norcross complexion blushes when she talks to Emily about their unforgotten loves.

"This makes me feel like a girl who played in the dirt and has been ordered to wash."

Vinnie pats her dry, rubs lotion on her white arms, and settles the fresh gown around her. Her sister's tender worry tells Emily she has not gained back the weight lost since March. Eating seems irrelevant. She is sick to her stomach more often.

"I think Dr. Fish has the perfect name, since he caught me swimming in the black waters."

"And reeled you in, praise God." Vinnie turns aside to wipe her eyes.

"'Revenge of the nerves.' My dreams are so populous—Father, Sam Bowles, Mother, Wadsworth, Gib, and now Phil. If dreams are couriers, then more messages await me than I can answer."

She looks at the photograph of Lord's portrait, a brilliant likeness that now hangs in the Salem courthouse. It is her bedtime ritual to gaze at the wise, powerful face, the high forehead, clustered with gray-white curls, the beautiful hands. If she stares at it long enough, she can re-animate it, teasing Phil's lips into a smile, working her fingers into the curls, bearing the full weight of his deep, soul-stirring glance.

"I wonder what he was thinking as he sat for the painter."

"He was looking from this world into the next. His face has such ascension. If I hadn't loved it, I would have feared it." *Those fingers touched me in secret places, and warmed my shy flesh. I held my face against that face, played with the watch fob, and unbuttoned all the buttons on his vest, wiped the tears from his eyes, and gave him all the pleasures I knew how to give.*

Vinnie turns her head and puts her finger to her lips. "Shh! Emily, do you hear that?"

They listen through the half-open door. The sounds from the library are faint but unmistakable. Excitement, ecstasy, the soft laughter that follows.

"We shouldn't listen, Em. We shouldn't even hear them." Vinnie shuts the door emphatically.

"Hush now. Austin and Mabel must go somewhere to be together, since they are loving outside the law. I'm hardly in a position to deny my brother the privilege." Phil's voice is in her ear, ringing changes on the letter O. "Did I ever make such sounds, I wonder."

"Well, missy, I can tell you that you are quite musical when—"

"*Thronged only with music, like the decks of birds.*"

"Is that a line from Shakespeare? It's nice, although I don't know if birds have decks." Vinnie giggles. "Did he mean 'necks,' do you suppose?"

"I was describing what it was to sing in Phil's presence."

Emily is somewhere else, the bower's soft, welcoming climate.

"I remember that dinner next door when we sang 'Broad is the Road that Leads to Death,' but I can scarcely imagine what tune would have suited your sweet soprano and his brazen trumpet."

Emily hums a few faint notes of a tune she composed long ago.

"Did you sing hymns?"

"We had a little hymn that nobody sang but us."

Itself to itself a timbrel, itself to itself a tune.

"I think what we are hearing from the library is not quite what I would call a hymn, although Austin sings lustily, and Mabel is a lark."

Emily winks, with a sly smile. "I suspect that she plays the organ rather nicely, too."

Her sister grins and claps her hands. "You are naughty! What would Phil say?"

"He would fill this room with his big laugh, and then he would make one of his own racy jokes."

She fears becoming a lost balloon, cast into the sea. After a sip of water, she grasps Vinnie's hand. "I must ask you for something important." Her voice bats against the cage of her weakness.

"Yes, dear." Vinnie takes Emily's cool ivory feet in her hands and massages them.

"Pay attention now, Vin. When I am gone, I want you to burn my letters. Without reading. All of them."

"Even Mr. Higginson's? And Loo and Fanny? And Phil's? Oh, Emily, why?"

"The letters have been a joy of my time on earth. But when I'm done, the letters must fly off into the flames. That is the end of their life."

"But you said that words begin to live when they were said."

"Yes, but I have never been consistent."

Vinnie sniffs and folds her arms over her chest, mimicking Maggie. "That is not a good answer. You have to think of something else."

Emily smiles at her sister. There's nobody like Vinnie in the world, and nobody she likes as well. "Dickinsons have never tolerated strangers knowing their private business."

"Tell that one to Austin when he sets off in the carriage with Mabel, for all the world to see!"

"What the good citizens of Amherst think is up to them. But words are slippery and open to many meanings. And I must protect people's privacy."

"You are thinking of Phil. His letters must be—must have been beautiful."

"If that's a hint for me to let you read them, I beg of you, please don't."

The letters parade in her head in sumptuous colors—rippling, bounteous, and bold. "I'll not soon forget Maggie's praising the judge's handwriting. She said the letters looked like they wanted to burst the seams of the envelope and shout with joy. Maggie has a poetic soul. I believe that the Irish are all poets, every last one."

"Yes, his words were beautiful, and I'll keep them until I'm ready to let them go into Eternity with me."

Her words, she knew from Mary Farley, were the last he ever read. Emily assumes that someone in his household has burned her letters. She hopes it isn't Abbie, but it doesn't matter now.

"Why didn't you marry him, Emily? He would have made you happy."

"He did make me happy, as I made him."

The hemlock branches ride up and down in the summer wind. She fingers the coral ring she wears on a chain around her neck, since her fingers have grown so thin. The gold bracelet sits on her nightstand, where she can reach for it and trace Little Phil's name.

"We talked of marriage in April of '82, although with Mother still here, the question of where to live remained thorny. He had already disposed of some property, and was easing into retirement. Then he had the stroke, and miraculously recovered. When I sneaked off to Salem, we approached the matter again—where to live, what to do about the Farleys, how he would cope with my need for privacy. He was a powerful persuader. No wonder men fainted in his presence."

"But you were stronger than those forces of darkness, and more stubborn."

"No, death was stronger than either of us. Phil knew it was coming for him. When he made his will, he wrote me that it made him feel both desperate and hopeful."

She falls quiet but doesn't cry—or can't. His voice abides in her ear, her body.

"I remember when he helped Mother and me write our wills. Mother was in pain, and had trouble concentrating. I hung on Phil's every word, wanting to please him. He was patient, and he held my hand and let me cry on his shoulder. Elizabeth, as you know, was one of the witnesses—her signature as elegant as herself. I was nearly forty-five years old, and I felt like a needy child."

Vinnie lights a lamp on the bureau. "You probably didn't notice, but I could tell then that he cared for you. After you and Mother had signed your wills, he came down to the kitchen and asked me for a cup of tea. He said that he and Father knew there was nobody in the world like you. I wish—never mind, Em. I just wish."

She busies herself straightening the bedclothes and fitting soft socks onto Emily's marble feet.

"After Gib died, I gave up hope, although I never gave up loving Phil. He was more frail than I knew, possibly than he knew. When he was with me, his mind fooled him. That is what minds do, perhaps what they are meant to do. On his visit in September he had talked of resuming work in the spring, just enough to be useful, not enough to kill him—or so he said. At that moment he sounded so like Father I thought he had swallowed his ghost."

"You were unlucky, I think." Vinnie's voice is shaky. "Mother. Father. Disease. Death. Abbie. Sue."

"No, we were lucky beyond imagining. To have known that ray of sun all my life, and to have loved him—how could that not be glory while I had it?" She moistens her handkerchief in her water glass, and holds it to her eyelids. "Vinnie, the letters? Do you promise to do what I asked?"

"I will. But I don't want to think about it right now. I want you to stay on this earth as long as possible." Vinnie kisses her on both cheeks, and leaves the room.

Emily is turning paler week by week, her skin transparent as tissue paper, the fine blue veins both an unreadable map and a sign of royal blood. She props herself upright and tries to walk to her writing table, but her feet refuse to hold her up. Talking about Phil has given her a happiness that reality now takes away.

She looks at the portrait. The mouth seems both solemn and merry. "Calvary and May wrestled in his nature," she had written of him. He had been tormented by Elizabeth's suffering, Emily's months of eye trouble. Father's sudden death. Gib.

But joy took him by the hand, and awakened him to new life.

She speaks to the well-beloved face: "Watch over me, my love. And tell me what to do with our story."

*

She sleeps, without the headache that often darts around her temples. When she awakes, she realizes that the answer has been in her mind for a long time.

In the ebony box where she keeps Phil's letters, lie the copies she has made of her letters to him. His words and hers rest embowered there, secretly communing in the dark. That knowledge restores her spirit, however frail her body has become.

Her plans are almost complete.

When she dies, Vinnie will find her poems in her bureau, in a chest—almost eighteen hundred of them, the work of her lifetime. Like a sower of seed, she has sent them to

Sue, Higginson, Loo, and Fanny. She has given forty little bundles of poems to Maggie, to keep in her trunk, safe in Emily's bedroom.

I am wise and sneaky as one of Vinnie's cats.

She'll ask Maggie to place her letters to Phil among her poems. Vinnie will read them, and Austin, perhaps Mabel, too.

Austin will know that Phil and I were their forerunners.

". . . *Tenderness has not a Date – it comes – and overwhelms,*" she wrote him the day before Phil's near-fatal stroke in 1882. He had survived to read the words.

Sooner or later, Emily whispers to the portrait, others will learn our truth.

24.

You will lift me back
Amherst, October 1850

P hil picks up Emily and settles her into the carriage beside
him. Vinnie and Sue Gilbert, the girls' friend, occupy the
back seat. Now that Emily is nineteen and Vinnie seventeen,
he no longer calls them his Little Playthings, although he still
feels protective of these lively petite young women.

"Now, Emily, we are going to go fast, so I want you to
hang onto me. Are you ready?"

"Yes!"

This is her first ride with Phil Lord, who is said to be
expert and thrilling in his handling of horses.

As they head south out of Amherst, the October
afternoon sunshine moves onto the flanks of Mt. Norwottuck
ahead, rising up beyond South Amherst's large farms. Phil
keeps the horses at a steady trot as they pass the little white
schoolhouse and the fields of late feed corn still awaiting
harvest. A mild wind moves through the drying stalks in
golden billows. They rattle like clapping hands. He flicks
the whip lightly across the horses' backs and they speed up.
Emily glances back at the dwindling village. Children are
playing in the schoolyard, an old familiar game. Could she
make their ring run backwards and unwind? She clutches his

pocket, and when they go faster, he tells her to wrap her arm around him, so that she won't tumble out. When she reaches across his back, she breathes in a scent like Father's, a wool coat fragrant with bay rum and smoke.

Is the wind blowing wildly, or are they making the wind? Behind her, Vinnie shrieks in delight. Emily turns to look at Sue, big-eyed and silent. Faster, faster, she thinks, and as if he can read her mind, Phil picks up the pace until they are flying up the side of the mountain, rounding the first curve on two wheels. Crows rise in a clacking mass from a nest of hemlocks. Sunlight slams against the trees, and Emily unties her bonnet and flings it away. Her glorious hair unpins itself in the wind. Another tickle of the expert whip and the road turns into a river of wind and light.

"Oh, time and I are flying!"

Who has the driver become? She shuts her eyes and sees Father and Austin, dark-eyed Sue, a black-clad minister, his lips open to thunder—and Otis Phillips Lord, poised on a branch with wide wings spread. Her clothes become feathers, then ribbons, then disappear. Only her arm clutching Phil's coat holds her to the earth. The horses' ears lean back, her hair lifts and swings in time with their manes. How they must love running until it seems they can run forever. Quick yellow leaves spin, fall and fly down the road up ahead. Or are they stars?

Behind her, Vinnie and Sue fade away, and the road vanishes until it becomes the dream of a road. The horses fly toward the stars, and now there are only Emily and the big laughing man in the warm black coat, speeding toward the edge of the earth.

Notes

1. *You Cannot Put a Fire Out*
   Amherst, September 1847
   I call Otis Phillips Lord "Phil," the name Emily called him.

2. *The Judge is like the Owl*
   Amherst, March – July 1862
   An account of the 1862 Amherst College Commencement and of Lord's and Beecher's speeches appears in Christopher Benfey's *A Summer of Hummingbirds*, chapter three (New York: Penguin Books, 2008).

3. *A Secret Told*
   Amherst, Boston, Cambridge,
   February – June 1864
   The letters of 1863–64 were written by the author.

5. *Let my first knowing be of thee*
   Salem, Amherst, Boston, December 1872
   The letters of November 20 and November 24 were written by the author.
   Dickinson described her response to Rubinstein in a letter to Loo Norcross, May 1873:

"He makes me think of polar nights Captain Hall could tell. Going from ice to ice! What an exchange of awe!" Dickinson's friend Clara Bellinger Green wrote years later, "Emily told us of her early love for the piano and confided that, after hearing Rubinstein . . . play in Boston, she had become convinced that she could never master the art and had forthwith abandoned it once and for all. . . ." Jay Leyda, *The Years and Hours of Emily Dickinson*, Vol. II, 273 (Hamden, Conn.: Archon Books).

6. *My House is a House of Snow*
Boston, Amherst, June 19 1874
No report exists of Judge Lord's attending Edward Dickinson's funeral on June 19; court business might have delayed his arrival until after the service.

8. *I died for Beauty*
Salem, December 1877
Mary C. Farley was Elizabeth Wise Lord's sister. I have called Lord's niece Mary Farley "Molly."

11. *A Shining Secret*
Crawford Notch, New Hampshire,
Amherst, August 1880
The letters in this chapter were written by the author.

12. *To Rock a Fretting Truth to Sleep*
Amherst, September 1880
The letter that ends this chapter was written by the author.

13. *These Fevered Days*
    Salem, Amherst, March – April 1881
    The letter of March 10, 1881, was written by the author, as was the letter from Abbie Farley.

14. *There Comes A Warning like a Spy*
    Salem, October 1881
    The letters of October were written by the author.

17. *Oh Shadow on the Grass*
    Salem, Amherst, April – June 1882
    The passages from letters of April 30 and May 1, 1882, are quoted in Millicent Todd Bingham's *Emily Dickinson, A Revelation* (1954), and are also in the digital Emily Dickinson Collection at the Amherst College Archives and Special Collections. The letter from Timothy O'Leary (3 June, 1882) was written by the author.

22. *The going from a world we know*
    Salem, Amherst, March – July 1884
    The poet's last letter to Lord was written by the author.

24. *You will lift me back*
    Amherst, October 1850
    This chapter re-imagines the poet's "Because I could not stop for Death" (Fr 479).

Acknowledgments

T hanks are due to many wise writers who gave superb counsel and editorial help:

Dick Todd, editor and writer; Shirley Abbott, a wise, seasoned writer of memoir and fiction; Jerome Charyn, author of the unforgettable novel *The Secret Life of Emily Dickinson*; Polly Longsworth, author of *Austin and Mabel* and *The World of Emily Dickinson,* who was generous with her time and her knowledge; Kitty Burns Florey, novelist and editor, for expert reading and editing, and for warm and humor-filled times with Fred the dog.

Thanks to good friends and fine readers:

Terry Y. Allen, Nancy Babb, Robert Bagg, Chris Benfey, Casey Clark, Nancy Coiner, Nick Czap, Peter Czap, Peggy O'Brien, Lisa Raskin, John Ratté, Mariève Rugo, Dick Tedeschi, Ernie Urvater, and Richard Wilbur for reading this novel in its earlier stages.

Lenore Riegel, for her kindness and encouragement.

Mike Kelly, Mimi Dakin, and the staff of the Amherst College Archives and Special Collections for their help with research.

Jane Wald, Executive Director of the Emily Dickinson Museum; Cindy Dickinson, Director of Programs and Interpretation; and my fellow guides for tolerating my obsession with Judge Lord.

Linda Roghaar, for expert advice from a savvy publisher and lover of books.

Artist Elizabeth Pols, for her superb cover design.

James Guthrie, for writing so well about Dickinson and the law, and about Judge Lord's friendship with the poet.

Kyle Wyatt and Alice Mullaly of the Central Pacific Railroad Photographic History Museum, for information about toilet facilities on passenger trains in the 1870s.

Rachel Liebling, for granting permission to use Jerome Liebling's photograph *South Parlor, Dickinson Homestead, Amherst, Massachusetts,* c. 1999 on the front cover.

Letters of Emily Dickinson from *The Letters of Emily Dickinson,* edited by Thomas H. Johnson and Theodora Ward, Cambridge, Mass., and London, England: The Belknap Press of Harvard University Press, Copyright 1958, 1986, by the President and Fellows of Harvard College.

Poems of Emily Dickinson from *The Poems of Emily Dickinson, Variorum Edition* edited by Ralph W. Franklin: The Belknap Press of Harvard University Press, Copyright 1998, by the President and Fellows of Harvard College:

Heaven is so far of the Mind	413
They dropped like Flakes	545
I live with Him – I see His face	698
As if the Sea should part	720
The Judge is like the Owl	728
There is no Frigate like a Book	1286
To pile like Thunder to it's close	1353
All that I do	1529

How fleet – how indiscreet an one   1557
So give me back to Death   1653

Portions of Dickinson's letters to Lord from Chapter V, "The Revelation," in Millicent Todd Bingham, *Emily Dickinson, A Revelation* (New York: Harper & Brothers Publishers), 1954; and the Amherst College Archives and Special Collections: amherst.edu/library/archives.

About the Author

S usan Snively is the author of four books of poetry: *From This Distance* (Alice James, 1981), *Voices in the House* (Alabama Poetry Series, 1988), *The Undertow* (University of Central Florida, 1998), and *Skeptic Traveler* (David Robert Books, 2005.) A guide at the Emily Dickinson Museum in Amherst, Snively wrote and narrated the films "Seeing New Englandly," and "My Business is to Sing," produced by Ernest Urvater, in the series "Angles of a Landscape." *The Heart Has Many Doors* is her first novel.

She has taught at Smith, Mount Holyoke, and Amherst Colleges, and has received fellowships from the NEA and the Massachusetts Artists Foundation. She helped to found, and directed, the Writing Center at Amherst College for twenty-seven years. She lives in Amherst, Massachusetts, with her husband, Peter Czap.

Snively has read her poetry, given talks on Emily Dickinson, and presented films widely in New England and elsewhere, and regularly leads discussions on the poetry of Emily Dickinson.

For the latest on the book, including events, contests, book club questions, and other happenings, visit her website at susansnively.com.

CPSIA information can be obtained
at www.ICGtesting.com
Printed in the USA
FFOW05n1047110315